The Adventures of Chip Weatherbe, MBA

A Lighthearted Story Of One Man's Daily Career Struggle

By

Michael F. Goyette

authorHOUSE

1663 LIBERTY DRIVE, SUITE 200
BLOOMINGTON, INDIANA 47403
(800) 839-8640
www.authorhouse.com

This book is a work of fiction. Places, events, and situations in this story are purely fictional and any resemblance to actual persons, living or dead, is coincidental.

© *2004 Michael F. Goyette*
All Rights Reserved.

No part of this book may be reproduced, stored in a retrieval system, or transmitted by any means without the written permission of the author.

First published by AuthorHouse 03/30/04

ISBN: 1-4184-0992-8 (e)
ISBN: 1-4184-0619-8 (sc)
ISBN: 1-4184-0618-X (dj)

Printed in the United States of America
Bloomington, Indiana

This book is printed on acid-free paper.

Dedicated to David and Amanda –
Do what you love, love what you do, and keep your priorities in focus.

Acknowledgments

Lead Editor
Alexis Black

Cover Design
RoessnerBenning Design (www.roessnerbenning.com)

Thanks to everyone who provided editorial input:
Melissa Goyette, Dave Androvich, Lisa Ashman, Mike Bloch, Jon Charnecki, Matt Charnecki, Dad, Dave Ferko, Ric Gowan, Michelle Goyette, Ed Kolodziej, Mom, Brian Reamer, Bill Rohrer, Eric Skinner

Special thanks to my wife, Melissa –
Thanks for supporting this experiment

Table of Contents

Beginning the Final Stretch - January 1

The Mission: The Sea Awaits 6

Case Study On What <u>Not</u> To Do: North South Air 13

Business Policy 20

The Tenacious Headhunter 26

Business to Business Marketing 30

It's a Mad, Mad, Mad Business World 35

The Call 39

The Interview – Charge! 41

What Do You Want to Be… 51

The Offer 55

The Resignation 57

First Day on the Job 60

The Group Project 68

Ted 71

The CEO: It's Good to be the King 78

C.A.T. 82

Germ Management (a.k.a. HR Run Amuck) 87

SIMM Meeting 92

What We Have Here is a Failure to Communicate (a.k.a HR Clarifies Germ Management) 97

This Situation is Crazy 104

Together All Contribute to the Organizational Structure 111

It's Not Harassment! She Just Thinks It Is 115

Diversity and Zero Tolerance: The New PP Program 119

Cafeteria Talk 124

The Soup Kitchen, Jack the Knife, and Big Mike & His Love Posse 131

Out of the Box Thinking 140

Germans and Airports 143

Radical Entrepreneurial Ideas: I Don't Know if You've Ever Really Considered the Benefits of Being an Alpaca Farmer 152

Cheerful Good-byes: The New Outplacement Program 160

Desperate Interviews: The Sea is Getting Rough 163

Why Am I Doing This? 167

Bern. Again 170

Incoming! (The Revised Evaluation Form) 174

Ted and Janice 186

Decisions, Decisions…Rajiv and Linda 190

Come Monday, It'll Be Alright… 195

Take this job and… 198

After the Storm: A Peaceful Sea (for some) 200

Prelude

E-MEMO

TO: Sales and Marketing Staff

FROM: Rajiv Chopra

SUBJECT: SIMM Meeting

    I was very disappointed with the team's showing at the SIMM meeting yesterday. Frankly, I was embarrassed. I expect more out of our group.

    These internal meetings are vital to the communication success of the organization. The information we provide is critical to the decision making of other groups. The strategic direction and therefore the future success of the organization lies wholly on our shoulders. We jeopardize GIT's very existence when we perform as we did. Assign your contribution to this meeting the highest level of seriousness and priority and be sure to produce accordingly. When the sales and marketing team drops the ball as it did, everyone takes notice.

    Additionally, you need to make every concerted effort to focus on what is important to conducting our business (i.e. serving our customers) and plan your activities accordingly. Focus only on those activities which contribute value to the forward progress of our company. The SIMM meeting is a clear example of this.

    To be specific…In the future, all tables, charts, and graphs will have a line size of no less than 1 pt and no greater than 2 point. All color slides should reflect our corporate colors. Further, use our logo wherever possible on all slides in accordance with the logo manual. Finally, make sure to run all slides and overheads by me before any presentation – I will be the final arbiter of what will be presented. You are all professionals, I expect you to use your best judgment. One might opine that I am being too harsh…rest assured… I am not.

    Dan: What is the status of the G1500 program? I did not see your status report this morning as we discussed. Why?

    Linda: Make sure to arrive on time for our next team meeting. If you need assistance in allocating your time, let me know. I might suggest taking a time management seminar. Check with Gracie on the availability of arranging such a class and inform me of your progress. Verify your receipt of this request by seeing me immediately.

Kelly: Schedule a meeting with Dan, yourself, and I to discuss the pricing on the C1500 quote. This should have been addressed last week. I am in a bit of a quandary as to why it was not…

Chip: I do not want a repeat of this performance next month. We hired you under the pretense that you would provide a specified skill set. One would hope that this does not turn out to be a poor decision, one which would require immediate reversal. Review the logo manual in detail and investigate taking a Power Point class. You need to become savvier with your presentation skills. Review with me any of your work that will be shown to anyone outside this office. See me immediately regarding this. I expect more out of an MBA.

Let's all get back on course. I expect everyone to be at the pinnacle of their performance next meeting.
Thx. – RC

And so it was that Chip carefully weighed the language in the E-memo from his manager Rajiv. As the words sank deep in his soul, the reality of his environment crystallized in his mind. With a horrifying awareness, he realized what he had done. He had been a big fish in a small pond, but had felt unfulfilled. He had attributed his wanting for more to the small size of the company and his income. He had made the decision to venture into the unknown. He left his comfortable, small company job in search of a career filled with passion, glory, power, and more money. Instead, he realized, he had entered a quagmire of detail, bureaucracy, and chart making. He realized that these corporate chains, these golden handcuffs that would surely imprison him and destroy his spirit, had been eagerly accepted and indeed fought for. He realized that after his relentless work and undying effort, he had finally gotten everything he had wanted; the job at a big corporation, the corporate ladder to climb, and the money. Gazing up the ladder with a dispirited heart, he realized he was on his way to the top. Chip Weatherbe, MBA, had finally made it.

Beginning the Final Stretch - January

Silence. No words, no sounds as he sits facing a very large, dark oak desk. He wonders why the desk is so big, the top coming nearly up to his chin and extending to 4' on either side of him. He considers the fact that he is 6', 210 pounds and yet feels so…small. The desk seems excessive. On the other side of the desk is an empty, large leather chair, a recliner with rollers. Again, excessive.

He notices a picture on the wall. The picture is of a sailboat on rough water with a caption that says something about finding new lands only if you're brave enough to leave the shore. The picture makes him feel anxious and it occurs to him that he has seen this picture before. Or maybe somebody said it to him once. He can't remember for sure, his thoughts are hazy. The room is otherwise a blur and seems to be empty.

A door behind the chair opens slowly. He doesn't remember the door being there a second ago. A woman emerges and takes her place in the leather chair. He knows she is attractive, although for some reason he finds it difficult to see her face clearly. Her question, however, is very clear.

"Where are the margin numbers I asked you for?"

The question is unexpected. She was supposed to ask why she should hire him. Wasn't this a job interview? Where did the margin question come from? His heart races as he searches for an answer. He feels an intense sensation of panic.

He notices the desk is now a large meeting table and the room is filled with people all staring at him waiting for the answer. Was I supposed to do an analysis? On what? Oh God! I forgot what I was going to say.

The woman asks, "What do you want to do?"

"What," he replies timidly. Despite feeling an overwhelming urge to run and hide, he remains motionless, paralyzed with fear.

"What do you want to do? Where do you see yourself in ten years? What do you want to be? What do you want to do." The attendees in the room begin asking the questions simultaneously. The group, the ranks of which have now swelled to well over a hundred by his best guess, are focused on him, waiting for his answer. If he didn't know better, he would swear that the entire world was listening, waiting.

I don't know, he thinks to himself. Don't tell them that, they'll never hire you. But it's the truth he reminds himself. Still, best to leave it unsaid; some truths don't need to be spoken. OK, keep it cool. I can wing it. Redirect them back to the margin question, that's easier to answer. Stand up and start talking. Command their attention. I need to... Rising slowly, he glances down. Oh God! Where are my pants? I have no pants on! What if they see me with no pants? What if...

Talking from a radio. Someone is talking about a stalled vehicle in the center lane on I-275. It's 5:00 a.m. Chip Weatherbe wakes in a sudden panic. The bed is damp with sweat. Time for another glorious work week. The dream fades as quickly as it appeared, retreating to a dark corner of unconsciousness, afraid to be confronted by the light. Rise and shine.

The routine is familiar. Get up, to the gym by 5:30 a.m. for a short workout, shower, a forty minute drive to work to get there a little after 7:00 a.m. Work until 5:00 p.m., then off to class or home for a rousing night of homework. Over the Christmas break he had almost forgotten the daily rituals. Today was the beginning of the first full week back in the saddle.

The after-work destination depended entirely on the day of the week. This semester Mondays and Wednesdays were school nights; classes to earn an MBA. Tuesdays and Thursdays were home nights, largely devoted to homework. The theory was, finish the homework during the week and leave the weekends free, although things never seemed to work out that way. Inevitably, someone from 'your group' couldn't meet during the week: they had kids to pick up and no babysitter, they had to work late, they had other classes on the nights you were open... the reasons for not meeting were endless. Not that this meant the weekends were any better for the group; they weren't.

Fridays were reserved for a night out with his fiancée, Stacy, assuming of course her schedule permitted. Saturday mornings typically focused on more schoolwork and the remainder of Saturday devoted to Stacy, housework, or one of his few hobbies. The house was starting to engulf more time. He had purchased it a year and a half ago, just after meeting Stacy. Since she had an apartment, they decided that after they got married, they would live in his house for one or two years until they found their dream home. At first, there was no work that needed to be done on the house. Then, Stacy started to spend more time there and the project load gradually increased. Since a month or two after their engagement, it seemed that every weekend required a large portion of his time dedicated to some home renovation task in desperate need of immediate completion.

Sundays were up in the air depending largely on his fiancée's schedule, the size of the current weekend project, miscellaneous work items that needed completion by Monday, and of course, more schoolwork. A small piece of available free time remaining had been spent recently in a job search, about three or four hours a week by Chip's estimation.

At thirty years old, Chip had been working full time since graduating from college, some eight years now. He had spent the three years following college at his first real job and had left there on good terms when it became clear that the only way to advance his comparatively low salary was to jump ship. He jumped for a twenty-five percent increase in pay, putting his salary where he thought he ought to be. The company he jumped to was a small automotive supplier with limited room for growth (financial or otherwise), but a comfortable environment. He had been at this company since the jump, working diligently to make a difference. His efforts had not gone unnoticed and he had earned a certain level of respect from his peers as well as a few decent pay increases in all but one of the five years. That particular year when no merit increases were to be seen, the company almost went out of business, having lost a number of key orders. Ten people were laid off that year and were never called back. However, the Company persevered and came back the following year, posting meager profits.

Chip reported directly to the President of the company, who was also one of the three owners. He liked the people he worked with and enjoyed the overall corporate culture. Although Chip worked hard, for the last year he often found himself bored with his job. He felt unchallenged and wondered more and more if he should explore the job market for something bigger and better. The image of the sailboat on the water searching for new shores always seemed to be at the back of his mind. A persistent voice was always pushing the issue – leave the shore, find new lands, be brave.

It was this thinking that lead Chip to spend time each week in his current job hunt, forwarding his resume to different contacts, responding to postings on various career web sites, and searching the local paper. He had started the hunt very casually about six months ago, which is to say that he began thinking about it. It wasn't until three months later that the first resume had been sent. Gradually, the search had intensified leading to a number of interviews and two offers, both of which he had rejected.

It was also this line of reasoning that had prompted Chip to pursue an advanced degree a number of years ago. As he had made the jump to his current employer some five years ago, he had decided that another degree was necessary to progress financially and professionally in today's competitive environment. He had talked with friends and acquaintances in the "business world" regarding ways to advance economically and the consensus was that a Masters degree was needed. That seemed to be one of the first questions a potential employer would ask, "Do you have a Masters?" No one seemed to suggest that a person was somehow a better worker if they had this degree, nor did anyone seem to be asking what that person did with the degree once it was earned. They only wanted to know if a candidate had one or not. At least, this was the discussion in Chip's circle of friends. And so, three years after earning his Bachelor of Science in Business Administration, he decided it was time to take the next step and earn the much prized MBA, a Masters in Business Administration.

Chip was pragmatic and viewed the MBA program accordingly. To his thinking, an MBA was simply a way to make more money. All talk to the contrary was smoke and mirrors. In today's market, an MBA was a necessary tool to simply keep pace with everyone else. It was three letters after your name which, if you could prove you had, might open a dialog with a potential employer or establish an improved negotiating position with your current employer. Although there was obviously some intrinsic value to the degree, the reasons anyone would do this to themselves were simple: to make more money or to get a better job. Of course, getting a better job meant more money and advancement in the company or the knowledge to do your job better were just different paths to the same goal – more cash.

He applied and was accepted into the MBA program at a university not too far from where he worked. He had opted to work during the day and take classes at night. This was an easy decision since trying to take classes full time was not financially viable. After all, there were mortgage payments to make, a honeymoon to save for, and a retirement to plan.

Nor was going back to school full time desired. The whole purpose of entering the program was to further his financial pursuits. Chip did not see how quitting his job or working part time would help him reach this goal.

It was now four years after making that decision that Chip found himself in the final stretch of the program; this was his last semester. Come April, he would have an MBA. He had started the curriculum off strong, taking two classes a semester for the first year. The second year he wavered slightly and only took one class a term. He had to drop the class in the fall due to his travel schedule at work and could only muster the motivation to take one class in winter. By year three, he could feel himself slowing down. Working a full day and then going to class or to the library to meet with the group was starting to become a grind. Chip knew starting out it would be difficult work, but knowing the path and walking the path can be different worlds; it always looks so easy on paper.

It was now Monday, the second week of January and tonight was the first night of class. Although class days were tiring, the time went by quickly. This semester, with the light at the end of the tunnel, time would fly and come May, life could return to normal.

Chip had the stair machine set for forty-five minutes – Mondays being cardiovascular days. Two large TVs, one in each corner of the gym, blared out the morning news as Chip unfolded his newspaper and glanced through the headlines: '…a bold cultural revolution…', 'Age-Bias claims jolt…', '…revolution spawns turmoil.' Over the sound of his own thoughts, Chip caught bits and pieces of the news anchor, "…more layoffs are expected later this week as…" and "…bought out by a German company…"

"…gets worse everyday."

Chip turned to the man on the stair machine next to him. He appeared to be in his mid to late fifties. "I'm sorry, what was that?"

"I said, it seems like the news gets worse everyday. Companies being bought out by overseas competitors. Economy bad. A lot of people getting let go in automotive," the man said between breaths. "Good people too. People who dedicated their lives trying to keep their company going. Then one day, they're told their services aren't required anymore and they're escorted to the door by security holding a box with twenty or thirty years of memories. Of course the people that are left standing…their workload is doubled."

Chip stared at the man, unmoved. "Doesn't somebody with that many years usually get a pretty nice retirement package? I would think there's a lot of people smiling when they get that phone call."

The man kept his eyes on the television, expressionless. "Yeah…well, that may be. But there are a lot of people that aren't. Try spending a few decades devoted to something only to be told that since you're part of the old corporate culture, you're the cause of all the company's problems and everything you can bring to the table really isn't that useful anymore. See if you're smiling," the man said glancing at Chip and immediately returning his gaze to the TV.

"Yeah, good point," Chip responded, masking his true sentiment and thinking to himself how enjoyable an early retirement would be. Besides, somebody who spent that long at a company made choices. They chose to stay in one spot, knowing that with the mere stroke of a pen, someone could end their time at the company. They had no one to blame but themselves for showing that kind of devotion. Chip glanced back at the man next to him. Not me, no way. No one's going to control how long I work. He returned his attention to the paper, forgetting about the man's comments. After all, being in a bad work situation, being at someone's mercy, wasn't something Chip would ever have to experience. He knew how the game was played. He was a smart MBA. No one was ever going to catch Chip with his pants down.

The Mission: The Sea Awaits

He flipped through the menu after ordering a Coke. Glancing around the crowded sports bar and grill, he noticed a large line forming at the door. Ninety percent white collar business people from local offices on their lunch. It's a good thing he got here early; otherwise he would have been looking at a minimum of one hour for lunch, not including drive time. Too long for Chip's schedule. He saw his friend Dave approach, looking thoroughly disgruntled. Chip had known Dave since freshmen year of high school, sixteen years now.

"Those bastards," Dave said, seating himself.

"And that would be your term of endearment for…" Chip asked.

"My damn customer…Hi, how are ya. I'll have a Coke , please…" he said, completely changing his demeanor and smiling at the waitress as she approached. As she walked away, he resumed his more abrasive tone. "Specifically, the buyer. I get so tired of these games sometimes. Day after day they jerk me around. I feel like I'm one of those guys that hands out towels in fancy restaurant bathrooms." And he added mockingly, "Done with your shit, sir? Care for a mint? One day I'm gonna walk into the buyer's office, open up his little book of purchase orders neatly on his little desk and piss on it."

"After they fire you, you can come and work for me. I'll need a good Sales Manager."

"I see. Well that gives me a warm fuzzy. Have you found the magical job where you're going to be rich, challenged, have fun, be happy…" Dave asked sarcastically.

"Are you happy with your job?" Chip asked, ignoring the tone.

"I love my job," Dave answered defensively.

"It doesn't sound like you love it," Chip challenged.

Dave shrugged and rolled his eyes looking to heaven for patience. "Some days are better than others. That's life, my friend. Some ups, some downs, all jobs, everywhere. You take the good with the bad. No job is perfect, no wife is perfect, no house…"

Chip only sighed.

"Tell me you know this. At thirty years old, please tell me you know this."

"Ok! Don't get your panties in a bunch. I know it. I just have this nagging feeling that I might be happier doing something else fifty hours a week instead of what I'm doing now. I keep thinking about starting my own business. Do something on my own…you know…me against the world. It's just been occurring to me more and more that I might be a lot happier if I worked for myself. I'm getting tired of busting my ass so somebody else can make money," Chip asserted.

"Then go do it. What's holding you back?" Dave asked curiously.

"I'm not exactly sure what it is I want to do. I've had a few ideas, but nothing I can really sink my teeth into. At least nothing I can survive on. I just know that I don't want to work for someone else the rest of my life," Chip said. "Now tell me you haven't thought about doing the same thing."

Dave submitted. "I have, especially on days like today. But I know that the grass isn't always greener. I know I'd have to work a lot more hours than I do now. Even if you hire people, you can't count on somebody else to run your business right out of the gate, if ever. You can't count on anyone but yourself. Remember, if you're not there, they're stealing from you. They're either taking product, cash or doing something other than the work they're being paid to do. They don't have the same investment that you have. If things go belly-up, what do they care? It's not their business, they'll just go find another job."

"Now there's an optimistic view of your fellow man."

"It's true and you know it. When I delegate some assignment at work now, it's like pulling teeth to get things done and I'm supposedly dealing with professionals at a big company," Dave said.

Chip pondered the argument as Dave continued. "You'd also make less money, at least for the first few years. And that nice little 401k plan you have, kiss that goodbye. I mean, think of this, you're putting in ten percent of your salary and your company is matching ten percent of that amount. Now that's on the low side; get into a bigger company and maybe they'll match upwards of sixty percent of that first ten percent. That's what I'm getting."

"Good point," Chip conceded.

"And you would be taking your work home with you every night…every single night. I have to believe there'd be a whole lot more stress in my life, less stability, and less certainty if I had my own business. Look, overall I enjoy the work that I do. Sure I get frustrated occasionally, but that's a function of dealing with other human beings, not of having a particular job. And when things get out of control at work, I can turn it off and go home for the weekend or take a couple vacation days. When you have your own business, you can't do that."

"You really think there's more certainty working in automotive? After all these layoffs everywhere? A lot of them white collar layoffs I would remind you. And not just the early retirement crowd either, some of the people I've heard about are new hires at some of these companies. You can't expect to be safe and secure anywhere, anymore. The company's gonna cut you loose at any minute it suits them. There's no loyalty on either side," Chip added.

Dave shook his head. "You know as well as I do that a large part of those layoffs are house cleaning. House cleaning under the guise of cost cutting. It's true that a few good people will get caught up in the net, but for the most part, the company is getting rid of dead weight. The bottom line is, if you're bringing something to the table, if you're valuable to the right people, you're safe."

Chip looked at his friend skeptically as Dave proceeded. "Maybe safe is the wrong word. I agree you're not really safe anywhere. But then again, somebody like you or me, I doubt we're in jeopardy of being completely taken by surprise and escorted out of the building some Friday afternoon. C'mon, are you gonna tell me that the company you're at now would ever get rid of you, let alone walk you to the door. You're way too valuable."

"But not irreplaceable," Chip interrupted.

"First, nobody is irreplaceable but you are not easily replaceable and somebody has to stick around to do the work. Second, they like you. And third, if they were going to get rid of you, chances are you would know that you had it coming."

"How would you know? You wouldn't necessarily know."

Dave nodded his head. "You'd know. Nassar knew. Deep down they all know. If they don't, then they're stupid and should be fired anyway."

It was Chip's turn to roll his eyes.

"That last layoff you guys had, you said yourself that out of the six people let go, only one of them was worth anything and he pissed off the head guy. Right?" Dave said.

"You're right," Chip conceded the point but continued to push the issue. "All I'm saying is that you are in greater control of your destiny when you work for yourself. You're not answering to anyone but yourself and your customer. You set the direction, the tone, the pace. No matter how much somebody likes their job, no matter how nice your boss is, in the end you do what you're told, you head for the door or you sit around being miserable. It's different when you're steering the ship."

"Okay, it's true that if you're not the lead dog, the scenery never changes. But don't kid yourself into thinking that a small business is the way to go, my friend. Most new businesses, and I'm talking upwards of eighty percent, fail in the first year or two. Everyone knows this, including the banks that are going to ask for some major collateral for a loan."

"Yeah, but the other twenty percent go on to be millionaires," Chip said quickly.

Dave sighed, ignoring Chip's statement. "And that little comment you threw in about answering to the customer, don't undervalue that little perk you have now working for someone else. Don't underestimate the value of being able to pass the buck when the shit really hits the fan. I mean really hits the fan. Working for someone else offers that kind of shelter. When you're steering the ship, its you battling the typhoon buddy. You're the one who's going to get wet. There is absolutely no one else to turn to."

Chip had no comment. He had heard these arguments before and knew there was some truth to everything Dave had said. But still there was that nagging at the back of Chip's mind. A little voice that said, don't be afraid, you can do it; leave the safety of the shore, sail into the unknown.

"Don't condemn the entire job market just because the particular job you're doing at the moment is wearing you down. I promise you, in six months you'll have a new job, more money, you'll be getting into it and we'll both have forgotten that we even had this conversation. What you need is a change ...and I'm not talking about the kind of change where you put your house up as collateral for a small business loan so you can finance a coffee shop that will likely close up in less than a year. I'm talking about a new job where you feel challenged and you've got at least a little room to grow. If you had a worthwhile change like that your outlook would improve," Dave said.

"My outlook is good now. I don't hate my job either. But the things I don't like about my job are common to every job where I have to answer to someone. If I'm going to put in the hours, the hard work, the pain, then I want to know that the payoff is going into my pocket and not someone else's," said Chip.

"You worry too much. Be happy. Be grateful for what you've got. You have a good job, you've got a nice woman, you're finishing your MBA, life is good," Dave said enthusiastically. "I'm telling ya, you need a change of scenery. You could easily get another fifteen or twenty grand on your salary if you moved to a bigger company. Plus, you would have more room to maneuver, more room to grow, better benefits... Isn't that why you're going for the MBA? How many times have you lectured me on using that degree as a tool to move ahead financially?"

"Often," Chip said. He envisioned another fifteen thousand on his salary, an increase that would certainly come in handy: money for the honeymoon, money to reduce his debt, money for his and Stacy's new house, more money for retirement, and on and on he dreamed. He certainly wouldn't see that kind of jump in pay starting his own business. In fact, he guessed, he would probably see a major reduction in pay, at least for the first few years. And if he stayed where he was, it could take years to reach an extra fifteen thousand.

"So what's all this crap about dropping everything you've worked so hard for and going in a completely different direction. Give it some time to see the fruits of your labor. You're almost at the end of the road and just when the payoff is going to take place, you want to bail on the plan. Be patient. That's it! You lack patience," Dave said emphatically.

"I have as much patience as you do."

"You probably have more," Dave laughed.

"You think an extra fifteen to twenty grand is possible?" Chip asked, knowing the answer already.

"I'm living proof, you know that. A full twenty may be a little stretch. Fifteen would be easy."

Chip considered the possibilities. It sure would be nice to have that little extra in the paycheck…

"Did you start classes already? This is the last semester right?" Dave asked, abruptly switching topics.

"Last semester…" Chip nodded. "Classes start tonight. Business Policy on Mondays, Marketing on Wednesdays."

"See? The light at the end of the tunnel."

Chip thought for a moment. "You're right. I'm pissing away my time chasing this self employment nonsense. And I did think of that. I've been getting back into search mode," Chip said, moving the conversation back to employers.

"Now we're getting somewhere. So how goes the search?" asked Dave.

"Ok. I need to spend more time on it though. I spent part of yesterday doing some searching," Chip said.

"Anything promising?"

"A few that looked…okay. I sent out three resumes to headhunters and another four directly to companies, nothing that really grabbed me though."

"Where did you search? How did you get the leads?" Dave asked, looking somewhat concerned.

"All the company postings and one of the headhunter ads I got from the Internet."

"That is so barbaric," Dave said, looking repulsed.

"Uh huh. And what exactly does that mean?" Chip said, somewhat irritated that his plan of action was being challenged, despite agreeing with the challenge.

"How many people worldwide do you think responded to those ads that everyone and all their friends saw?" Dave asked.

Chip paused. There could be just a couple, then again there might be thousands. "Not all those people are qualified," he defended weakly.

"Fair enough. Have you gotten any bites?" Dave said, dropping the challenge, evidently tired of the pursuit.

Michael F. Goyette

"One from a company I responded to a week ago. Selling something," Chip said, mumbling the last words.

Dave stared at him in disbelief. "You're going on the interview and you don't know what the job is for?" he asked, shocked and concerned.

"Yeah" Chip said smiling.

"You're not serious are you?" Dave asked.

Chip laughed.

"You're not serious. Why are you jerking around with jobs you know you're not going to take?" Dave asked, shaking his head.

"I wanted to see what was out there. I haven't had an interview in years. I look at this as a warm up, a little stretch before the big game," Chip replied.

"Oh," Dave said, looking somewhat relieved. "Well here's a question to keep in mind when you're warming up. Every job has its bad days. Every job. Ask them to describe what that bad day looks like. Does a bad day include more political infighting? Does a bad day involve the same unhappy customer who calls every week? Does it involve you explaining to the customer why your shipment is late? I was interviewing someone the other day and they asked me that question. I thought it was a pretty good question. Their response or lack thereof can tell you a lot."

"Good idea," Chip said.

The waitress refilled their drinks and took their order.

"You know what bothers me the most about interviewing?" Chip asked. Dave shook his head while sipping his drink. "I feel like I'm voluntarily putting myself under a microscope and saying 'look at me and judge whether or not I'm good enough to join your little team'. I feel like I'm in high school again trying to get a date."

Dave was shaking his head vehemently. "Don't look at it that way. Look at it as a conversation between equals where you are both trying to determine if there is a match. You need to find out as much about them as they do about you. Remember, they want to make sure they hire the right person for the job. It's in their best interest to see if there is a legitimate fit. And you have to show that same kind of diligence. You owe it to yourself to make sure the fit is valid. And that's different from just selling yourself. Turn it around and make them show you why you should grace them with your talent," Dave suggested.

"You think that will work?" Chip asked.

"Sure, why not? Go in with a little attitude. Nothing too pushy, just assertive. Remember, looking too confident is better than looking too desperate. Just like getting a date. No worthwhile babe wants to date a desperate guy. You know that… from high-school," Dave said laughing.

"Shut up," Chip responded, as Dave laughed louder.

Dave made a face like he was going to cry, sniffling slightly for effect. "Hello, my name is Chip. I love you. Will you please hire me?"

"You bastard," was Chip's only response.

"All right. So let's bring closure to this discussion. This is your mission my friend: Stop your belly aching, find something you love to do, and go do it. And you can start by finding a new job at a bigger company for more money. You're the man. Give'em hell!"

Case Study On What <u>Not</u> To Do: North South Air

Hard times. A somber mood. The few around the table who had been there awhile were numb. They sat expressionless waiting for the next wave of bad news, the next axe to fall. Many had already jumped ship. Some had packed their parachutes and were waiting for the right moment to jump. Some were just waiting. For what exactly, no one seemed to be able to say. A miracle turnaround? Some divine intervention that would alter the course of the airline to a brighter horizon? A headhunter to call and hand them a new tomorrow? No one knew for sure, but there they sat…just waiting. Some were bitter. How unfair that they should have to be put through this. How unjust! They didn't deserve this! It didn't used to be like this. Return the cheese they cried in unison, return the cheese!

A small, but growing few were enthusiastic about their future. For the most part, these people had been brought in immediately following a massive house cleaning. The house cleaning couldn't be avoided. After all, the airline was having a lot of problems, problems which were clearly caused by the previous regime and therefore could be solved by eliminating those decision-makers. The dinosaurs were replaced with fresh, new minds filled with new, diverse ideas. People who cast aside the old, people who thought outside of the box.

Of course, the team had one thing in common, they were all still employed at North South Air. Despite the company's struggles to maintain its very existence, they were still there and had not yet moved on. Most of the others with any kind of foresight had left.

But now, just as it seemed inevitable that the doors would close permanently, North South came under new management, hand picked by the board of directors. A President, fresh from over twenty years in the Automotive Industry. He knew that cost cutting was the only way to survive. A Vice President of Operations, straight from the Pharmaceutical Industry. "R&D" she chanted, "R&D! R&D will save the day". A Vice President of Finance, direct from Wall Street. "Do what you will" he said, looking down at the others, "…just give me the bottom line and returns I want. We need to maximize shareholder wealth."

They were only missing some market insight. Easily corrected they knew. Simply outsource it.

It was the dream team if there ever was one. Maybe this was the change that some were waiting for. Maybe these three would deliver the company from disaster. Of course, aside from their experience flying from point A to point B, the three had no experience with managing an airline. The three were all seasoned veterans in their respective industries. And since they were successful there, then it only followed that they should have no problem being successful here. After all, it was just another business. Didn't the principles of sound business apply? However, being the cautious and prudent business individuals they were, they had taken a number of steps to help ensure their success.

First, they hired a General Manager to run the day-to-day operations, enabling them time to focus on the big picture. The headhunter they went through to hire their manager assured them that this guy, Bob Gibbons, was the right guy for the job. "If you think I'm good, wait'll you get a load of Bob. You ain't seen nothing yet!" the headhunter had promised passionately. Bob was an MBA with 15 years experience in the airline industry and according to the headhunter, could do anything. So for a small fee of $45,000 to the headhunter and a salary of only $94,000 per year for the new guy, the trio had themselves another savior.

The Vice President of Operations was skeptical. The salary seemed somewhat low. "For a guy that's supposed to be this great, you would think he would command a higher salary. Is that salary in line with others in the industry?" she asked.

"Bob's philosophy is that he shouldn't be making millions while the company is hurting financially and we're laying people off. He says he's willing to sacrifice his own salary for the first couple years until we're on our feet. His comment was something to the effect that these presidents and CEO's that made a fortune off the backs of others made him sick. He's a very grass roots, practical kind of guy. He could be a great PR tool," responded the President.

With no objection from the VP of Finance, North South had a new GM.

Then came the task of defining the market environment. The new leadership was sure this task could be outsourced. And so, under direct orders and only one week in his new position, the new General Manager hired BKR Marketing Services. The trio persuaded Bob to search out an objective marketing view. They told Bob that a full "market analysis" was needed to ensure success. They also indicated that they thought an experienced researcher should be able to complete an analysis of this nature in no more than two or three weeks. Although the new leaders weren't exactly sure what the marketing analysis would encompass or how it would help them once it was complete, they were certain of one thing – it was absolutely required in order to establish the strategic direction of the company.

Bob knew just the person to handle it – Barb Rawson. Bob knew 26 year old Barb from an advertising class he had taken during his MBA program. Barb had dazzled the instructor with her unorthodox concepts and eye-catching slogans. She had of course, received an "A" for her efforts. Inspired by her success in advertising class, Barb went on to establish her own consulting firm, whose mission was to save ailing companies through brilliantly conceived and flawlessly executed marketing strategies. Barb had been in business for almost a full year now, touting a pristine track record of success.

And so, six weeks after Bob was hired and a mere five weeks after BKR was contracted, a meeting of the minds was held at NSAir to discuss the future of the company. The three leaders and a number of key managers turned out for the unveiling of the new plan, the plan that would save them and catapult the company into undreamt financial success.

With both the numb and the energetic, the determined and the hopeless, the old and the new all present, the market research and strategic direction was defined.

"Thank you for coming to today's meeting," Bob began. "As you know, we have had some financial difficulties over the recent years. In fact, we were close to closing up shop completely just a few months ago. In response to this new competitive environment, we have enlisted the services of BKR Marketing. BKR has done extensive research in our industry and is here today to share their findings and make a number of recommendations to help us define our path. I'll let Barb tell you a little about herself and some of her past successes. Barb, the helm is yours."

With a simultaneous smile, wink, and nod at Barb, Bob surrendered the spotlight and let everyone know, in the cheesiest possible way, that Barb was "The Woman".

Confidently, she took center stage. Her brilliant smile, the bright clothes she wore, the bounce in her step, and her tone cried out, "Look at me!"

"Thanks, Bob. First, I'd like to welcome you all and thank you for letting us be a part of your new beginning. After conducting extensive consumer marketing research over the last few weeks, I'm convinced that you folks have a great chance of being a dominant player in this market. Like Bob said, I'm Barb Rawson and this is my partner Paul Copowitz. Paul and I studied together in the Master's program. Paul is currently doing extensive research and pursuing his PhD in Marketing," Barb said, fully anticipating a round of ooh's and aah's, which, much to her dismay, never materialized.

Barb continued and summarized for the group her background in marketing research, advertising, and sales. She listed all the classes she had personally taken in these areas and even had a handout showing her grades in each class. Having firmly established herself as the resident marketing expert, she unveiled her findings and outlined the obvious solutions to all of NSAir's problems.

"You'll find attached a summary of the findings we uncovered. So often consulting firms point out the problems and rarely offer solutions specific to your needs. You won't find that with BKR Marketing. For each finding, we have a recommended course of action that is very specific. In fact, we will, over the course of the next few weeks, outline a specific strategy and assist you in its implementation. We don't just fix problems, we find solutions – marketing solutions," she said triumphantly, throwing her chest out and looking into the distance.

The President glanced down at Barb's business card. Her message was reinforced in brilliant colors and dramatic script...

BKR Marketing
The marketing solutions people.

Barb began to outline her findings one by one, articulating each as if it were an ancient prophecy handed down through the millennium, with the sole purpose of making its way to the present in order to deliver NSAir from its current financial bondage.

Finding 1 – Substandard Customer Service

"The first thing we discovered was that people feel they are not treated with respect when flying. Typical customers feel like the airline doesn't care about their needs. They have somewhere to be at a certain time. The airline doesn't care. They are uncomfortable in their tiny seat. The airline doesn't care. They are tired from a busy day of business travel. The airline doesn't care. This is a common complaint in the service industry. And isn't that reasonable? Think of your own situation, aren't you put off by someone at the ticket counter who seems like they don't care that your flight was delayed or canceled?"

Slowly, lights began to go on in the minds of the group. Nods of approval cascaded throughout the room. Surely these were reasonable and truthful statements.

"We think the solution to this problem is really very straight forward," Barb said.

Recommendation for Finding 1: Slogan campaign – Tell me, I Care

"You need to show you care about your customer," Barb proceeded to describe. "The customer feels like they are treated like a number, like their business doesn't matter, like they can easily be replaced. The customer does not feel like their needs are being addressed. This is an obvious problem with what I consider to be an obvious solution. We developed a new slogan to overcome this perception: "Tell

Me, I Care." "I Care" will tell the customer that…well…you care," Barb said, smiling brightly, tilting her head to one side.

The heads in the room nodded. All was being made clear. If only NSAir had gone through this exercise earlier. If only they had found Barb sooner.

Riding her wave of glory, Barb continued. "Notice our choice of words…'Tell Me, I Care.' To care is not enough. You need to let the customer know they can talk to you. You need to let them know that you feel their pain. When they hurt, you hurt. You need to say to them, 'Tell me, I'm there for you' and they will open up. And when they do that, they don't feel so much like a number anymore." Barb looked in the distance again, seeing the brighter tomorrow. "The slogan will be prominently displayed at every terminal, on every brochure, in every advertisement. Everyone will have a pin with the slogan, to reach out to everyone they meet."

Finding 2 – Product Offering

There seems to be confusion with the customers regarding our routes. Many customers don't understand that we offer international travel to both Canada and Mexico.

Recommendation for Finding 2: Slogan campaign – We fly both ways

"This one is self explanatory," she said, seeing no need to elaborate further.

Finding 3 – Airline Name

"We need something exotic. There is a tremendous amount of competition these days to grab the attention of folks," Barb said. "We see an opportunity for differentiation through the product name.

Recommendation for Finding 3: New Name

"We propose a new name for the airline. Something trendy, European sounding. Something with pizzazz. We give you…" Barb walked to an easel covered with a large sheet. She grabbed the sheet and dramatically pulled it away, revealing a large poster board with the airline's new name. The name was written in brilliant colors and dramatic script, the combination of which conjured pictures of a twisted, nightmarish carnival out of a Stephen King novel. Each letter was colored differently leaving one on sensory overload.

P̲i̲ ̲a̲Z̲a̲ Airlines

"…Pizaza Airlines!" Barb finished.

Before the room had time to react, Barb was on to her fourth and final finding. Hit them with everything at once, she thought. Don't give them time to even think.

Finding 4 – Lighthearted Approach

"Finally, people are still nervous about flying. We need to help them relax. The best way to do this is through humor. Like Southwest used to do. Their use of humor not only attracted customers but made the customers' flying experience a joyful one. They backed off of that after the events of September 11, but we think it's time to reinstitute some of their great ideas."

Barb's partner Paul sat quietly through the entire presentation, smirking at his audience. He nodded knowingly, understanding that these poor sheep were lost and were now being shown the way.

The Vice President of Finance interjected. "Isn't that somewhat risky. It may be a little early to bring humor back into flying. Aren't people still a little to nervous for that yet?"

"That's exactly why we should do it now. We need to be the first back to market and establish ourselves as the leader." Seeing that her words were not being fully embraced, she pushed forward. "I understand your concern, however, we have seen the results of a number of focus groups that suggest that people are ready for a little levity on the plane. To not add humor is a short-term approach. We need to think strategically, look over the next five to ten years. The airline that can establish a positive relationship and earn the flying public's trust first, will likely be able to dominate in the long run."

Barb continued for another hour summarizing findings, showing industry charts and graphs, outlining customer demographics, and concluding her information dump with a very glib, "Any questions?"

The pep talk appeared to have been effective. Her enthusiasm seemed contagious. The group had seemed to grow in its general approval. She thought she saw a final approval of her plan in the faces of those present. She thought for a moment that their eyes glimmered with hope. "But wait!" she said to herself, looking deep into the eyes of one or two of the team. A few stray hold-outs remained! And the President…no sign of acceptance or rejection. The deal had not been finalized. How could this be?! The hold-outs could ruin everything. They would raise objections. They would rock the boat. All her work could be defeated by these few nay-sayers. Their words would be a poison, sending death to her out of the box ideas. Couldn't they see the vision? The finish line was in sight. Would Barb stumble? Would she, could she convince them of the sheer, simple genius of her plan?

One of the younger managers, frustrated at the shallowness that he perceived existed in the presentation, put his thoughts before the jury. "I don't want to rain on this parade, but what about fixing some of the other problems. First, we have a shortage of pilots and crew, which constantly causes flight delays. We're always having mechanical problems with the planes, further delaying flights. For some inexplicable reason, we can't keep track of passenger tickets from the time of purchase to boarding. We're short staffed at ticket counters. The people we do have there are under-trained and overworked...I'm not sure that the solutions you've presented here today address any of these issues."

The group froze. Nervous glances could be seen around the room. Barb glared at the boat rocker. An unbeliever. How dare he! She felt her heart race.

The General Manager glanced at the President. "What are your thoughts?"

All eyes were fixated on him. He stared at the manager who had raised the objection. Without saying a word he began clapping; slowly, deliberately. A message sent to squash those who did not embrace the new beginning, the new ideas, the out of the box thinking.

A few started clapping with him. The clapping slowly grew in its intensity, growing into a thunderous roar. The team was cheering, shouting. "We can do this!" "We are number 1!" "Pizaza Airlines! Pizaza Airlines! We will find the cheese!" they chanted together. The team was fired up. A new battle in the skies would begin and the rejuvenated warriors were ready for it. Yes. This indeed was the sign they had waited for. Delivery to the Promised Land was at hand.

The manager who had voiced his objection quietly sank into the shadows, never to be heard from again.

Barb was radiant with pride. She had done it, once again. She had saved a company from almost certain death. She bowed as a tear of joy ran down her cheek.

Business Policy

Business Policy. One of the final classes of the MBA curriculum and in theory, the culmination of all the other courses. It would provide the student with the opportunity to use everything he had learned in all the other classes in "real life" scenarios. This was week one of a sixteen-week semester.

Chip arrived thirty minutes before class and settled himself into his desk to review his schedule for the upcoming week. The classroom slowly filled with an assortment of people: men and women, various races and colors. Almost everyone was dressed in what appeared to be white collar work clothes, predominantly business casual although he noted a large number of suits, ties, and jackets. At least a quarter of the people were talking on their cell phones while another quarter waded through their calendar or messages on their PDAs.

As seemed typical, the class was roughly half men, half women. Ages ran from the mid twenties to a few who might have been in their late forties or early fifties. This latter group always raised a question in Chip's mind. Why do something like this now? Why spend your entire day working and then go to school at night at this point in your life? Could it make that much of a difference to their salary? Would they learn anything really valuable from a textbook that twenty or thirty years of experience should have already taught them? Obviously, they could always learn something new, but why this format? Why not some very specific training on some specific topics? Chip remembered his undergraduate classes. He remembered learning a lot of things he hadn't known before. Then he remembered going into the workforce and forgetting most of those things since he didn't use any of them in his daily routine. In any event, Chip concluded these people must be getting something out of the program, otherwise they wouldn't be here.

The professor entered the room and greeted everyone with a friendly "Hello" and a "Sorry I'm late, I'm running a little behind schedule today." He removed his coat and immediately walked to the front of the podium.

"I'm Brian Simpson and this is Business Policy. Welcome," the professor started. "If you're not registered for this class, welcome, however you may want to find the class you are registered for," he said light-heartedly.

The professor looked to be in his early forties. He wore a mock turtleneck with a button down sweater vest, a pair of faded blue jeans and despite the below zero temperature, he wore sandals with no socks.

"Today we'll discuss some housekeeping issues: expectations (both yours and mine), the class structure, the grading policy, and a number of other detail items. I'll hand out a syllabus, which we can discuss. It's very straightforward, no surprises. But before we do that, I'd like to get started by talking about the MBA program overall. This university has been offering an MBA program 'at night' for a number of years now. As you know, although the classes are offered during the day at our main campuses, all classes are offered at night at our satellite locations in order to accommodate working professionals like many of you. The program is based on many assumptions about what you want. In structuring the classes, we have tried to keep in mind that most of you work during the day and many of you are sacrificing time away from your families or other priorities in your life in order to earn an MBA. In order for us to continue to provide a quality product that you are willing to obtain through sacrifice, we at the university need to have a clear understanding of your wants and needs. This understanding of wants and needs, by the way, is exactly the understanding that every organization needs to have when it presents a product or service offering to its customers. At least, it needs to have it if it is going to succeed," he said, moving to a table next to the podium. He sat on the table, crossing his legs, and resting his arms on them as if preparing to enter some meditative yoga trance.

"So, I would like to begin by posing two quick questions to you, my customers. Why did you take this class and why did you enter the MBA program? And this is not a 'can you read the professor's mind' exercise. I don't have a preconceived answer; I'm looking for your candid input. Although if history is any indication of the future, I suspect I know some of the answers we might hear today," said Professor Simpson.

A woman in her early twenties, three rows away from Chip, raised her hand.

"Yes. What's your name?" asked the professor.

"Kimberly" replied the woman, bubbling with energy but camouflaged under a mask of extreme professionalism. Clearly, Kimberly was mentally prepared for another semester of academic challenges. She was dressed in a dark blue business suit, blonde hair down to her shoulders, with only a hint of light makeup. It appeared she had just come from an easy day at the office. Her hair was fully intact, clothes shown no sign of extended wear and her attitude…who could possibly have this much energy at the end of a work day, Chip wondered. Chip glanced around the room. Most of the faces were tired. Most of the clothes were wrinkled, showing they had been worn since early morning. The few that were dressed in suits had removed the jackets and loosened the ties.

Professor Simpson engaged Kimberly. "Kimberly, why did you take this class and why…"

Kimberly interrupted, not wanting to hear the remainder of the question. "Well, to answer your first question, I registered for this class because I wanted a class that would integrate everything I have learned over the past two years into a cohesive, hands-on, practical approach to succeeding in today's business environment," she answered with eyes distant, almost reading to herself. "In answer to your second question, I think it's important we get an appreciation of the experiences of other people so we can better ourselves and our work environments," she said, beaming with pride at her answer.

"Thank you Kimb…" Before the Professor could finish, Kimberly resumed her answer.

"Also, this experience teaches you to think outside the box. You learn to question traditional thinking and you learn to think problems through using very diverse ideas from people who may have different views than you. It's important to look at problems from different angles to find the best solution. And this environment is the perfect setting to do that in, where unique perspectives can flow freely, where all diverse ideas are valued and where you can really challenge the status quo," Kimberly finished.

Idiot in training, Chip thought to himself. It wasn't that anything she said was wrong, per se, it was more in the presentation; trite, scripted, rehearsed; perfect for towing the company line and *not* thinking outside the box. In fact, he thought he had seen her first answer, close to verbatim, in the course description. Her message walked the straight and narrow path, following exactly what a university professor or maybe the MBA program advertisements laid before her. Or maybe that was the pitch she would use in front of a potential employer. Not a bad tactic, he considered. It was difficult to pinpoint the exact source of the perceived rigidity of her speech, but Chip was sure of one thing, in their desperate attempt to be inclusive, her words left him with the impression that any ideas deviating from the strict party line would be rejected outright. Indeed, they would likely be met with hostile rebuttal if significantly different.

Professor Simpson responded, smiling politely and in a mild tone, "Thank you, Kimberly. Anyone else?"

Kimberly showed an expression of mild disbelief. How could an educated man like this Professor Simpson apparently not grasp the complete depth and breadth of her answer and seemingly show no interest in exploring it further through detailed discussion and analysis. Surely there must be something wrong with him.

Chip opted to share his own view of the MBA program. Raising his hand, the Professor acknowledged him. "Yes. What's your name?"

"Chip Weatherbe."

"Why did you register for this class and why are you in the MBA program?" repeated the professor, appearing thankful that Chip did not interrupt.

"Because it was required and to add twenty grand to my salary," Chip said. Half the class chuckled lightly and nodded, a few "Amen's" and "that's it" cascaded throughout the room. The other half of the class maintained frozen stares, completely unamused by his apparently flippant comment.

The professor smiled and pressed forward, evidently interested in exploring this answer. "Ah, a pragmatist. Let's open a dialog and examine your second answer. What makes you believe that getting an MBA will achieve 'twenty grand' as you put it?"

Chip shared his thoughts: his view on using the three letters, MBA to assist in advancing financially.

Kimberly was appalled and decided it was time to jump into the fray. "That is so shallow and I think typical of a lot of people who don't take these classes very seriously. You shouldn't even be here if you feel that way. That type of attitude lessens the credibility of the program. I also think self-improvement is a very common goal for people in this program. People who are looking for an enriching and diverse life experience. I, for one, take this very seriously and think there is a tremendous amount of value in this program."

"So do I," Chip replied, "At least twenty grand worth of value."

A few 'You're too low' and 'Raise your expectations' comments could be heard through light laughter.

As Kimberly was about to retort, Chip pushed on. "And...One of the ways to measure how serious someone is about a degree like this, especially one you earn after work, is to identify what they have to sacrifice in order to achieve their goal. In that light, I'll bet I'm sacrificing just as much as you are in order to get this degree and therefore I'm just as serious." A passing thought hit Chip which he decided to explore. "I mean, we're both sacrificing fairly precious "after work" hours to pursue this degree right?"

Kimberly stared at Chip, offering no verbal response. Her clenched jaw and glare spoke volumes. Chip continued. "What I mean is, we both work a typical, grinding nine or ten hours a day before we do this at night, right?" Chip nodded trying to solicit a response. "You have a regular day job right?"

Her glare intensified. "If your question is, do I work for a living, the answer is yes. I work very hard during the day. I've just chosen to focus my efforts during the day on completing this degree. Keeping your focus is important in today's business environment," she said harshly.

"So is multi-tasking," Chip added quickly. A full time student. No wonder she's so bubbly at this time of day, thought Chip as he continued his discussion. "And you don't always have the luxury to focus like a laser on one problem or issue at a time. Sometimes you have to juggle multiple activities. But on to your other point, in terms of self improvement, I can think of a lot of other ways that are cheaper, more efficient, and have just as good or better results other than the MBA program to 'improve' myself."

The professor interjected. "If I could step in and play Devil's advocate for a moment, Chip, I'm sure there are numerous reasons why someone would enter the MBA program. Isn't it conceivable and indeed probable that someone has chosen this path in order to enrich their life and 'better' themselves, if you'll allow me to use such a subjective, ambiguous term?"

"No question that it's conceivable but I'm not so sure it's probable. This program isn't cheap and it takes a lot of time to do a decent job. There is a large investment of time and money. Now, I'm not a finance guy, but I'm thinking there's gotta be a major payoff somewhere. So when you start talking about self improvement as the return on investment...it just seems a little too idealistic in light of all the other avenues you could choose for self improvement. I mean, there better be a lot of improvement for the time and money spent. I suppose it's conceivable that if you have a lot of spare money and time, your acceptable return might be somewhat low but I doubt that's probable."

"Doesn't your company pay for the program?" the professor asked.

"Yes, but I'm taxed on it and my company does expect a payoff in the form of better ideas, more productivity, better problem solving...something. And then there is still the issue of time which I think is somewhat precious to just about everyone."

Kimberly was beside herself. The comments she was hearing were too outrageous for her to not respond. How could she tolerate such unorthodox views, knowing how wrong they were? "These classes give you information that you need in the business world. These classes teach you how to solve problems so that when you're done, you can outperform those who haven't taken the classes. You gain experiences that you may never otherwise get. You learn to think and to appreciate different, diverse ideas."

"I agree that you expand your experience base by examining other people's experiences. I agree that you can get good "technical" information that is useful and I believe you broaden your view and problem solving ability by sharing ideas with others who may have a different view. All I am suggesting is that all these things contribute to you achieving more money. Further, I would suggest that the case work we do is done in a vacuum where we can choose to disregard variables that we don't like and "focus" on one thing at a time. The real world doesn't work like that. Variables come out of nowhere that demand your attention. Often, solving these problems has no upside while leaving them unchecked creates a tremendous downside. You don't get a real feel from case studies about what it is like to be in that situation. Now, case work is probably the next best thing to actually going through a situation, making it extremely valuable, but it is still a sheltered environment. So in terms of teaching you problem solving, it has its shortcomings. It is a good tool, a useful tool. But it is a tool to create dollars. With the competitive environment the way it is out there…with companies looking specifically to hire MBAs, getting this degree is a way to differentiate yourself from your competition in order to get an always limited resource…namely money. I cannot imagine how money wouldn't figure into the equation."

"There are other ways to make money, if that's your only goal," Kimberly added.

Chip hadn't really considered this argument, but rolled with the punch. "No, but it is a stable and conservative approach."

Wanting to regain control of the discussion direction, the professor again interjected. "We have tried to create a program that is marketable for people like Chip while at the same time making it a rich, enlightening experience for people like Kimberly…"

He continued to elaborate on drawing out customer needs.

"Unlike some of the other classes, there will not be regular tests or quizzes. There will be one final paper and presentation of that paper submitted at the end of the semester. It will be a team project and will represent seventy percent of your grade, with the presentation and paper carrying an equal weight of thirty-five percent each. The remaining thirty-percent of your grade will be based on class participation. Each class, we will have an open discussion on a particular topic…"

The Professor went on to describe the details of the class as Chip's thoughts drifted to his own situation. Kimberly was wrong. This was about making more money. Okay, maybe she got something out of this that went beyond a career tool, maybe everybody did. Great. It didn't change the fact that he needed this to compete for the dollars he sought. And if not this, then something else to differentiate himself; a higher degree in something, more training, connections… The self employment or come up with an idea no one else has thought of approach hadn't taken him anywhere. Better to take the safer path: higher education. The MBA just happened to be his poison of choice, he thought to himself.

Dave was right. Take this tool and run with it. Finish this endeavor, move to a new company, get a major bump in the paycheck and never look back.

No need to worry. Advancement would come. More money would come. Better benefits would come. Just keep working hard, put in the hours, pay the price now and something would come up.

The Tenacious Headhunter

The clock read 7:20 a.m. when Chip arrived at work. Running a little behind today; another late night on the phone with Stacy going over wedding plans and talking about their days. At 7:25 he received his first phone call, just the tip of the iceberg. The phone rang relentlessly after that, one customer after another. A spare part needed to be sent UPS same day, a customer line went down and they needed someone from service immediately, a quote needed to be e-mailed by noon in order to even be considered as a supplier. Overlapping the calls, an endless stream of people walking into Chip's office: we're late on a list of spare parts orders, we're late on a strategically key equipment order, we can't expedite parts from our suppliers since Jim (also known as the Purchasing Department) called in sick and no one else knows who to contact, where's my review, I need that presentation by today, and on and on. The next time Chip looked at the clock, it was 11:20 am. Another full morning. The time flew by virtually every day.

The job was okay, as far as jobs went. The pay was all right; not as much as he thought he was worth and not as much as he suspected the market would bear. The work was somewhat enjoyable and fairly important, being eighty percent customer interface work: quoting, presentations, phones calls, customer meetings, sales calls, as well as a host of other activities that would directly affect one of his automotive customers. The remaining time was spent on internal paperwork and meetings, most of which Chip was sure the organization could do without. What attracted Chip most to the job was the people he worked with and the overall environment. Although he was always to work early, if he needed to come in late, it was typically no problem. Leaving early occasionally or taking some last minute personal time never seemed to be an issue. He did his job as he saw fit and called his "boss" when he occasionally required some higher authority. When the boss did interject his thoughts and decisions it was always done in a spirit of team effort rather than a dictatorial mode. The overall flexibility was extremely enticing.

Michael F. Goyette

But despite all this, Chip wanted more. He worked hard every day. He occasionally worked long hours. He made a difference where he was. But after all was said and done, he was a big fish in a small pond. He couldn't help but think of other opportunities, other possibilities and ways to spend his work week, others ways to invest his hard work that might have a bigger payoff. Despite the flexibility and comfortable environment, Chip had his sights set on more money, more responsibility, more growth, a greater challenge, a reduced likelihood of closing up shop...basically a bigger, more stable pond.

And why not, he asked himself. Why shouldn't I push for something better, something more? I'm getting my MBA and I could be just as happy somewhere else making more money and growing in my career, he thought to himself. Besides, this is getting boring. He felt he could do his current job half asleep. I need to make a change now, so in five years I'm not still doing this same job with only a little additional pay.

At 11:30 sharp, the office cleared out, leaving Chip to himself for at least the next half-hour. Chip could feel the onslaught subsiding, a chance to catch his breath. In all likelihood, Chip could accomplish in the next thirty minutes more than he would the last two hours of Friday afternoon. What a morning. I have got to find something else, he thought again. This pace is insane; so much to do, in no time and with next to no resources. How could it get done? The same as it always got done; by doing the best you could with what you had. The same way he had been doing it now for over five years.

Someone, anyone, take me away from this. I'll take anything with more money and a change of scenery. Someone just please respond to one of my resumes.

At that moment, the phone rang. Chip laughed at the irony. My guardian angel no doubt.

"Chip Weatherbe speaking," Chip answered.

"Chip Weatherbe please," responded a gruff, assertive voice.

"Speaking," Chip said.

After a brief bout of coughing and hacking, the voice continued. "Chip, this is Bernard Jones of Bernard Jones and Associates. You can call me Bern, Chip. I got the resume you sent for the Sales and Marketing position," Bern said, talking a mile a minute.

Chip was stunned. A higher power must be listening. He became suddenly alert. Listening carefully, he prepared to put his best professional foot forward. First impressions are everything, make this count. Impress this guy.

The man on the other end of the line continued to cough. The rough voice reminded Chip of someone who had been smoking since he was seven years old. It sounded older, grandfatherly. A picture of the boxing coach from the movie "Rocky" entered Chip's mind and remained for the duration of the conversation.

Chip envisioned a short guy with a skullcap yelling, "You can take him, Chip, you can take him."

"Yes. Thanks for calling…" Before Chip could complete his thank you, Bern was off and running.

"Yeah. Chip, listen. Resumes are only used to weed people out. No one's ever been hired because of their resume. Lots of people have been put in the circular file because of it, but nobody's ever been hired. All those books out there about knocking 'em dead with a killer resume, it's all a bunch of crap. You know that don't ya Chip?" Bern asked, rhetorically.

Chip listened closely, trying to discern what Bern was talking about. He searched his mind, trying to remember the exact contents of the ad to which he had responded. He thought the way Bern had started the conversation was odd. Chip glanced around nervously to see if anyone was around to hear the conversation. Fortunately, there was not.

"Well, I…" Chip started to speak and was again abruptly interrupted.

"Yeah, listen. I think we can get ya into this company, Chip. But first we need to talk about a few things. So many kids go into interviews and screw 'em up. Ya gotta put your best foot forward, Chip. Nobody's gonna just hand you a job and say, 'Here it is'. Ya gotta fight for it. Now I'm gonna bend over backwards to fight with ya kid, but at some point you're gonna have to fight on your own," said Bern. Again, the vision of Rocky's coach filled Chip's mind.

Chip remembered sending his resume to Bern but couldn't recall if a specific position had been cited. Chip suspected that none was; he had a fairly clear memory of all the headhunters he had sent information to. Still, he couldn't be sure and didn't want to be caught in the middle of a lengthy discussion on the topic if people began returning from lunch early. Chip wanted to postpone the conversation to a more appropriate time when he wasn't surrounded by his boss or worse yet, coworkers. He tried to interrupt and propose another time for the discussion.

"Bern, can I call you back…" Chip started but Bern was still going strong.

"Chip, listen. This is a great opportunity. Do ya have a dark blue suit? You gotta look your best. When you look your best, you feel your best. You gotta look and feel confident. No earrings. You don't have an earring do you, Chip? Not one of those little hoop earrings. Every time I see a guy with one of those hoop earrings I think of a goddamn pirate. I keep looking for the parrot on his shoulder. Waiting to be boarded, all that kinda pirate stuff. Nobody wants to hire a pirate. You know what I'm talking about, don't ya, Chip?" Bern rambled.

Pirates? How did we get to pirates? What was this guy talking about? Chip was growing increasingly anxious and annoyed. He wanted to end the conversation and attempted another interruption.

"Excuse me, Bern…" Chip tried. Although Bern wouldn't let Chip finish a complete thought, he appeared to have read Chip's mind.

Michael F. Goyette

Bern continued. "Listen. I'll call you back later tonight. I know you're busy. Give me your number at home. No cell phone. I hate talking on those cell phones. You can never hear. Always breaking up," Bern said.

Bern accepted the number from Chip and as abruptly as the conversation had begun, it ended. It occurred to Chip that he had had a similar conversation with a used car salesman once. The word slime came immediately to Chip's thoughts and he couldn't escape the feeling that he needed a shower; no guardian angel, for certain.

His own words ran through his mind…someone, anyone, take me away…Chip had been right. "Something" had come up. Well, like they say, be careful what you wish for, you just might get it.

Business to Business Marketing

He strode down the hall, head held high, grinning inside, inspired by his own existence. If the world could bring forth a man like him, then there was indeed hope. He smiled inwardly that all these lost sheep had come to him for an education, for enlightenment. Come to him to tap his business knowledge and expertise. Come to him for his guidance. Guidance that he would only provide to a chosen few who would have to earn his wisdom.

Any of the common folk could read the textbook. But this was insufficient, only a piece of the puzzle which, by itself, could not possibly present the full depth and scope of the larger picture. Only his expert input could provide the all encompassing understanding that would be required to legitimately earn the title of MBA.

Of course, this true knowledge, this understanding of the business world could not be given away for free, lest where would the value be? How could he define the value of his real knowledge as anything above zero if it were just handed out, like a casual 'good morning'? No, his coveted information that these future MBAs sought would have to be worked for, they would have to sweat for it. Tears would need to be shed to acquire it. Leave the textbook to the forsaken, the great unwashed; those not worthy of his effort.

Exactly how the wisdom was earned was another matter. The 'how to' was an enigma to the vast majority of students. How did you get him to share his secret wisdom? There was no criteria, no path outside the syllabus to explain how to receive this wondrous gift of insight from the Teacher, and the syllabus seemed to fall short. Sure, some students occasionally stumbled across an approach that yielded favorable results. Some stayed after class, almost pleading for information. Some talked to him at the coffee machine at break, explaining at length how useful the information he had just covered would be to them at work. Some, he just took a liking to and allowed these fortunate, chosen few to find shelter under his wing.

If all else failed, there was always breast size. Large breast size to be specific. Red or blonde hair preferred, wedding ring optional.

He barely acknowledged most students as he passed, offering only a quick nod and sometimes not even that. Hello's evidently weren't to be given freely either.

The classroom door. He peered inside. My flock. His heart swelled with pride. Another group had again come to him. They were talking loudly as he stepped quietly closer to the door. Somewhere, in some dark, hidden recess of his mind, the talking was briefly translated into an ovation, thousands of grateful students cheering him for having the goodness and courage to stand before them and share his latest theory on business. Immediately, however, the illusion was dispelled, and replaced by a strong desire to instill discipline in his followers, to impose order on the environment. To send a message and let them know who was in charge.

The lights in the room turned on and off three times. The room fell silent. He smiled inwardly - they know to follow me, they always know.

"Did he just turn off the lights to get us to quiet down?" a lady sitting next to Chip whispered.

"Yes, he did. I feel like I'm in first grade again."

"I think this is going to be a long class," she said.

He marched to the front of the room, smiling arrogantly, even flirtatiously with the better-looking women in the room. "Let's have everyone's attention," he said, sizing up his new flock. "Everyone excited to be here? Try to stay focused on what I'm saying. I don't like repeating myself," the Professor began, taking his customary place at the front of the room.

Excited to be here? Chip glanced at the people around him who seemed to share puzzlement at the statement.

The Professor resembled Captain Kirk; Kirk in his older days, with a toupee plus ten pounds. Chip estimated he was in his mid forties. He was dressed in khaki pants, a beige turtleneck sweater and a somewhat worn sport coat.

"I'm Doctor Roger Martin." Placing the appropriate stress on 'Doctor', he paused slightly, allowing them to digest the significance of his title, to feel the power it possessed. "I have a Ph.D. in Marketing and Economics and I've been teaching young minds like yours for the last decade."

Chip looked around the room. At least one third of the class appeared to be over forty. The youngest people in the room looked to be in their mid twenties.

The Doctor stood at the front of the class, placing a foot on an empty chair next to him and resting his arms on his knee. He smiled a knowing smile. He knew what they were going to say, he knew what they were thinking. He always knew. "I know some of your bodies are a little older, but your minds are still young and empty of real knowledge; that's why you're here. If your minds are filled with anything, they're likely to be cluttered with misinformation. You're aspiring MBAs and you seek the seed of business knowledge to be implanted by qualified, learned men such as myself. Most of you will take this knowledge and use it frivolously chasing the almighty dollar. Hopefully, some of you will use it for more noble purposes and perhaps even enter the world of academia one day. My goal will be to teach you to think. Specifically, to think strategically."

Finally, someone will teach me how to think, Chip laughed to himself. Thank God.

"My extensive education and academic experience puts me in a truly unique position to deliver…" the Professor began. Almost on queue, Chip began to tune out. His thoughts turned to work, to job hunting, to Stacy, to the wedding. It was so easy to tune out during most of these discussions. Occasionally, a discussion piqued his interest and might be found useful at work, although more often than not it seemed to be a lot of the same stuff. Stuff to learn for the test or to drop into the final presentation. Stuff that if the Professor saw you focusing on or at least mentioning would score you points. Maybe a third of what the Professor said was important to achieving this goal. Another third might actually be useful. The remainder was quickly forgotten and never missed.

He noted that he was much better at this perceived game now than he was as an undergraduate. He could listen for the key information, key words, key phrases and be no worse off than the gal (like Kimberly) next to him who wrote down and committed every detail to memory. No worse off at least, from a grade standpoint.

His thoughts turned to the call from the headhunter. No follow-up call as promised.

"…choose groups today…" the Professor continued. Chip made a quick note to himself…Choose group-today and switched quickly back to the headhunter, a multitasking trick he had honed at work after years of non-value added internal meetings.

Stacy had told him to forget about the headhunter. Based on the single fact that he had not called back as he said he would, she concluded that he could not be counted on and so, erase him from further discussions. Chip's knee jerk reaction was to agree. Why waste time with someone like that? Besides, he seemed very odd.

"…no midterm exam, but a final paper and presentation due April 25, as per the syllabus. I will however, meet with each group bi-weekly to review your work and guide your thought process…" Chip heard, taking a copy of the syllabus.

Still…why not hear him out. What could it hurt? Take a chance and see what happens. All that would be lost is maybe an hour of his time.

"…passing out an article on K-Mart…". Why always K-Mart, Chip wondered. Why did the professors seem to make a bee-line straight for K-Mart? The financially troubled company seemed to have been on the preferred target list since his undergraduate years. Although Enron and Tyco had recently popped on the radar screen, the punching bag of choice still seemed to be K-Mart. Chances were that Professor had used K-Mart in the past and was intimately familiar with different analyses' and conclusions offered by previous groups. That fact, combined with K-Marts problems and bad press provided the professor a perfect vantage point from which to cast stones at the ailing company, all the while keeping himself safe from the brighter students who might offer ideas he had never considered; a situation that would be completely unacceptable. Of course, he had likely used the case in classes other than Business to Business Marketing: Marketing 101, Business Policy, Advertising, Advanced Marketing. Hammering K-Mart could be done under numerous flags. Tying the company to the current course goals would rest on the shoulders of the students under the strategic guidance of the Professor.

Time crawled slowly forward into the third hour of class. It was now close to 8:30.

"...and select your groups now. Identify each group member on a piece of paper as well as your final presentation topic and submit it to me. I'll be the gatekeeper for final approvals. Once I provide my acceptance of your proposal, you can be excused for the night," said Doctor Martin.

Chip glanced around the room. The question was simple: whom do you want to see or communicate with for an hour or two over the next sixteen weeks? Wedged in that time frame you would also likely have a couple Sundays containing three or four hour blocks to either get things back on course or pore over the details of a final review.

The whole process of choosing a group was really a crapshoot. You never knew whom you were going to team up with. In all likelihood, you didn't know the people around you, so you grab the two to five people (depending on the designated group size) sitting closest to you and hope for the best. If you knew people in the class, you might be able to minimize your chances of creating a team that would consume all your free time or get entangled with individuals with whom you didn't see eye to eye.

The people you chose could be taking classes full time. They would likely have significant time to devote to these projects; evenings and weekends would more than likely be fair game. The people could be very detail oriented, wanting to review every comma and period contained in whatever paper or presentation was put together. They would likely propose meeting before or after class and probably once or twice on the weekends. Overkill as far as Chip was concerned.

Or maybe a couple in the group might consider themselves "managers", big on outlining plans and wanting to oversee the work in progress, but never really bringing anything of value to the table.

Of course, there was the outside chance, and it had happened before, that the group clicked immediately, the work was divided fairly, and the project came together with minimal meeting time. Chip was lucky enough to have been involved with groups of this nature three times during his MBA journey. This time, unfortunately, Chip didn't see anyone he knew or had worked with in the past. In that case...cross your fingers.

It's a Mad, Mad, Mad Business World

The ceiling was still, he noted while lying in bed staring; a static point of reference in a constantly changing world. A refreshing change. In spite of the perceived constant upheaval he saw everyday, he could always count on the ceiling every night. To be there, unmoved, unchanged.

What a stupid way to look at a ceiling. But then again, better than thinking about tomorrow, about another work week. The thought of another five-day grind tied his stomach in knots. It was Sunday night at 10:30 and another week sat looming, waiting to be embraced. The weekend had come and gone at a breakneck pace as usual. He had left Stacy's apartment an hour ago in order to give him a few minutes at home to adequately prepare for the upcoming week. The week-ends flew by and with the wedding preparations well under way, Saturdays and Sundays were little more than a blur.

Time to get some sleep.

Chip laid in his bed, contemplating how to slow down the progression of time and optimize the few moments a week he had to himself. Just as he turned out the light and began to dream, the phone rang.

"Hello?" Chip answered, waking suddenly.

"Chip Weatherbe please," said a gruff voice.

In an instant, Chip recognized the voice as Bern's. Chip wondered why a headhunter would be calling at 10:30 on a Sunday night, especially someone older like Bern. He must have achieved some level of success by that age to warrant not working on Sunday night. Was this what he had to look forward to after 35 years of hard work; working at 10:30 on Sunday night? Would every week for the next three decades fly by until one Sunday night he would find himself making phone calls at 10:30 at night for work? Didn't this guy have a wife to talk to? Kids? A hobby? A favorite TV show? Wasn't there anything else this guy could be doing on a Sunday night other than making these calls? Chip put these questions on the back burner for later analysis and refocused his attention back to the current conversation.

"Hi Bern, thanks for calling me..." Chip was cut off before he could finish; par for the course it seemed when talking to Bern.

"Chip, listen. I talked to the President of the company and he really wants to meet ya. Do ya have a navy blue suit? Wear a navy blue suit. You wanna look the part. Nice shoes too, wing tips. Wing tips are the only shoes to wear during an interview. Make sure they have a nice polish on 'em. They gotta shine. When they shine, you shine. I want you to go in Tuesday morning at 10:00..." Bern continued, when it occurred to Chip that this was only the second conversation he had had with Bern. Bern knew nothing about Chip other than what was on his resume. Furthermore, Chip knew nothing about the job (or Bern) other than the brief description in the newspaper. Chip decided it was time to take control of the discussion.

"Bern, can you tell me a little more about the job?" Chip asked. This was the first full sentence he had ever said to Bern. A sense of relief and accomplishment overwhelmed him.

"Chip, this job is for you. You know the only person qualified to do any job is the person doing it or the person who just got done doing it. Nobody else is qualified. Do you think anyone is really qualified to be President of the United States? Does anybody really know what it takes to be President of the United States other than the President himself or the guy who just got fired from being President? No! It's the same with every other job. You can do this job, Chip. You're just as qualified as anyone else going for it." Bern said.

A red flag went up in Chip's mind. It sounded like Bern had anticipated a negative reaction and was already addressing the objection. Chip couldn't decide if he was annoyed or entertained by the conversation. In any event the discussion had again moved to left field. He tried to regain focus.

"Bern, what exactly does the position entail?" Chip asked, becoming more aggressive with his tone.

"Chip, don't talk. Listen." It was apparent that Bern wanted to remain in the driver's seat.

"Okay."

"You're gonna be selling computer systems to the Big 3. Multimillion-dollar contracts. Big software systems, Chip. They're looking for a seasoned veteran. Someone who'll knock their socks off starting day one," Bern continued.

Chip had no experience selling computer software or hardware. Although he was confident he could learn, he wasn't sure he could hit the ground running. He decided to share his lack of credentials with Bern.

It was Chip's turn to interrupt. "Bern, in all candor, I don't have a lot of direct experience with selling software or hardware systems. I know I could learn..."

Bern tried to interrupt but Chip was ready and persisted, talking slightly louder to drown Bern out. "I know I could learn and I know I'd be good at it, but I'm not a seasoned veteran. If they're comfortable with that, I'm happy to talk to them," Chip finished.

Obviously the comments fell on deaf ears. Bern was relentless. He continued, "Chip, you gotta go in there and tell 'em, 'You ain't seen nothing yet'. You remember Al Jolson, Chip? He was before your time but Al Jolson used to say, 'You ain't seen nothing yet'! And that's what you're gonna tell 'em. 'You ain't seen nothing yet'! Says here on your resume that you're an MBA, right? I thought MBA's could do anything. Unless you know something I don't!"

"I'm finishing up my MBA and I'm not sure..." Chip said.

"Well that seems to be the problem! You're not sure of anything. You can do better than that, kid. If you're gonna walk the walk, you gotta talk the talk. Don't be afraid to step up to the plate kid," Bern lectured.

It was getting late and Chip had a long week ahead of him. The conversation seemed pointless. Chip made another desperate attempt to get back on track. Perhaps another angle might be the correct approach.

"What about salary and benefits, Bern? My fiancée and I are interested in the healthcare benefits offered," Chip inquired.

Bern exploded. "Chip, you can't let a woman tell ya how to run your career. My last five wives tried to do that. And I said no way! You gotta stand on your own at some point and lay down the law. You can't let your wife or mommy or daddy or friends tell you how to manage your career!"

The conversation had gone from mildly dumb to insane. Last five wives? How old was this guy? No wonder he's calling on Sunday night, Chip thought. And Bern's entire tone, how presumptuous! Chip knew it was not only time to end the conversation, but to end his short-lived relationship with Bern. It was clear that Bern was drunk, had a screw loose, or was very bored. Chip didn't really care which it was, as long as he could put some distance between himself and the tenacious headhunter. He decided to stretch the truth slightly.

"Bern, since I sent you the resume, my current employer has come through with a nice raise and promotion, so I think I'm set where I am for the next couple years," he explained.

Again Bern erupted. There seemed to be no end to his fiery effort. "Well, I wish you would have told me that! What the hell am I wasting my time for! I'm working for you, my friend. Now Chip, listen. Opportunities like this don't come along everyday! This guy I'm talking to, he ain't the type to sit around waiting for Chip Weatherbe to decide what to do with his life! And he sure as hell ain't gonna wait for your little honey to make up her little mind! This is the opportunity of a lifetime!"

Half believing at any moment that Rod Serling would step out of the closet with his cigarette burning to announce entry into the Twilight Zone and half believing that this was just a bad joke, Chip ended the conversation.

"Bern, I've got somebody at the door. Thanks for calling and keep me in mind for future opportunities. Thanks. Bye." With that, Chip hung up.

Somehow, Chip's life didn't seem quite so grinding after talking with Bern. In fact, it looked pretty good.

The Call

Time for lunch. Chip listened to his voice mail at home, looking for a response to any of his recent resumes he had sent. One new message: "Hi, my name is Terry Stilling from the Career Resource Development and Change Management Team at GIT. You recently responded to our opportunity listing for a Marketing Manager and I wanted to call you and set up a time for you to come in for an interview. If you are still interested in the position, please call me back at…"

Chip wrote down the number and decided to return the call offsite on his cell phone. Finally, a bite.

After driving to a nearby shopping center parking lot for a little privacy, he returned the call.

"GIT, Terry Stilling speaking."

"Hi Terry, this is Chip Weatherbe. I'm returning your call from earlier."

"Thanks for calling me back so quickly, Chip. You recently responded to our ad for a Marketing Manager. I wanted to see if we could set up a time for you to come in for an interview."

"Absolutely," Chip replied excitedly. Finally, someone showing interest. Marketing Manager – the title had a nice ring to it. And at a large company like GIT no less. The title would most likely come with real money, at least more than he was making now. It was a manager position, so no doubt he would have a team of people reporting to him. How many? Eight? Ten? Was it a Marketing Manager for all GIT products or just for a specific division or product line? Marketing Manager for all of GIT! What an opportunity. What a real salary!

But what about a Marketing job? Is that something he really wanted to do? What would it entail? Whatever it was, he was confident he could do the job.

Chip's mind raced as he tried to keep pace with the explosion of possibilities he saw before him. He could see everything falling neatly into place: a new challenging job, the money he was looking for, and he and Stacy could probably afford to move right after the wedding instead of waiting two or three years. The job might even require international travel. How would Stacy feel about that? If the money were right, she would get used to it. Didn't GIT have offices in Germany and Japan? Would he be in charge of worldwide marketing operations? Probably not, not with a title of Manager. Maybe that was the next step – Marketing Director of Worldwide Operations.

Or maybe he would spend time in marketing – a year or two – and then move into Sales Management.

Hadn't GIT had some financial difficulties recently?

Chip overwhelmed himself with possibility after possibility. The world was truly his oyster. The potential was blinding. So blinding in fact, that the questions about GIT's financial stability and his ponderance on what the job entailed, quickly disappeared from any further thought.

"How does Friday morning look like for you? Friday at 8:00?" Terry asked.

Chip quickly checked his palm pilot. A few meetings but nothing he couldn't skip. Looks like a vacation day.

"Friday at 8:00 a.m. looks good."

"Good. You'll meet with Rajiv Chopra and Kelly Hayman and possibly one other person. Come through the front lobby and call Rajiv when you arrive. Do you know where we're located? Take…"

Finally, progress, movement forward. He would finally be challenged and make some real money. He could finally set sail into an ocean of unknown, exploring a new job, a new career, a new company, and experience the financial and skill set growth that he knew he was destined to achieve.

Finally, the ship would leave the dock.

The Interview – Charge!

Chip pulled into the GIT parking lot at 7:50 a.m., just in time for his 8:00 interview. According to his human resource contact, he was to meet with his potential "boss", Rajiv Chopra, at 8:00 a.m. and Kelly Hayman at 9:00. He entered the building lobby at 7:55. The lobby was nicely decorated with two leather sofas and a leather chair surrounding a rectangular, very low, glass table. The day's edition of the Wall Street Journal lay on the table. There was no receptionist, only a note on the wall which read: **Please use the company directory to locate and phone your party. If you cannot find your party, dial "0" and the operator will assist you.** A small table with a beat up paper directory and a phone were located beneath the sign. A locked glass door lead to the office area. The lock was opened by a badge slide located on the wall next to the door.

Chip dialed Rajiv's number. No answer. He's likely getting his coffee or running a few minutes behind. When voice mail picked up, he left a message. "Hi Rajiv, this is Chip Weatherbe. It's about five minutes before 8:00. I wanted to let you know I'm in the lobby and ready to meet at your convenience. Thanks."

He seated himself and began glancing at the paper, pretending to read it. He stared blindly, running mentally over the interviewer's potential questions and his possible responses.

After some time, Chip glanced at his watch which read 8:05. Give him a couple of minutes. A man entered the lobby from the outside. Chip looked up anticipating that this was his contact. The man offered a brief 'morning', slid his ID badge through the lock and entered the office area.

8:10 a.m., no sign of Rajiv. Two more individuals entered from the outside. Chip looked up from his paper and greeted them with a quick nod and good morning.

8:13, still no Rajiv. Chip began to wonder if maybe he had gotten the time or day wrong, perhaps the wrong building. He put the paper down and pulled out his

PDA to verify. Indeed, according to his schedule, he was in the right place at the right time. What if I entered it on the wrong day initially, Chip thought to himself. There was no way to verify at this point. The original paper that the meeting was first written on was likely at the top of a landfill somewhere. He thought of calling his HR contact to verify the interview. A fairly drastic and potentially incorrect move if his new boss was just running a few minutes late he decided. Call the operator instead. No, give him a minute.

8:17. Chip walked over and dialed the phone. No answer. Give him until 8:30. And stop looking at your watch, he scolded himself, it's just an interview.

At 8:23, Chip checked his watch again. Damn it. It always seemed to Chip that the time leading up to big meetings, presentations, or in this case an interview, was the killer. The actual event itself was easy; it was all the mind games you played with yourself beforehand that wore you down. Waiting like this gave you to much time to wander from the original focus. Growing tired of waiting, Chip decided to push the situation forward. Someone must know this Rajiv guy. I'll just flag someone down and ask, he thought to himself.

He peered through the glass door leading to the office area. He saw a hallway leading some forty or fifty feet to what seemed to be a large open office area with multiple cubicles. Immediately on the other side of the door to the left he could see two cubicle walls about four and a half feet high, behind which, to the best of his view appeared to be two work areas. An opening between the two walls was clearly an entrance or exit, depending on which way you were going. He couldn't tell if anyone was sitting in the work area. Immediately on the right he saw what looked to be a reception desk with no occupant. Directly behind this was another cubicle wall, only this one taller at about six feet. Chip couldn't see much on the other side of the wall but assumed that an office was located there.

He gave a quick knock on the glass. At the cubicle to his left he noticed a woman's head slowly rising above the cubicle wall. The head only rose far enough for him to see the woman's eyes. She wore glasses and held a phone to her ear. After staring at him for a moment, her head quickly dropped behind the wall again.

All right, nobody wants to talk right now. Come on honey, be brave and open the door.

After another minute, the woman's head returned, this time rising well above the wall. The woman passed through the cubicle exit and walked toward Chip showing no emotion. She was attractive and tall at about 5'10" with blonde hair. She was dressed professionally in a woman's business suit and carried herself with poise. In her hand was a black Franklin Planner. She opened the door and smiled on command. "Hi, I'm Kelly Hayman. You must be Chip Weatherbe." Kelly said, shaking Chip's hand.

"Hi Kelly, nice to meet you," Chip replied with a smile.

"Have you been waiting here long?" she asked, dispassionately.

"Since 8:00. I thought the first meeting was at 8:00. According to the HR contact I was going to meet with..." Chip glanced at his palm pilot and searched for the name, despite already knowing it. "...Rajiv Chopra? Did I get the time or date wrong?" Chip asked lightheartedly.

Kelly responded coolly. "No, I'm sure you got it right. If it's okay we'll change the schedule slightly and you and I can meet now, before your meeting with Rajiv."

"No problem."

Kelly abruptly turned. "Let's see if we can find a conference room." Chip followed her a short distance past her apparent office. On the right, next to what appeared to be the reception desk, a room labeled CRA-4 sat empty.

Chip followed Kelly in and moved to the side of the table facing the door.

"Sorry to keep you waiting," she said, closing the door behind them and taking a seat. She showed little emotion while she removed his resume from her planner and began the interview.

"I have the resume you sent in...but maybe you can give me a summary and tell me a little about yourself," Kelly said.

Chip began reviewing his career and academic credentials, highlighting recent achievements and activities. He had what he felt was a successful eight years since graduating from college: a consistent rise in income and responsibility; enough underdog success stories to make himself sound interesting, even a few creative ideas that actually panned out into real business strategies. He spent the next ten minutes or so sharing this information with Kelly.

"...I've been at my current employer now for about five years..."

"Why are you leaving?" was Kelly's first question.

Direct and to the point, Chip thought. Now this is the kind of interview you can work with, get rid of the pleasantry questions and go straight to the heart of the matter: why are you leaving the job you're already at and why should I hire you? He also sensed a level of curiosity.

"The company I'm at has been great, but it's a somewhat small company; not much room for growth, financial or otherwise. So I guess I'm looking for a new challenge in an environment where I can grow a little."

"Exploring new lands..." Kelly said.

"Something like that," Chip replied.

"Why do you think this job will..." A knock on the door interrupted Kelly mid sentence. The door opened and a man entered. An Indian, on the shorter side, maybe 5'9", well dressed in business casual – trendy business casual – entered the room. The glasses on his boyish face added to a portrayal of intelligence. When he spoke, he carried an air of innocent charm, charisma and confidence.

"Sorry to interrupt," he said smiling.

"No problem," Kelly said, turning to face him. Chip noticed her attempt at a fabricated smile.

The man entered the room and offered his hand to Chip. "I'm Rajiv Chopra."

"Chip Weatherbe. Nice to meet you," he said, shaking Rajiv's hand.

"Whenever you're done here. I'd like to have a few minutes with Chip and get us back on schedule. I'll be in my office for the next half hour or so," Rajiv said.

Chip found Rajiv's tone and remarks somewhat odd. It almost seemed that Rajiv was suggesting that Kelly had somehow slowed the interview process and had gotten them off track. Kelly provided no indication that she heard this veiled accusation and responded politely "I'll let you know."

Rajiv paused for a second, staring at Kelly. For a brief second, Chip noticed a small change in Rajiv, in the eyes he thought to himself. A slight flare of irritation or annoyance. The first thought that came to Chip's mind was, he wants to rip her head off. He wondered why? Certainly Kelly's response was appropriate. Again, if Kelly saw the same change in Rajiv, she offered no sign. The whole exchange enabled Chip to catch a glimpse of something else in Rajiv, something behind the pretty boy face and harmless appearance, something buried beneath the surface, a sort of subtle manipulative, controlling approach fueled by a hidden anger. It was just a first impression based on nothing more than an initial, knee jerk feeling. Whether Chip saw it in his demeanor or heard it in his first few words, he couldn't say. In fact, that little something that was hiding was so obscure that Chip immediately silenced the faint voice at the back of his mind raising the question – what does this guy want from her?

"Let Gracie know," Rajiv said, sounding overly accommodating. And with a quick, and somewhat fake "thanks," Rajiv turned and walked out.

Kelly stared after Rajiv, wearing no emotion or expression. She slowly turned back to Chip, showing her consistent professional face. "Anyway…" she said looking down at her notes. "Do you have any other questions?"

Her tone was somewhat inconsistent with her expression and it was clear to Chip that there was some underlying tension or issue between her and Rajiv. Not that it mattered. Stay focused on the interview he thought to himself. Her question took him by surprise; they really hadn't discussed his abilities or the job content at all. She had been in mid sentence asking a question when Rajiv walked in. She now seemed content to abandon the discussion. Why was she cutting the interview so short? Time to investigate a little deeper. After all, if he was going to be working with her, this was a perfect opportunity to begin a meaningful dialog and get to know his potential coworker a little better. It would also be useful to have a little information about the job before talking to Rajiv.

"Can you describe the position? What are your expectations?" Chip asked.

"You'll be tracking cost, pricing, and margin information on all the products in our area. You'll also be tracking competitors and whatever information we have on their quotes..." Kelly trailed off somewhat and seemed to catch herself from saying something she shouldn't. "You'll be working for Rajiv so he can probably give you greater insight into what the roles and responsibilities are. I'm sure he'll outline his expectations."

What was the point of this interview, he wondered? It didn't seem that Kelly wanted to move forward with this discussion. Chip wasn't going to let her off that easy. He had spent a lot of time getting to this point and he was going to make sure the effort was worth his while.

"Okay. What can you tell me about GIT in general? How has your experience with the company been," Chip inquired.

The question seemed to take her off guard slightly. She began to say something, but stumbled. When she finally answered, her words were measured and precise. "Every job has its ups and downs, you just have to choose one that works for you. This one has worked for me," she said, closing her planner. Obviously, the conversation was over.

"Let me take you over to Rajiv," she said, standing up.

Chip followed her out of the conference room to Rajiv's office, some ten feet away and across from the work station where Kelly had originally appeared.

"Wait here," she said assertively, stopping next to the reception desk. Chip noticed a nameplate on the desk – Gracie Smyth. The chair sat empty, pushed in. Gracie apparently wasn't in yet this morning.

Chip heard Kelly talking to Rajiv, explaining that she could not find Gracie but that she had concluded her discussion.

"Great. Have him come in and sit down," Chip heard Rajiv reply.

Kelly emerged from the office and with a quick, "nice meeting you, you can go in," she walked down the hall and out of sight.

"Come in and have a seat," Rajiv said as Chip entered the cubicle. "I'll be with you in just a minute." He continued to shuffle through a number of papers on his desk, not bothering to look up.

"Looks like it's going to be a pretty nice day today," Chip said, trying to make small talk and break what seemed to be an eternity of silence.

Rajiv only stared at the paper in front of him and offered no reply, no acknowledgment that he had heard Chip speak.

When he did look up, he smiled graciously and chuckled, talking to Chip like he was an old friend he hadn't seen in months. "Sorry about that. There's always some crisis that needs addressing," he said. "I'm sure you know how that is."

Rajiv's demeanor and tone were naturally friendly, making Chip question his earlier impression. "I understand, I live with it everyday," Chip said.

The conversation rolled smoothly from there, creating a genuine, amicable dialog. Soon, Chip's earlier thoughts of Rajiv had faded. Rajiv's knowledge of his business was impressive. He knew his customer, he knew his competition, he knew his own company, the products, the structure, and the strategic direction. His talking about what he knew, asking Chip questions and attentively listening to the answers was all perfectly balanced. This guy knew his stuff. Chip could see why he had attained this respectable level at such a young age.

Their discussion primarily focused on Chip and his skills. Rajiv was encouraged that the MBA was close to completion and commended Chip for having the discipline to stick with the program in the evenings after work. Gradually, after about half an hour, the conversation began to come to a close when it occurred to Chip that he still didn't know a whole lot about the job, just scraps of information. It was time to dig a little deeper.

"Can you tell me a little more about the job? I think I understand from a broad perspective what the job entails, but can you give me any additional insight as to how you see the job fitting into the organization? Do you see the position growing..." Chip asked.

Rajiv nodded his understanding. "The position up to now has focused on activities that one might associate with a traditional Business Analyst – tracking our products as well as those of competitors, tracking market pricing, understanding our business, etc. We have a need to grow that position into something more. We need someone who will not only understand the nuts and bolts of GIT's business, but also be able to take that knowledge two or three steps further and understand what the market is doing by comparison and define our future direction. You will be responsible for setting a new course. I really see endless possibilities."

Rajiv's enthusiasm was contagious. Chip again saw unlimited potential. "Do you have any specific goals or plans in mind?" Chip asked.

"That's what a smart MBA like you is supposed to tell me," Rajiv said laughingly. "Where do you see yourself in the next two to three years?" he asked, abruptly veering from Chip's questioning.

"First, I see myself succeeding in this job; reaching the goals that we jointly set for the next twelve to eighteen months. You're hiring me to bring a specific value to the table, so in all fairness to you and GIT that should be my primary focus. In the future, once we grow this position, I can see myself possibly managing a team that might be dedicated to these pursuits and activities. Some type of customer interface position, possibly sales management is also a direction I would like to explore. For the immediate future however, I think it's reasonable to keep this position as the first priority," Chip said, watching carefully for Rajiv's reaction.

"That's good to hear. I see that as a prudent way to move forward. For now, you're going to be the Marketing Manager. Later, we certainly have room for you to move if that's the direction you desire. A sales type position may be a good fit," Rajiv said, rising and walking to the door. "I don't mean to cut this short but I have a meeting to run to. I'll have Kelly walk you to Human Reources. I think they have some paperwork they need you to complete," he said, rolling his eyes and patting Chip on the back. "Always bureaucratic paperwork."

Kelly appeared from her work area. "I'll take you over to HR."

Chip followed Kelly through what seemed to be a maze of hallways, often saying hello to some passerby. As they walked, Kelly described the areas they passed through, telling Chip what the department did, who ran it, and who she knew in that area. As she continued talking, Chip felt confident that things had gone well. He saw Kelly's informal tour of the office as a positive sign. Although he wondered if the job was something he really wanted to do, he decided that the growth potential was worth whatever temporary function he found himself in first. If he really hated what he was doing, it would only be for a while until he advanced or found another area in the organization that he liked better. This was just one small hoop he had to jump through to get what he wanted, he thought to himself. Wasn't it? Chip pushed that question to the back of his mind and tried to refocus on the conversation at hand.

"...this is the HR department. Janice Stalls is in charge of this group," Kelly said whispering. She glanced at Chip and smirked as if there was some inside joke she wanted to share but thought better of. For a second, she dropped her professional demeanor, a refreshing change.

They reached a small office at a corner of the building. There was no name on the open door. Kelly walked in while knocking. "Hi. We have an appointment with a Scott Snow in Human Resources this morning. Is this the correct office?"

A young man sitting behind the desk stood up to greet them as they entered. Chip wondered if was a new hire himself; he certainly didn't look old enough to have too many years of experience, appearing no older than nineteen, maybe twenty. "Actually we're not called HR any more. We are the Career Resource Development And Change Management Team. I think everyone should know that by now," he said with a smile and caustic edge in his voice. "But I think you've got the right place."

Kelly stared at him blankly, coldly. "Okay. Well, if we've got the right place then I'll leave you two alone. You can walk Chip to the main lobby when you're finished?" Kelly asked.

"Sure, no problem."

Kelly turned to Chip, smiling. Her expression had softened from the conversation with the HR guy. "It was a pleasure meeting you. I'll be in touch," she said as she walked away. Chip shook hands with Kelly and moved his attention back to the HR guy.

"Hi. Scott Snow. Nice to meet you," Scott said while extending a hand to Chip.

Chip responded in kind. "Hi. Chip Weatherbe." The Career Resource Development And Change Management Team, what an inflated title for Human Resources, he thought.

"Have a seat Chip," Scott said

Scott appeared to be very young, maybe one or two years out of college. He wasn't dressed in the standard "business casual" attire but wore a new, pristinely pressed olive colored suit, tie, starched white shirt and cuff links. His hair was perfectly styled, suggesting that considerable labor hours, gel, and possibly large amounts of hair spray were involved in creating the current effect.

His office was small, barely accommodating the desk and the two occupants. It looked like it may have been used at one point as a large storage closet. An older looking desktop computer sat on a thin work counter mounted to a partition standing against the back wall. Beyond this small counter, there was no real useful workspace.

A paper inserted in a clear plastic stand on the counter read:

GIT Core Values
Diversity
Tolerance
Harmonious union with the environment
Life Balance for all employees

"I know what you're thinking...the office is pretty small, right?" Scott asked, obviously noticing Chip's surveillance of the room.

"Not at all, it looks fine," Chip said politely.

"I'm moving tomorrow..." and after a dramatic pause added, "...in the window office immediately next to Janice." His remarks were clearly spoken to have an impact. He stared at Chip, looking for a response.

"Great," was all Chip could offer. He sensed that his statement was not the one Scott was seeking, owing to the look of slight annoyance on Scott's face.

"Janice is the Human Resource Director. I report directly to her and she reports directly to the Fausto Fernandez. I'll be sitting just down the hall from him. So I'm definitely somebody you want to stay on the good side of. Keep in mind, your future employment is in my hands," Scott added, laughing like he had just told a joke. Chip saw it as a desperate attempt to prove his value, surely a sign of insecurity and reflective of inexperience.

Chip responded lightheartedly, raising his hands as if surrendering. "Oh hey... you're the man." Scott smiled and nodded. "Of course, usually if you're the man, you don't have to tell people you are, they just know. But to each his own, right?" Chip said laughing.

Scott seemed to have heard Chip's message and appeared somewhat embarrassed. He moved quickly to his next subject. "Let me start by telling you little about myself. I'm in the process of completing my undergraduate work. This internship is an integral part of my extensive education."

An intern, Chip thought. Why am I wasting my time with an intern?

"At the end of this program I will have a dual major in Human Resources and Organizational Behavior and Development, not your typical single path major," Scott said with pride, apparently again searching for some pat on the back for his outstanding work. "After I complete my undergraduate, I intend to pursue a Masters in both areas."

"Very impressive," was the only response Chip could stomach. What do you say to someone so intent on explaining their worth?

"Now on to some vital paperwork. I need you to fill out this employment application. As part of the application, please provide for me your three major strengths and three major weaknesses. Also, identify a recent problem at work and how you handled it. These are important questions and tell an employer a lot about the person they are dealing with," Scott said.

Three major strengths and weaknesses? How academic, Chip thought. What a complete waste of time. Would this information really contribute to the decision making? Most likely not. More than likely, no one other than perhaps Scott would read it. Well, that's the game. The best response is to keep the answers short and simple

"I have some important work to get done for an upcoming directors meeting that I'm involved with. So I'll get to work on this…" he started, hesitating slightly, waiting for Chip to answer some unspoken request. "…would you mind stepping out in the hall to complete the form, the things I work on are highly confidential. You can knock when you're done."

Chip smiled. "Sure. No problem," he said, rising from his seat and walking to the hall. Scott followed and closed the door behind him. What an inflated sense of self worth, Chip thought. Not only was the guy arrogant, he was clearly misguided as to his place in the company. Rajiv would be the decision-maker in this case. Kelly would likely provide input and influence the decision. To what extent he wasn't exactly sure, but Scott…well, Scott would likely not even be asked to supply input. He was just somebody to collect the paperwork. Poor kid would have a rude awakening one day. Then again, maybe he had already woken up to his real position and this was his way of handling the news. Inflate your worth often enough and maybe people would start to believe it.

Chip walked to his car, two and a half hours after beginning his interview. This isn't what I want to do, was his first thought. Quickly followed by, this could be a good stepping stone into another management position, one with more responsibility, or some other area. Spend some time as a Marketing Manager and grow the team or move into a higher management position...with a car, expense account...then who knows. But how long before that happens? A year? Two years? Three? And what would he be doing in the meantime? The job sounded more like a Business Planner or Analyst than a marketing function, he thought. Despite Rajiv's vision of growth, the job sounded extremely mundane. And I'm replacing a guy with six years less experience than I have. What does that say? I'm overqualified and chances are good I won't be happy doing the job. But the pay is good: the bump in pay I'm looking for. One promotion into sales and I'd be sitting pretty. On the other hand...

Something didn't sit right. It wasn't anything Chip could put his finger on. It was no particular fact, no exact conversation, nothing he could get his arms around and consider. He thought about his discussion with Rajiv; he was professional, but Chip didn't get a comfortable feeling about the conversation. Maybe it was the way Rajiv had asked the questions, with some hidden suggestion of accusation. No, surely that was Chip's imagination. Maybe it was the way Chip had answered the questions; he didn't feel like he had adequately represented his real knowledge and skills. No, his answers were fine, it was something else. Was it Rajiv, Chip questioned. No, it was the entire interview, start to finish that set him at unease: the late start, Rajiv, the arrogant little HR guy, the job itself, the building, the weather...Whatever the case, it just didn't feel right.

Kelly seemed nice: very professional, likable. He felt he could work with her when a thought occurred to him – what is all this about feelings? Look at the facts and decide from there. Forget the feelings; use logic and be objective. The interview hadn't gone bad. They seemed somewhat interested, at least interested enough to make it conceivable to believe that they might make an offer.

Chip dialed Stacy's number at work as he drove away. She would have input.

No, he shouldn't second guess himself, the situation was fine, stick to the facts, not feelings. The job was a decent job at a decent company with decent benefits. Nobody flinched when he outlined his salary requirements; they must be too low. Despite this, the salary was fifteen thousand higher than where he currently was at, exactly what he was looking for. This was a big company he could move around in, good benefits, good money. Yes this was a good job. He paused. But still...

What Do You Want to Be...

"I forgot to ask, how did your interview go?" Stacy asked excitedly. "I was so distracted today I forgot to ask. Why didn't you remind me?" She sat with her back leaning against Chip's chest, his hands gently massaging her shoulders. They rested cozily on the sofa in front of a blazing fire, wine glasses in hand. A Friday night wind down from another week.

"It went...okay," he reported dispassionately, not breaking stride with the massage.

Stacy sat up and turned to look at him questioningly. "It went 'okay'? What does that mean? Is it something you're interested in? What about the salary? Who did you interview with?"

"Easy, one at a time. I interviewed with my boss to be, my immediate team mate and some very arrogant, very green little guy from Human Resources. The HR guy wasn't much more than a paper shuffler and order taker. If this Rajiv guy says yes, I'm in. They're okay, I guess. I know I can do the job..." Chip said.

"But what...?"

"I don't know... it's okay I guess," Chip said, struggling to find the enthusiasm and passion he had felt only days before when he had first found out about the interview. It seemed to have been completely extinguished after his face to face conversations with Rajiv and Kelly.

"You keep saying okay and 'I guess'. That doesn't sound encouraging. Isn't it something you want?" Stacy asked.

"It's something...I can do. And the money is good. It sure would help us out."

"How much?" Stacy asked holding her breath.

"About fifteen thousand more than what I make now," Chip answered.

"Yes!" Stacy replied excitedly. She stared at Chip and saw that he shared none of her excitement. "What's wrong? It's not something you want to do?" Stacy lost her initial excitement, but managed to remain patient.

"I don't know. For one, the job seems like a lot of numbers work for a marketing position. Rajiv was fairly evasive about what marketing goals he wanted completed. He kept throwing the marketing question back at me, saying that I was the expert and he was turning to me to grow that area. Absent any new and exciting marketing plans I bring to the table, this is just a business planner position. It concerns me that I have no one reporting to me even though my title is manager. Rajiv says the team will grow in the near future but I'm sure he won't put that in writing. The lady I'm going to work with seems pretty sharp, but I wonder about the guy I'm gonna work for," Chip said, staring into the fire, looking for some guidance or direction that was not forthcoming.

"What's wrong with him? He's an idiot?" Stacy asked.

"No," he replied, remembering his first uneasy impression. "He seems like he knows what he's talking about. He's very assertive, aggressive…you can tell he's very politically correct: everything you would expect from a manager climbing his way to the top. It's just his personality, you're left with the impression that he's at least got the potential to be a little sneaky."

"If you're uncomfortable about the job, don't take it. Something else will come along," Stacy said disappointedly, resuming her position lying against Chip.

"Well, it could be a good opportunity. We could use the money. And just because I'm in this position now, it doesn't mean I have to stay there forever. Once I'm in I can move around in six months or a year. It is a big company," Chip argued.

"Are you replacing someone? Isn't this a new position?" she asked.

"I'm replacing someone. On the other hand, from the way Rajiv describes it, he wants the position to grow into something bigger than what it is now. He wants it to be a Marketing Manager. He even admitted that the job was a…what did he call it…a Business Analyst but he wanted to expand the scope of responsibility." Chip said.

"Perfect opportunity. It's a fresh start. I'm thinking that means you lay the groundwork for any successor. You're not having to clean up anybody else's mess or try to live up to someone else's reputation. Nobody knows what this new position should be. This is your chance to define it," Stacy said. Chip stared at Stacy skeptically. "Okay, how could you not agree with that?" she added.

"There's still some expectation based on what my predecessor did, although it doesn't sound like he lived up to expectations. Also, new positions are easily erased," Chip said.

"Okay, don't take it then," Stacy said, growing somewhat annoyed.

"Still, the money would be nice. I wouldn't be able to cover that ground staying in the job I'm in now. The 401k is better too. The health coverage is better. I would also pick up an extra week vacation since they get the week between Christmas and New Year's off," Chip said.

Stacy offered no input.

"On the other hand, I did a little research on them and hear they're having some financial problems. There's been a rumor that the group I'm talking to could be on the chopping block at some point," Chip continued.

"Do you know that for a fact?" Stacy asked.

"No, nothing is guaranteed."

Stacy sighed slightly. Chip could sense the conversation was frustrating her. "Turmoil is opportunity for someone aggressive like you. If they get sold, it's likely to be to a bigger company that wants to dominate in that product. That means they'll put money into the company after they buy it. And if none of that works out, you're still working for a large, respectable company for more money. You can take that experience and leave in a year. Somebody would scoop you up," she said optimistically.

"Or they could cut serious heads, then sell the group off. Or vice versa. If I..." Chip began but was quickly interrupted by his bride-to-be.

"Okay, look. What do you want to do?" she asked, exasperated. "It's either something you want to do fifty hours a week and you're going to go after it, or it's not something you want and you'll keep looking until you find something. Don't take something you're going to be unhappy with. If you do that, in six months or earlier, you'll be in the same place you are now," she said, pulling away from him until she sat opposite him on the couch.

"It's not that easy. It's not that simple of a question. This is a big decision. There are a lot of things to consider..." he said, raising his voice slightly.

Stacy shook her head and rolled her eyes. "That is not the problem. The problem is, you don't know what you really want to do. You haven't decided what you want to be when you grow up," Stacy said.

Chip bristled. "Ouch, that hurt," he said, glaring at her.

Stacy noticed his expression and opted to back off slightly. "I didn't mean you're not grown up, you just haven't decided what it is you really want to do... as a career."

Chip remained somewhat defensive. "Well it's kind of hard when you have bills to pay. I mean, I don't think the things I want to do will pay for a new house or a honeymoon or kids or retirement or..."

Stacy smiled. "And what are those things that you're dying to do but you're sure won't pay the bills."

Chip stared at her, quickly trying to search for an answer. Her smile broadened. "Well..." he started. Seeing his struggle for some answer, for any answer, made Stacy laugh, making Chip more determined to offer up some response. "Real estate! I want to buy and sell real estate! I want to rent out houses."

Stacy laughed louder. "Oh God! You do not! You just think that will make you money so you can start your own business – whatever that means! Tell me you really love dealing in real estate and being a landlord." She waited momentarily, but saw no reply was forthcoming. "The bottom line is, you think it's a way to get out of working for someone, but it's not something you're really interested in, it's not something you're passionate about. Tell me I'm wrong."

Chip could offer no response. Everything she said was right. But how did that change the current decision? Defining a career path that he was passionate about, something he would love doing could take awhile and would involve risk. In fact, a change like that might never happen. And during the time he was finding or making this dream career happen, bills would still need to be paid and he would therefore still need to work. And if he was going to be unhappy working fifty hours a week somewhere, shouldn't it be somewhere where he could optimize his pay? If he was going to be unhappy anyway, why not be compensated for it while he continued his search for something better.

This argument brought him back to his current path and the current question: Do I take this job for more money while I search for what I really want to do, or do I make fifteen grand less while I'm looking?

Well, when put in that context, the answer is clear – take the job.

But still…

The Offer

Chip played the messages on his answering machine.

Message 1: "This message is for Chip Weatherbe. This is Kelly Hayman from GIT. We recently sent you an offer for the sales and marketing position we discussed and we haven't heard back from you. If you would, please call me at your earliest convenience to discuss. I can be reached at …"

Chip listened carefully to the message again and wondered if he had missed something. He had not seen a written offer and in fact, had not received any feedback . Had it gotten lost in the mail? Had he inadvertently thrown it out with all the other junk mail? No, he decided. He had never received an offer. He decided to call immediately to clarify the situation. He dialed Kelly's number.

"Kelly Hayman speaking."

"Hi Kelly. This is Chip Weatherbe. I'm returning your call from earlier," Chip said.

In an assertive, very professional, bordering on cold tone Kelly said, "Hi Chip. Thanks for returning my call so quickly. Chip, we hadn't heard back from you regarding the offer we sent. We were wondering if there was a problem with the offer or if you intended on accepting it." The last sentence sounded almost accusatory.

Chip responded in a like tone, "Kelly, I'm glad you called to talk about this. I haven't received an offer, either verbal or written, nor any feedback from our last conversation. I was beginning to wonder if you were still interested in filling the position."

Kelly responded, "Someone from Human Resources was supposed to call you. We also mailed the offer last week via Federal Express."

"I never spoke to anyone and I never received the package," said Chip.

Chip's comment was met with a deafening silence. Chip wondered if she had hung up. "Hello?"

"Oh, I'm still here," Kelly answered. Her cold, professional voice continued. She added, "Let me call HR and see what's going on. You haven't received anything? No one has called you other than me? Rajiv didn't talk to you yesterday?"

"No," Chip said plainly.

For a slight moment the professional calm seemed to waiver in Kelly's voice, being replaced with a frustrated resignation. "Okay. Someone will get back with you."

"Okay. I look forward to hearing back from someone," Chip said. And as he was hanging up, he could have sworn he heard the echoes of some profanity being uttered on the other end of the line.

The Resignation

Paul stared at his computer screen in intense silence. He read through one of those chain e-mails that started with one person and built momentum until it seemed like everyone in the company had either replied to the message, forwarded the message, gotten a cc: of the message, or had been referenced in the message.

The initiator was sales, a heated message outlining how thoroughly incompetent manufacturing was for having been unable to meet the customer due date. It wasn't bad enough that the product would not ship for at least 3 weeks past the due date but apparently no one from manufacturing had seen fit to raise a flag and notify sales. Consequently, here sat sales getting a phone call from the customer the day the product was due, asking for a shipping tracking number. Sales would have to break the bad news to the customer and field questions like "If you knew it was going to be late, why didn't you let us know?" So an e-mail was sent internally to weed out the guilty. Manufacturing of course responded, citing engineering's inability to supply accurate drawings and an updated bill of materials. They did not have the information they needed and therefore, how could they be expected to build the product at all, let alone on time. This was something that engineering had known about for weeks, manufacturing claimed. Engineering answered the accusation by referencing conversations with sales, explaining that they were unclear as to the customer specifications and requirements. These open questions should have been cleared up two months ago, allowing engineering ample time to supply the appropriate drawings. Sales rejected the argument and cited an earlier e-mail indicating that the product had been supplied in the past and that drawings should already exist. Purchasing threw their two cents in. Manufacturing reiterated their position...And on the notes went, concluding with a request for Paul to support the proposed solution.

Paul removed his glasses and rubbed his tired eyes. It was only 8:00 am and already he had a headache. What a way to start the day. Oh well, another day, another problem that needed solving.

He glanced up as Chip entered his office. "What?" he barked dramatically.

"Well, who pissed in your Wheaties, Captain?" Chip answered.

"Everyone! Now what do you want?" Paul said, emphasizing "you".

Chip felt a nagging of guilt for what he was about to do. His current employer and specifically Paul, had treated him well over the last few years. At least as well as their means would allow. He had a stable environment, a team he worked well with and a lot of flexibility. That didn't change the fact that there was no-where to go from here. Financially, he would likely only get meager increases from now on. He had pretty much reached the top of what they were willing to pay. There might be some added incentives here and there but nothing amounting to what he could achieve in a single jump to somewhere outside the company. His job was set, the organization wasn't big enough to have multiple departments that allowed movement. If he stayed, they needed him where he was. If he stayed, he would likely work in that same position until the owners decided to sell the company or just close up shop. More than likely, they would sell. Probably to a larger competitor or to a company looking to add their particular product to their portfolio. Then all bets were off. Job security, flexibility, financial growth all became unknowns; no different than the situation he was moving into now. Except with this move, he knew there was a financial increase. But aside from the money, better to take your destiny into your own hands, he thought. Better to incur the risk on your own terms, on your timeline rather than someone else's. He had a single sheet of paper in his hand. The letter of resignation. Cold and to the point – 'Please accept this letter of resignation. My last day is…'

"I got a phone call yesterday," Chip said.

Paul stared at Chip for a moment and raised his eyebrows slightly asking the question…and? without speaking. He then glanced at the sheet of paper in Chip's hand and a light seemed to go on in his eyes. He put his glasses back on and returned his stare to the computer screen.

"And…?" Paul said calmly without looking at Chip.

"And it was from a company named GIT …they had a job offer…" Chip trailed off, finding it difficult to just say 'I resign' and hand his boss the letter of resignation. All the times Chip imagined walking into his employer and letting them have it for the years of injustice and oppression faded and were replaced by a feeling that he was abandoning ship just when he was needed. But when wouldn't he be needed, he argued with himself. There was always a problem that needed his input, required his involvement. There would never be a good time to leave. And after he did leave, someone would fill the void; everyone is replaceable.

"And you told them to go pound sand…that you love it where you are and you're never going to leave, right?" Paul said smirking, never looking at Chip and beginning to type his response to the e-mail.

"I told them I'd accept the position," Chip replied.

"Well, what did you go do something stupid like that for?" Paul asked rhetorically.

"For more money and growth," Chip replied candidly.

"I pay you money!" Paul announced.

"You do, just not enough," Chip said lightly.

"Is it ever enough?" Paul asked.

Chip considered the question. No. It was the wrong question to be asking he decided. He was young and talented. This is what you are supposed to do to grow your salary and career. You would have lots of time later in life to ask yourself those questions; after you got the house you wanted, after you put the kids through college, after you had enough for retirement. Not now. Now was the time to grow. To explore new jobs. Now was not the time to settle. The decision was the right one.

In his final weeks at the employer he was leaving, Chip found that although he was once a central player at the company, he was only a ghost now. People still said good morning and stopped him in the hall to congratulate him, but the feeling of being part of the team was gone. People smiled politely when he offered his input but it was now out of tolerance rather than interest. The people coming to his office to ask for answers dwindled by the day. Indeed, he was now at sea, only waving to those still on shore.

First Day on the Job

The office seemed familiar to Chip: a large room, large desk, and large leather chair. Of course, all offices start looking the same after a while. Maybe he had seen something like it in a dream once. He couldn't remember; not that it mattered.

It was a fairly large office, at least compared to the few offices he had seen at GIT. The room was large enough to accommodate six people comfortably; one behind and two in front of the desk. At least another three people could fit easily around a small meeting table located opposite the desk. It was larger than Rajiv's office and decorated with a number of paintings and award certificates. A large brainstorming white board hung on the wall, devoid on any content at the moment, except for a small box outlined in the upper left corner labeled "concept incubator".

How does a concept incubate just by being written down on a white board, Chip wondered? A catchy phrase if nothing else.

A large framed poster was the focus of the wall next to the meeting table. The poster read:

Open Dialog Checklist

✓ Make clear your intentions – Intentions are just as important as actions and results.
✓ Listen – Apply edge of seat test
✓ No position – Don't engage in narrow thinking by adopting any position or by forcing someone else to take a position
✓ No interruption – It's not polite to interrupt while people are sharing
✓ Silence is okay – But we prefer to have people sharing
✓ Listening is important

Michael F. Goyette

- ✓ Share your assumptions
- ✓ Entertain new assumptions
- ✓ No ping pong – Once you find that someone disagrees with you, agree to disagree and end that particular discussion
- ✓ Challenge ideas, not people
- ✓ Be sensitive to how other people might perceive your statements and actions. Even if you are well intentioned, you could be offending or harassing someone. Harassment will not be tolerated.
- ✓ Risk free – There is no risk associated with sharing any of your feelings.
- ✓ Ask for what you need – Whether the person you're talking to can supply it or not, you'll feel better expressing the need.
- ✓ Honest and Open
- ✓ No fear, no rank
- ✓ No winners or losers – We don't win or lose, we just share
- ✓ If an idea doesn't fit in with the current topic discussion, place it in the concept incubator for later consideration
- ✓ No demand for results – Sometimes just expressing our feelings can be valuable

And Above All...

Tolerance and Respect – Respect the diverse opinions and individuals around you. Intolerance will not be tolerated.

"Hi, I'm Janice Stalls. I'm the Vice President of the Career Resource Development And Change Management Team," Janice said, bubbling with enthusiasm and shaking Chip's hand.

"Chip Weatherbe, nice to meet you," he responded.

"Welcome to GIT, Chip," she said. "I wanted to spend just a couple minutes with you before you get started on your new path and share with you GIT's core values and guiding principles. I think it's these values that make our organization a benchmark for others to follow."

Janice handed him a laminated piece of paper summarizing GIT's core values: Diversity, Tolerance, Harmonious Union with the environment, and Life Balance for all employees. No other explanation or detailed description was provided. Any reference to serving the customer was noticeably absent.

"We have a tremendous amount to offer here at GIT: Organizations representing the inclusive, diverse culture we at GIT promote; change management counselors to assist you in this stressful transition; a real focus on giving back to the community and environment; fun group activities like Paint the Town," Janice said, smiling broadly.

"Paint the town?" he wondered out loud.

"Yeah! Paint the town! The GIT team identifies one or two houses in economically challenged areas in need of some finishing touches and we paint them. It's a great opportunity for you to give back to the community and to get to know your fellow co-workers outside the work environment. As you can see, it also ties directly to two of our core values: harmonious union with the environment and life balance. I'm hard pressed to think of a better way to be in harmony with the environment or to balance your life than to give back to people in need."

"Sounds great," Chip said, working to sound somewhat enthusiastic. He wondered what he was giving back, to whom and why.

"I'd like to show you a brief video of Nigel Warren Jones III, our Vice President of European operations," she said, quickly changing subjects and walking to a television and VCR in the corner of the office. "It's from a speech he gave a week ago at our European office. We just got the tape in yesterday, so this will be the first time for both of us. In fact, I think it's the first time anyone outside the immediate meeting attendees have seen the video. I've been told by our office in Europe that his speech is breathtaking."

Janice put the tape in the VCR. Chip was already feeling somewhat anxious. It was now 10:00 and he hadn't accomplished anything. He had arrived at 8:00 as instructed and sat for almost an hour waiting for his Human Resource contact. After a twenty minute tour of the rest rooms and cafeteria, he sat back down and waited another forty minutes for Janice. Three hours of downtime if you assume a start time of 7:00 am as Chip was accustomed to. Lighten up; it's only the first day, he thought. The pace is bound to pick up. He tuned back into the tape, missing the grand introduction of Nigel, but in time to hear the substance of his speech.

"…You will see different and diverse teams in every building. This will bring new ideas and a sense of inclusion for all," said Nigel, complete with an ear catching British accent.

"…GIT will be an icon of diversity. The old white male culture will disappear and in its place will be a tolerant culture, one that celebrates our differences and encourages people from all backgrounds to participate in policy decision making. No longer will a small group of people dictate to us how to run our business and how to run our lives…"

The comments received a standing ovation, drowning out the speaker in mid sentence. The crowd cheered, smiling, clapping loudly. Chip wondered why the audience was so enthusiastic. Surely these comments were inflammatory; words to divide rather than unite. Certainly the phrases would be seen as caustic rather than healing. Clearly the words were accusatory; identifying one group based solely on age, skin color, and gender as the basis for some ill-defined and unwarranted "guilt". He also wondered if the audience realized that a white man in his late fifties was providing these remarks. As the camera panned the audience, a few could be seen clapping half-heartedly, offering each other frowning glances. Obviously, they did not share the exuberance of the speech.

Listening to the speech, Chip joined these few in their complete lack of enthusiasm. Many of the comments made him feel uncomfortable, leaving him wondering why someone at this level didn't take every opportunity to focus on the positive: to deliver an uplifting message and to offer an inspiring vision. Why not offer words to motivate, when it occurred to Chip that possibly some of the attendees *were* motivated by the retaliatory verbiage. He glanced at Janice who was transfixed on the television, smiling with pride.

Despite her happy expression, she seemed to hear his thoughts and turned the tape off.

"I just remembered, I have a meeting in ten minutes I have to prepare for," she said with a plastic smile. "And besides, it probably wouldn't be fair to the rest of the folks at GIT if you saw the speech first. We don't want anyone having an unfair advantage."

"Fair enough," Chip replied, guessing that the rest of the speech was much of the same and not feeling the least bit interested in hearing more. Although he was turned off by the comments, he wasn't completely shocked by their appearance. Today's environment seemed to embrace any statements with any mention of the word diversity, irrespective of the context in which they were used.

"One quick final note…one of your responsibilities as a GIT employee is to recognize diversity in the world around you. Specifically, we expect you to open a dialog with your Guidance Manager on how you will achieve this. Depending on schedules, you can have this discussion one-on-one or in a small team; there are advantages to both. Of course, in a small team, there is a tremendous amount of synergy between different people, promoting team cohesiveness," Janice said, standing and walking to the door of her office. Chip followed her out, wondering when the real work would begin.

"I had Gracie schedule you introductory meetings with a number of key people you should establish a dialog with," Kelly said, walking with Chip back to their computers. "You've obviously met Rajiv. He's out until Thursday but he wanted a meeting with you next Monday to talk about goals and objectives. This is what we call our Designated Work Area or DWA. It's part of the greater Designated Work Environment or DWE as we call it," she said as they stood staring at their desks. A long, L shaped shelf, fastened to the wall served as a desk. Kelly's computer was positioned on the base on the L, forcing her to sit with her back facing the entrance and Chip. What would serve as Chip's DWA had a computer some five feet away from Kelly. No partition stood between the two.

Chip glanced at her questioningly. "DWA?"

"I know. There's a few people in the company who have a little too much free time on their hands, coming up with one acronym after another," she whispered, seeming somewhat disgusted and at the same time showing a level of resignation. "Oh, and remind me, he left a few things for you to take a look at by next week," she said smiling and pointing to a large pile of disorganized paper next to Chip's desk.

"From Rajiv?" Chip asked. Kelly nodded. "My first homework assignment," Chip said lightheartedly.

Kelly smiled and responded only with silence. Chip wondered at the significance of this lack of commentary. After a moment she continued. "Okay. I've also set you up with two of the key Account Managers. There's also Mark and Andrae, two more Account Managers you should talk to. You should probably spend some time with each of them. You'll get more information spending an hour with them then you will spending a week digging through that," she said, again pointing to the pile of paper.

"You'll meet Ted Friday. He's our Chief Engineer. He's been here forever and knows everything about every product we've ever made." The look of disgust returned. Obviously, she was a person with strong opinions on the people around her. "I even got you an appointment with the CEO, which is no small task. Although it helps that Janice is pushing her new, 'Get to know the little people program'." Kelly giggled.

"The little people program?" he asked, already having a good sense of where she was headed.

"Janice wants the CEO to mingle more with the little people to show he cares. You met with Janice this morning, right?" Her tone suggested she was looking for some further insight on his impression of Janice. Chip thought it better to keep all opinions to himself this early in his stay and offered only a quick, "Yes I did."

Kelly continued on, listing the meetings for the week and identifying which names were politically correct for Chip to remember.

"They're all important to some extent. You're a bright guy, you'll figure out who…"

"Is this the new Account Manager?" A woman in her late thirties approached their work area. She was thin with short blonde hair, glasses and a somewhat homely face.

"Chip, this is Gracie. She's our closest neighbor," Kelly said, pointing to the desk just outside of Rajiv's office.

"Hi. Chip Weatherbe. Nice to meet you," he said, shaking her hand.

"Nice to meet you. I'm Gracie. I'm the Sales and Marketing Department Admin," she said smiling. "If you need anything, I'm right over here, just give a call."

"Thanks, I appreciate it."

"I'll be back in awhile, I have a doctor appointment," she offered, walking to her desk, picking up her coat and departing quickly.

Michael F. Goyette

"I don't want to taint your opinion of anyone, but watch what you say around her. She likes to think she's the eyes and ears of Rajiv and HR."

"Really?"

"Yeah, she's kind of the HR cheerleader. Every chance she gets, she touts whatever nonsense is being spewed. I don't know why she does it. It's not like she has any friends in HR. No connections and apparently no vested interest in supporting anything they say," she said, shaking her head. "She obviously believes in her heart every company line that is thrown out. Librarian," Kelly sneered.

"Librarian?" Chip wondered out loud.

"Her nickname. Doesn't she remind you of a librarian: very plain looking with a very blah personality? She's just so…plain."

Chip hesitated. Best not to jump in the gossip game at all, let alone on your first day. Best to take the high ground. "I can't really say, I just met her."

"Good man. Stay out of the dirt. At least until your feet are on the ground," she giggled. "We've got a few minutes before lunch. Let me introduce you to the Account Managers."

Chip followed Kelly to a group of six workstations, which created a large square area. Two of the works areas seemed to be completely vacated. Of the remaining four, only one was currently inhabited. A table in the middle might have acted as a meeting table if not for the clutter of parts, drawings, folders, and papers completely covering its supporting host.

A man in a shirt and tie with his suit jacket hanging neatly from a hanger on the wall next to him occupied one of the areas. Sitting with his back to all approaching visitors, he seemed intent on his work.

"Hey Dan, do you have a minute?" Kelly asked.

"Hi Kelly. I'm just getting ready to go to the customer, will it take long?" he replied, glancing back and returning his gaze quickly to the computer screen.

"I just wanted to introduce you to our new Marketing Manager, Chip Weatherbe."

Dan spun quickly around and rose from his seat. "Hi, I'm Dan Bridges. Nice to meet you."

"Chip Weatherbe, nice to meet you."

"Can we talk when I get back? I'm a little pressed for time now," Dan said.

Chip quickly replied with a 'no problem'.

"I checked your calendar and scheduled a meeting for you and Chip tomorrow at 3:00," Kelly said.

"Perfect," Dan said putting on his coat. "Welcome aboard."

"Thanks."

The office seemed deserted as Chip and Kelly headed back to their desks. Chip noticed more than a few cubicles completely void of any trace of recent use.

"The place seems empty," he observed.

"Typical around lunch."

Chip looked at his watch. Lunch already? The morning had flown by. As they rounded a corner, a woman approaching quickly from the other direction almost ran them over. Her brown hair was straight, falling just past her shoulders. Upon introduction, one might have focused quickly on her soft attractive face. However, her tight white shirt and an even tighter black skirt, emphasized every curve of her petite figure, distracting the onlooker from anything above the shoulders.

"There you are. I was just at your desk. You want to grab lunch?" the woman asked Kelly. Her voice was seductive, matching her appearance.

"Yeah. Let me grab my purse. Oh, Chip, this is Linda," Kelly said.

Linda shook Chip's hand. "Hi, Chip, nice to meet you," she said, smiling flirtatiously. Her delicate touch held Chip's hand long enough to make him feel uncomfortable. Despite trying to stay focused on the introduction and his next dialog, he found himself pausing momentarily in thought to glance at her chest. In the second this took place, Chip noticed that her shirt was close to being see-through. At least, see-through enough so that Chip could see her lace bra underneath. Although her chest wasn't what most men would consider big, the tightness and transparency of her shirt called out for immediate male attention.

"Hi, nice to meet you," Chip stuttered.

"I'll go grab my purse and I'll meet you out front," Linda said. "I'm sure I'll see you around Chip," she said, walking away.

His eyes followed her down the hall before she turned the corner, forgetting that Kelly was still staring at him. "Is she an Administrative Assistant?" Chip asked.

Kelly offered an evil grin. "What makes you say that?" Chip felt immediately like he had been set up. Obviously by Kelly's demeanor, she was not an Admin. He sensed that Kelly wanted him to think this and wanted further conversation on the matter.

"Nothing," Chip said innocently. "Was it a wrong assumption?"

"She's an Account Manager," Kelly continued to smile, staring Chip directly in the eyes. "Why did you think she was an Admin?"

"I don't know…" Chip stumbled, trying desperately not to say anything that would offend her friend. Kelly continued her devious smile. "…um…the way she was dressed was…"

"Was like an Admin and not an Account Manager," Kelly finished his sentence laughing. "Don't worry, everyone says that. And all the men stare. But what was it exactly about the way she dressed that made you think that?" she asked, finding obvious pleasure in pushing the discussion.

Chip felt his face flush. "You're a real shit disturber aren't you?" he said lightly.

Kelly's only response was to laugh harder and ask the question again. "No really, what made you say that?"

Seeing there was no diplomatic way to retreat and realizing that Kelly wanted to play, Chip dove in head first. "Maybe it was her see-through top," Chip replied.

Kelly lowered her head and giggled loudly. "Over lunch, I'll let her know you were admiring her chest."

"You're a very bad person and I have work to do," he said, feeling embarrassed.

"Don't worry," she said, hitting Chip's arm. "I've been telling her for a while that if she wants to be taken seriously, she has to dress seriously, not like she's going to a bar."

Chip said nothing. Too much had been said already, at least enough to get him in hot water on his first day.

Kelly was laughing again. "You look terrified. Don't worry, your secret fantasy is safe with me."

Chip shook his head and took a seat at his desk, ignoring the bait.

"I think Rajiv has a thing for her. He's real subtle about it, but you can tell. He tries a little too hard to be inconspicuous. Of course not everyone admires her. There's at least one guy around here who thinks she dresses a little over the top and doesn't mind saying so. He thinks she should be at home baking cookies or something. His ideas are a little outdated. Like I said, you'll get a chance to meet Ted on Friday."

The Group Project

God, this is stupid! What a colossal waste of time! The entire conversation was pointless and yet they had been going over the same ground for the last two hours. It was now the third week of class and they had met as a group once a week, Thursday evening, since week one. Each meeting ended roughly the same: the conversation spiraling round and round and then ending abruptly with no real direction or agreement being established. He glanced at his watch – 9:00 p.m. He loosened his tie and rolled up his sleeves, trying to achieve some small level of comfort in the clothes he had been in for the last fifteen hours. He knew he would be in them for at least another hour.

After four days on the new job he felt mentally drained; the last thing he wanted to do was spar with this group. Four days and he hadn't really interfaced with Rajiv yet: no direction, no goals. Not wanting to appear helpless without guidance and more importantly, trying to avoid complete boredom, Chip had taken it upon himself to set his own path. He wondered why he felt so tired. He hadn't really put himself at a grinding pace. He had spent a lot of time sitting in on meetings, reading through presentations, introducing himself to various people and trying to bring himself up to speed on GIT's products and overall business. Be that as it may, he didn't feel like he had accomplished anything. Maybe that was it: information overload. So many details in such a short time. But in spite of the quantity of information, he felt bored. Bored and tired. Give it some time, he thought. You have just transitioned from being a key go-to guy to being a nobody. Give it a chance, it's only been a week. In no time at all, you'll be challenged, invaluable. Once Rajiv defines what he is looking for, the pace and challenge will pick up.

"…I just think we need to spend more time assembling and agreeing on the information we're going to include in the final presentation. We have to show him our progress on Monday and I think we need more than this. I have a wedding

Saturday, but we can meet Sunday morning and go until whenever we finish," Kimberly said.

Chip rolled his eyes and sighed, forgetting about work and sitting back in his chair. "Oh Jesus! Look, there's no reason to meet on Sunday. In fact, there is really no reason to continue our meeting now, let alone every Thursday night. Everyone knows what they're expected to bring to the table on Monday. We all just need to go away and do it! We can meet twenty minutes before class and compare notes. According to the syllabus, all he is checking this Monday is our one page outline to see if we are on the right track. We're going to have a five-minute conversation with him and that will be it. I think things would go a lot smoother if we each worked on our own piece of the puzzle separately and touched base every class for a brief update. I think trying to meet as a group and create everything from scratch, as a team, is just a waste of time."

Kimberly ignored him. This was her typical response to Chip; at least it was the response she had desperately tried to implement starting the first day they were rudely thrown together in a group by the Business Policy Professor. Immediately on the heels of the "Why get an MBA" discussion, the Professor thought it would be a growing experience (as he put it) for both Chip and Kimberly to be on the same project team. "The diverse views that you each bring to the table should ignite some fascinating discussions," he had said. Chip had noticed the grin on his face as he said this. That bastard.

Why did these professors think that putting two polar opposites in the same group somehow automatically meant meaningful discussion? More often than not, Chip had found, after hours of the two polar individuals battling it out, the moderates in the group would eventually want a "compromise" and suggest adopting some "agreement that everyone could live with." In the end, this would be some watered down proposal that no one was really happy with and in fact was not nearly as profound or substantive as going with one of the polar ideas. Of course, adopting one of the polar views had two fundamental problems. First, at least one member of the group would be pissed off that their idea was completely snubbed. Second, the idea could be one hundred percent wrong, thus putting the entire team out on a limb. If the idea or proposal being brought forth was good, the team would almost certainly have a home run and get an A. On the other hand, if the idea was off track, it was likely to be way off track and potentially doom the entire team. A moderate idea that, in the end, took no stand and offered nothing of controversy was inevitably the safest route.

"I think we can all agree that some team interaction between classes is useful but likewise, we probably don't need to devote entire weekend days to the project at this point. I think we can find some middle ground," said Tony, a middle aged, middle level manager offering a middle of the road proposal. Spoken like a true moderate. No real solution had been offered, just a vague suggestion of compromise; a compromise that should make everyone equally unhappy.

Kimberly frowned. "This is pointless," she said.

"Finally, we agree on something," Chip chuckled lightly.

Kimberly couldn't resist a smile and the group laughed nervously. "What if everyone sends their portion via e-mail to the team by sometime Sunday afternoon. That way, everyone can review the information before class on Monday," Tony offered.

Kimberly lightened. "That would give everyone all day Monday to review the material."

"And we could still meet a few minutes before class, like Chip said, to discuss and offer feedback," Tony said while nodding at Chip, sounding overly accommodating and very enthusiastic. "Is that okay with everyone?"

Although the two others in the group nodded and agreed, it seemed more out of resignation than actual support. They were right, Chip thought. Just agree and end this nonsense already. Of course, on the surface the plan sounded fine, a real "let's meet half way strategy". In reality, Chip knew that Sunday afternoon probably meant Sunday night and that meant he would only have Monday to review all the information; maybe Monday at lunch for twenty minutes. Kimberly, no doubt would have the entire day Monday for review and would likely have endless suggestions for improvement that she would want to spend an exorbitant amount of time discussing and coming to a consensus on - the difference between a full time student and a working student.

Not that it mattered. A decision had been reached, finally. Best to let sleeping dogs lie. Chip quickly offered his concurrence of the plan. Now he could go home and relax for a few minutes. Then he would get up the next morning and do it all over again. What an existence, he thought. Work, work, sleep and work more. Then again, no one ever said being the captain of your own destiny was easy.

Ted

Chip approached the office and knocked lightly on the open door. A man sat at a desk with his back to the door. As he heard the knock, he turned. The man was in his late fifties and had a neatly trimmed white beard, but no mustache. His short hair was also white and he wore a small pair of bifocals. His neatly pressed white dress shirt and tie were covered by his long blue, buttoned lab coat which, despite its many years of wear, was clean and pressed. A number of mechanical pencils and pens filled a pocket protector in the coat's breast pocket, all neatly arranged and properly organized by function and size: mechanical pencils to the left, eraser in the middle, and pens to the right. The tops of all these delicate instruments were precisely aligned. A name on the lab coat read: Ted.

He stared at Chip without saying a word. "Hi, I'm Chip Weatherbe. I'm the new Marketing Manager. We had an introductory meeting scheduled for 8:00. Do you have a few minutes?" Chip said, walking into the office and shaking Ted's hand.

"No," Ted said, somewhat whining with a pained expression.

"Oh, no problem then. Should we reschedule for Monday?" Chip asked.

"No," Ted repeated in the same voice.

"Ok…Did you have another time in mind?" Chip asked, remaining polite.

"No," Ted replied shaking his head.

Chip stared at Ted. He saw in Ted's demeanor and tone that this obvious runaround and uncooperative behavior was intentional. Chip briefly considered his next move.

"Well, I'll tell you what. We had the meeting scheduled for 8:00 today, so let's keep it there. Mind if I sit down?" Chip asked while taking a seat and making himself comfortable.

"Yes," Ted answered, although more assertively this time.

"So, I understand you're a seasoned veteran around here, Ted. Everyone I've talked to says you're the only person in the organization that truly understands our products and customers. They say, if you're trying to fix a problem and all else fails, call Ted," Chip said smoothly.

Ted sat back in his chair smirking and folded his arms. Chip wasn't sure if he had gained any ground but decided to push forward. After all, at least Ted wasn't demanding that he leave. "So you're the new Marketing Manager?" Ted asked.

"That's right," Chip replied.

"Who or what do you manage? I mean, other than yourself and whatever it is you spend your time on," Ted asked grinning a devilish grin.

Chip smiled. It appeared that Ted wanted to play a little before discussing business. "At this point, no one. Although we are expecting to grow the department and I anticipate once that happens, there will be a number of people on my team," Chip replied calmly.

"Grow the department? No kidding. I had heard that we're discussing getting rid of a few people. In fact, I had heard that as early as next week they are going to announce a hiring freeze and then possibly lay a few people off. People who are overhead…like marketing people," he said with a smile. "So it's interesting that they hired you, let alone hire more people like you," Ted said raising his eyebrows. "Don't you think?"

Chip paused and considered the statement. He had overheard a couple people at the coffee machine earlier that morning whispering the same thing. At the time, he had written it off as office gossip, but now he wondered if there was a grain of truth in the tale.

"I hadn't really heard anything…" Chip started.

Ted interrupted. "So why do you call yourself a manger if you don't manage anyone but yourself? I mean, if that's the criteria for being a manager, then can't everyone call themselves a manager?" Ted asked.

"I…" before Chip could finish, Ted jumped in again.

"Forget about that for now. Maybe you can help me answer a question that's bugged me for years," Ted asked, apparently preparing for another assault.

"I'll certainly try," Chip said, maintaining his composure.

"What do Marketing and Human Resource people do?" Ted asked, leaning forward and resting his elbows on his knees. Chip felt his blood rise slightly. Although he knew that Ted was playing with him, it never made this conversation any easier. He had addressed similar questions in the past from other peers and each time he had succeeded in earning at least a little respect for his answer. Despite that success, the knee-jerk frustration at hearing the question just wouldn't go away.

Ted continued. "I understand what an engineer does. He designs stuff. I understand manufacturing. They make the stuff that engineering designs. I understand what a salesman does. He lies and sells the stuff that manufacturing made. I even understand what the God forsaken bean counters do. They count the money that comes in from sales and then they don't share any with engineering, all the while expecting engineering to design more stuff. But for the life of me, I can't figure out what Marketing and Human Resources do." And after a slight pause, he added, "They are the same aren't they? And aren't they mostly women? I'm surprised to see a guy in this position."

Chip resisted a powerful urge to reach across the office and slap Ted. Taking a moment to compose his emotions and not to be discouraged by the blatant prompting, Chip answered.

"No. No, they're not the same and there are a lot of women in both areas. But let's tackle one question at a time. Let's start with what marketing does. In your scenario, marketing tells engineering what to design," he stated dispassionately.

Ted sat back again in his chair, folding his arms and laughing. "Is that so? I don't seem to remember the last time a marketing person gave me an idea for a new design. In fact, come to think of it, I never remember even getting any design changes from Marketing. I remember getting some very pretty, very colorful brochures that didn't say a whole lot. I remember seeing some pretty graphs once that I assume came from our Marketing group, but I don't remember any design ideas."

"Well, that's because you didn't have me around," Chip said matter-of-factly.

Ted smiled with a raised eyebrow. "Oh really?"

"You see, the way I look at it, the role of strategic marketing is, to a large extent, to define the needs, wants, and trends of a market and feed this information back to the organization so the fine people in engineering know what direction they should be headed. Otherwise, you may end up spending a lot of time and money developing products that the market is not interested in buying. Sure, you may design something everyone is impressed with. It may be the greatest thing in the world. Hell, it may even work," Chip chuckled lightly and despite Ted's smile, he couldn't help but notice the slight tinge of red in his cheeks. Chip pressed on. "But without knowing that someone is going to buy it, it's likely to be wasted effort. You'd just be pissing your money away and with as tight as money is now, I don't think any company can afford to spend time and money going off in the wrong direction," Chip said.

Ted appeared to be considering what Chip had just said. "I thought Sales told us what the customers wanted and needed?"

"No, Sales just lies and sells the stuff that manufacturing made. I thought we just established that," Chip said, looking overly confused for effect.

Ted laughed. "Very good, young man, there may be hope for you after all."

Chip continued. "Now you might think that's pie in the sky stuff; not very specific, right? So let's take it down to the next level – defining the wants and needs of specific customers within that market. And this by the way is where Sales comes in. We need to answer a few questions: What are the specific customers looking for in terms of requirements, both short and long term? Furthermore, we need to look at the wants and needs of our customer's customer. In what direction are the forces outside the customer moving? In other words, in what direction are the people that buy our customers' products, that impose legislation on our customers, or that compete with our customers…in what direction are these forces pushing the people that buy our stuff? Once we've answered some of these questions, then we identify what we as GIT can bring to the table to meet those wants and needs."

Ted interrupted. "Whatever happened to making something no one thought of and selling it to them. Did people really know that they needed the Internet? Or did someone create it and sell it?"

"You're right. No one said they needed or wanted the Internet, but there was a need out there to share large amounts of information quickly, to communicate faster than the current methods of the time. The Internet was the response to this need," Chip answered.

Before Ted could jump in again, Chip continued. "Now once we've done all this and decided what to offer the customer, we identify a specific reason or reasons why the customer should choose us and our product over the competition. We need to show exactly what we are bringing to the table and clearly explain what benefit the customer will derive from our offer. Now I'm not talking about just a description of the product and its benefits, I'm talking about what the customer gets out of it in terms of their specific wants or needs. We call this the value proposition. It's the story we're going to tell the customer. This is a big part of what strategic marketing is about. It's not everything, but it's a big part of it. Strategic marketing…"

Although Chip had initially captured Ted's attention, he now seemed bored. Ted leaned forward, again placing his elbows on his knees and interrupted Chip. "Why did they hire you, knowing that next week they're probably going to get rid of you?"

Chip was silent.

"Now, Ted. They wouldn't do something silly like that," Chip said, concealing the knot growing in his stomach.

Ted chuckled. "You obviously are not familiar with our new management. Have you ever met the new CEO? Or that bastard Brit, Nigel Warren Jones III?" Ted asked with an exaggerated look of curiosity.

"No," Chip replied cautiously. He hesitated slightly. "I saw part of a video with Nigel and I think Kelly scheduled an appointment for me to meet with the CEO Monday at Rajiv's request. Why? Is there something I should know?"

Ted laughed and turned back to his desk. "Good luck, Mr. Marketing Manager, good luck."

Chip started to say something but decided against it. "Well, thanks for the insight, Ted. I'm sure we'll see each other around."

Michael F. Goyette

"See you around Marketing Manager," Ted replied.

Chip rose and left Ted's office, feeling more uneasy every minute.

Maybe it was time to have a conversation with Rajiv. Earlier, Chip had seen him walking to the coffee machine. He had offered Rajiv a nod and good morning and had received no response, no recognition from Rajiv that a greeting had been uttered. Rounding a corner, he saw Linda walking away from Rajiv's office and Rajiv staring after her. The fact that he was staring at her as she strode away was embarrassingly obvious.

"Hi, Rajiv," Chip said approaching him.

Rajiv's eye's jerked quickly from Linda. For a brief second, Rajiv looked extremely guilty. The guilt was quickly replaced with a look of annoyance, bordering on anger. Caught you, Chip thought.

"Have you had a chance to review the 2003 competitive market share data and update all charts and graphs showing our position in the market?" Rajiv said, staring combatively at Chip.

Chip was taken off guard. Where did that come from, he thought. His mind raced, searching his mental archives; had there ever existed such an assignment? What was Rajiv talking about? "I can certainly do that." Chip replied and after a short response added, "What is the timing on that? How soon do you need it?"

Rajiv let out something between a sigh and a disbelieving laugh. "Chip, we need that information for the upcoming SIMM meeting. You know that. It's critical information that we need to supply. You haven't compiled that information yet?" he said accusingly.

"I have to apologize, no I haven't. I wasn't aware…"

Rajiv stared at the floor shaking his head, appearing wholly disgusted with what he obviously considered as blatant stupidity standing before him. "Chip, you need to drive this process. We need a go-getter who is going to grab the bull by the horns. If you wait around, things just aren't going to get done; this isn't going to work. You need to take the helm. Get on it right away. Let me know your status by close of business today," Rajiv said.

Chip's initial surprise was quickly wearing off and was replaced by a natural desire to defend oneself and deny responsibility when pushed so abruptly. "Can you provide some insight into this upcoming meeting? I'm unclear of the expectations…" Chip started, again being interrupted by Rajiv.

"I'm surprised Kelly hasn't reviewed this with you. Get with her. She can fill you in on the details. Let's touch base at close of business today. We really need to get moving on this. I need you to make it happen. You're steering the ship," Rajiv said, turning and retreating to his office.

Chip was in shock. What was all that about? There had never been any conversations about preparing for any meeting, he was sure of it. As quickly as he thought this, his mind took an abrupt turn and he began to second guess himself. Had he missed something? Missed an e-mail maybe? He didn't recall any conversation about a...what did he call it...a sim meeting?

He needed to talk to Kelly quickly, get her reaction to the situation, and obtain any information she may have. Approaching his desk he saw her staring at her computer, a travel cruise website on the screen. She quickly changed the screen to a spreadsheet when she heard him getting near.

"Do you know anything about a..." Chip began to ask.

"...a SIMM meeting," Kelly finished in a monotone voice and never taking her eyes off the screen.

Chip felt a slight burden lifted off his shoulders. At least she was aware of the meeting. "Yeah. Rajiv said you might be able to give me some details on what to prepare," Chip said.

"Probably not," she replied coolly. Before Chip could say anything, she continued. "I can tell you what was covered last meeting and some of the questions that were raised," she said, turning to look at him. "It was a big circle jerk," she said in a hushed voice.

"Ok..." Chip said hesitating, ignoring her commentary. He could feel his frustration mounting. If this was so important, why couldn't Rajiv or Kelly rattle off the top of their head what was required? Kelly's impression of the meeting certainly seemed different than Rajiv's. "Will the meeting minutes from last time outline the expectations for next time. I'd hate to be unprepared and end up looking foolish."

"Do you really think he gives a crap?" whispered Kelly, so matter-of-factly and so quickly that he wondered for a moment if she had really heard the question correctly, until he noticed that she swallowed hard after the question. It was as if she had just said something she really hadn't intended to say. For a split second, Kelly looked unsure of herself. Chip had opted to take advantage of the situation and probe the question.

"What do you mean?" Chip asked.

Any hint of shaky confidence on her face was quickly replaced with an overconfident smile. Chip observed that she had a certain knack for doing that, changing masks on a dime.

"What do you think of Rajiv?" Kelly asked, avoiding Chip's question altogether.

This was obviously a trap. From her smile, Chip could tell that whatever answer he gave would likely be wrong. He decided to proceed with caution along the safest path.

In an upbeat tone Chip whispered, "He seems like a good guy. He's tough, very driven. He seems like he really knows his stuff and knows what he wants. Looks like he's well respected..." Chip trailed off his sentence looking for some guidance

Michael F. Goyette

from Kelly. He wondered if he was inaccurate in his assessment. The broadening smile on Kelly's face told him he was.

Kelly nodded. "In two or three months, tell me what you think."

The CEO: It's Good to be the King

The king's guardian sat in vigilant silence at her rigid DWA, waiting intently, unyieldingly to deliver one of her preordained messages: "Mr. Fernandez is not available right now," "I'm sorry, you'll have to make an appointment," or her favorite, "I'm sorry, no one sees Mr. Fernandez without first checking with me." This last message she reserved for the lower folk, the ones she knew would have no recourse other than to leave quietly after the lashing she would give them.

The years had apparently not been kind to her. She looked as she may have at one time been attractive, perhaps even beautiful. However, a few extra pounds detracted from what could have been an appealing figure. Years of smoking and tanning booths had left her looking leathery and plastic and provided a yellowish tint to her highlighted hair. The unnecessarily tight skirt and blouse did not help the appearance. An occasional smile might have softened her otherwise hardened expression, but protecting the entrance to the master's chamber was not a task to be taken lightly; there was no place for smiles in this line of work.

The counter in front of her contained a small plant and a name plate which read "Bertha Potter" and underneath the name "Executive Assistant to the CEO". A welcoming bowl of brightly colored candy, positioned on the counter next to her face, was in stark contrast to the scowl she wore. A small card next to the jar read, "Please, take one! ☺"

"Can I help you?" she snarled.

"Hi. I'm Kelly Hayman and this is Chip Weatherbe. Chip has an appointment to meet with Mr. Fernandez. I made the meeting…"

"I'm sorry, Mr. Fenandez is not available right now," she said, glaring at Kelly and Chip. "You will have to reschedule," she added, resuming her work.

"All right," Kelly said, making no attempt to hide her irritation. "Can we make it tomorrow at the same time?"

Bertha responded without looking at them, her eyes now fixated on the computer screen, complete with glare shield. "Mr. Fernandez's schedule is booked for at least the next six weeks. You should contact this desk in four or five weeks to reschedule."

The brush-off was unmistakable. As she was finishing her "go away, I'm busy and don't need to be talking to you" speech, two men appeared from the doorway behind her. Both were dressed in suits, one in gray and one blue. Bertha heard them, glanced in their direction and proceeded to glare at her guests. Kelly nudged Chip and offered Bertha an exaggerated smile, moving to intercept the CEO.

Bertha's face glowed bright red. Tilting her head to one side and no doubt, thinking wholly unpleasant thoughts, replied to Kelly with an evil stare.

The tall man in the blue suit said good bye to the other as he approached Kelly and Chip. "Hello. I, am Fausto. I am happy to meet you." He stated suavely and fairly dramatically shaking Kelly's hand. He had an accent, the exact origin of which was difficult to pinpoint. He might have been from Latin America or possibly Brazil or even Spain. Are you here to see me?" he asked, smiling at Kelly. If Chip hadn't known better, he would have sworn that Fausto was gazing into her eyes.

If Kelly saw the same look, she offered no indication. Ignoring Bertha, she answered Fausto. "Actually, Chip is a new employee and was scheduled to meet with you this morning at 9:00," Kelly replied politely, but not over-anxiously, appearing completely at ease conversing with the pinnacle of the food chain.

Fausto made no attempt to hide his disappointment, going so far as to slump his shoulders forward and let out a sigh. Kelly allowed herself to smile at this overly dramatic display, missing Bertha rolling her eyes.

Quickly recovering his enthusiastic expression he turned to Chip. "Hello. I, am Fausto. I am happy to meet you," he said, shaking Chip's hand and holding his arm with his left hand. "Come with me."

"I'll talk to you later," Kelly said to Chip, as she turned and departed quickly, not wanting to risk overstaying her welcome.

Chip followed him to his office, leaving Bertha to stew in her failure to guard the most precious entrance to the king's chamber. Such insolence from the little people! Such arrogance! Didn't they know that he was busy...that she was busy? Didn't they know that they needed to check with her before seeing the master? Didn't they know proper procedure? This insult would not go unanswered. First and foremost, she would allow him two or three minutes maximum, then interrupt with some urgent matter, sending the little worker on his way. But something more was necessary at this point. They had pushed her into a corner and left her no way out, no alternative. She had given them the answer that little workers like them required and they had ignored her, pushed her aside like she was some common secretary and went directly to Him. She would have to proceed prudently, sensibly, in the only way that a slap in the face like this warranted. Sure, they would be angered by it, they would get their collective hands slapped, but that was not her concern. No indeed, that was not her concern. She needed to send a strong message: Through this gate, none shall pass! No, they most certainly would not like what she was going to do. But how else would they learn? How else could they grow? What other recourse did she really have? It was time for her to write…A Memo. Followed by…A Call. Both would be directed to their boss. They had left her with no reasonable option. Yes, she decided, this egregious action required A Memo and A Call. She would do both immediately. Then they would know, they would know…

The office was ornately decorated. A large round oak table surrounded by four leather chairs was positioned in the left center of the room. An immense desk dominated the wall with the window. For a second, the desk reminded Chip of a dream he had once had, the details of which he couldn't remember. For some reason, suddenly but briefly, he felt anxious. A large leather chair, obviously Fausto's, was positioned between the desk and the window and two smaller leather chairs directly in front of the desk. The wet bar located on the left wall behind the table was absent of any visible alcohol, but plentiful in bottled water and sodas. To the right, two leather sofas created an 'L' shape with an oak coffee table in the middle.

Chip entered the office and turned to see Fausto close the door behind them. Immediately a life size, framed photo of Fausto next to the door captured his attention. The bottom of the frame began about four feet from the ground, the top extended to the ceiling. The picture showed Fausto smiling and pointing at the observer.

"You like my picture?" Fausto asked, staring adoringly at himself.

"Yes, it's very nice," Chip answered politely. That is out of control, he thought to himself. He glanced around the room and noticed the walls on either side of him were covered with smaller framed photos, all containing some rendering of Fausto: Fausto skiing, Fausto boating, Fausto standing next to a Porsche, Fausto eating a hot dog at a fair. In each he was smiling, knowing exactly where the camera was at all times. Although some of the photos that Chip could see had other people in the pictures with him (Fausto shaking the hand of Michigan's Governor) the vast majority shown only Fausto.

As Chip surveyed the room without moving, he noticed that they were both still standing in front of the larger than life picture, Fausto still staring at it.

Chip remained motionless, wondering what he should do. Neither moved. Chip stared at the picture, trying to look at Fausto out of the corner of his eye. The CEO remained motionless, transfixed on his own image. Finally, Fausto whispered, seeming to converse only with himself, "I am Fausto." Chip was at a loss. How does one respond to such a blatant statement of fact, other than with a 'yes, you are'. Where do I go with this, he thought to himself. Was it a question? Was he supposed to respond?

Lifting the burden of decision making off Chip's shoulders, Fausto finally offered some guidance. "Come, we shall sit and talk."

Fausto took a seat at his desk and Chip followed suit on the opposite side. Through the windows behind Fausto, Chip could see part of a courtyard complete with trees, a number of picnic tables, and a walking path; a refreshing view compared to the high gray office partitions dominating the rest of the facility.

"You like the view?" Fausto asked. He was smiling enormously and nodding his head at this point, seeming to read Chip's mind; his expression eagerly awaited Chip's confirmation.

"It's very nice," Chip responded. And before he could stop himself, the next comment flew out. It was the first thought that came to Chip's mind. It was one of those harmless but inappropriate comments that one typically regrets before they can finish saying it. Before the words were out of his mouth, Chip was already thinking of ways to backpedal. "It's good to be the king."

How could he have uttered something so stupid, so trite? He knew his comments were not professional; fun, but in no sense professional. He understood that he had an audience with one of the most powerful people in the company and may only have that audience for less than a handful of minutes. He knew that the window he had to make a good impression, to sell his talent and capability, to leave a lasting impression was brief. Whatever few words he offered would need to count. And yet, knowing all this, he had let slip the tremendous opportunity before him and chosen instead to toss out a very old and overused joke. I could have at least pulled out something new and updated to lead with, he thought to himself.

If Fausto shared Chip's thoughts, he offered no sign, showing instead an even broader smile and booming with laughter. He nodded and pointed a finger at Chip. "It's good to be the king," Fausto said. Fausto's cheery spirit and laugh was contagious and Chip immediately found himself repeating the comment in unison with Fausto, laughing just as hard.

The office door behind Chip opened and he turned to see Bertha enter.

"Mr. McPherson on line one, Mr. Fernandez," she said, glaring at Chip.

Fausto rose. "I have enjoyed our little talk," he said, still chuckling and walking around the desk to Chip. He shook Chip's hand. "Please, if you need anything don't hesitate to call me…" he said, trailing off, his eyes wandering to Bertha's behind as she walked out of the room. His eyes snapped back to Chip. "It's good to be the king," he said, laughing loud again and slapping Chip on the back.

Chip left the office, reflecting on the situation; it certainly must be good.

C.A.T.

Chip approached a door at the end of a long corridor. The hall and door were off the beaten trail. A number of lights were burned out, leaving the area looking dark and cavernous. A sign on the door read:

"Please submit all questions in writing via E-Mail to CAT. Identify clearly if the problem is a hardware, software, or printer problem. Be specific! Your request will be prioritized and we will respond as soon as possible."

The note was signed – CAT. The door had no window on it and it was locked.

This was ridiculous. He was already beginning his third week of work and he still wasn't able to access all the information he needed to prepare for the SIMM meeting. Every time he thought he had a handle on the information required, Rajiv threw something new his way. This week it was information off the mainframe. Rajiv's request had been clear, however, after hunting the information for two days, becoming completely frustrated that it was nowhere to be found and receiving only blank looks from everyone he asked, he finally approached Rajiv to share the obstacle.

"It's all in the mainframe, Chip," Rajiv had said in a condescending tone. "You should know that by now."

"How do I get access?" Chip had responded, feeling smaller and more insignificant by the moment.

Rajiv had shaken his head and sighed dramatically. "It's a very simple process. Kelly can guide you through it. Check with her immediately."

Chip had completed the required paperwork to gain access, but still didn't have it. He needed to move quickly now, the SIMM meeting was only days away.

Chip knocked hard and waited for a response; no answer. He knocked again; nothing. Kelly hadn't been kidding when she said the IT support team was tough to communicate with. Chip glanced around, searching for another entrance, phone, or some other way to circumvent the door. As he was looking, he noticed a small lens mounted in the upper right corner of the wall and ceiling. I'll bet that's a camera, thought Chip. Those arrogant bastards are not only screening their calls, they're screening their visitors. This was too much. Chip stared at the camera and pounded on the door.

Chip finally heard someone approaching from the other side. A man in a CAT baseball cap opened the door. He was very thin, black, wore a blue T-shirt covered by an unzipped, beat-up old spring jacket, faded jeans, and glasses. He looked to Chip to be in his early thirties.

"Yes?" he said, with no expression, staring at Chip.

The hint of annoyance in his voice was almost funny to Chip. Wasn't this guy supposed to be servicing him and assisting with any computer questions and problems? Evidently customer service was not at the top of his priority list. This was going to be a tricky discussion. Try a lighthearted approach, Chip thought.

"Hi. I'm Chip Weatherbe from Sales and Marketing upstairs." Chip said extending his hand. "Well, who did you piss off to get stuck down here?" Chip asked jokingly.

The man remained expressionless, shook Chip's hand, but did not give his name. "This is by design, not by dictate. CAT's design. Did you read the sign?" the man replied, pointing to the sign on the door. "Now if you'll excuse me, I have work to do. I don't have time for this idle banter with you," the man said as he began to shut the door. Chip had made it this far and wasn't going to surrender any ground now. He quickly slid his foot forward, preventing the door from shutting. The man looked at Chip in surprise.

"I know you're busy, but I'm having some problems accessing the mainframe and it's holding up my work. I've left at least five messages over the last week and haven't heard back from anyone. Do you have a couple minutes now? I would really appreciate it. Thanks," Chip said pleadingly while walking into the room.

A shocked expression covered the man's face. "You think you can just walk in here and start making demands? This is unacceptable. What's that sign say?" the man asked, pointing again to the sign on the door. "CAT doesn't take walk-in demands. Send me another e-mail, maybe I'll respond," the man said while holding the door.

Chip stood in the room, refusing to move. An office partition blocked Chip from moving straight or left. He could only move to the right with only enough space between the partition and the wall for one person to walk at a time. The partition extended about ten feet to the right from where Chip was standing.

"You misunderstand. I'm not making any demands. I was told that if I had a computer problem that no one else could possibly fix, then I was to come here and talk to the only computer team in GIT that knows what they're doing. So, in accordance with what I was told, I have climbed the mountain of computer wisdom and knowledge in search of the best that GIT has to offer," Chip said with a smile.

The man stood staring blankly at Chip for a moment, then started laughing. "You hear that shit?" the man yelled over the partition.

Another man's voice responded. "I heard it. And it's the best *anyone* has to offer, not just GIT."

The man who had opened the door for Chip stopped laughing and looked again at Chip. "That's right, the best *anyone* has to offer. There is no problem that we can't solve. We are the masters of this organization. Without us, this facility would not function. There would be no GIT without us. Isn't that right?" the man said, talking over the wall again.

"It's getting a little deep in here," the voice on the other side of the wall responded. The man in front of Chip started laughing again.

"Then I heard right and have come to the right place," Chip said, walking down the length of the partition and turning into a small room about twenty by twenty.

"Hey, you can't just walk in here," the man who opened the door said. "Everything in this room is highly confidential. CAT allows no one in here."

Chip now had full view of the room. There were two desks, computers, and computer pieces scattered everywhere. The second man was sitting at one of the desks, typing on a keyboard. He was white, dressed in jeans, a casual button down shirt, and wore glasses. He glanced up when he saw Chip, however, seeming completely disinterested, returned to his work.

"What is the CAT, you keep talking about," Chip asked.

"Not *the* CAT. Just CAT. That's like calling you *the* Chip," the man who opened the door responded indignantly.

"I see. And what does CAT stand for?" asked Chip.

"Computer Assistance Team," the man at the desk replied casually.

"You'll refer to us as CAT," said the man who opened the door.

"I see." It's no wonder I got no response, Chip thought. The egos here are astounding. "And what do I call you?" Chip asked.

"I'm Darrell. That's Jeff," said the man in the jacket, pointing to Jeff, sitting at the desk.

"How'ya doing?" Jeff said.

"Now about this computer problem…" Chip said placing his laptop on the only cleared surface in the room.

"And you think we're gonna fix it just like that?" Darrell asked.

Chip smiled at him. "That's right."

"This guy has balls," Darrell said, laughing again.

Jeff rolled his chair over to the laptop. "Who was assigned this?" he asked Darrell.

Darrell typed something into one of the many terminals scattered around the room. "Bob was. I guess we know why it didn't get done."

Jeff sighed. "Okay. Let's see whatch'ya got," he said.

"I thought I had access, but it comes crashing down every time I go into the mainframe to get a price or cost information. Then Kelly said I needed another password, which I don't yet have…"

Jeff turned the laptop on and began working on it.

Chip looked around. He saw an endless array of Dilbert cartoons posted up and multiple charts and references to SETI. Chip thought he would play to the computer guys for a minute and establish a good communication. Part of establishing a good communication link, thought Chip, was making a topic connection with the other person. Start talking about something they are interested in and the communication can blossom from there. After seeing some of the paraphernalia in the room, he thought he had a good starting point.

"Why CAT?" Chip asked Darrell.

"You don't like our name?" Darrell defensively.

"I was just thinking you could call yourselves something like CRASH."

Darrell bristled. "We don't crash down here and we can't be responsible for every idiot around the building who doesn't know what they're doing with their computer."

"No, no. CRASH, as in Computer Resource And System Help. But I see the perception issue. Then how about something like CADAVRE, Computer Assistance Desk and Anti-Virus Resource Employees." Chip paused a minute seeing if Darrell would catch on, which apparently wasn't happening. Maybe the references were too obscure. "You don't play computer games do you?" Chip asked.

Darrell stared, not knowing how to respond. Then Jeff spoke up. "Quake III Arena."

A light went on in Darrell's head. "CRASH and CADAVRE. Quake III is old news. You've been living in a cave if you think Quake represents state of the art games. But I like the way you think, my friend," he said nodding.

Jeff laughed lightly, shaking his head and appearing fairly disgusted. "You are so gullible. He's stroking you so the next time he comes down here you'll give him what he wants. He's probably from Sales and Marketing."

Chip laughed and patted Jeff on the back. "Your man here is smarter than he looks," Chip said to Darrell.

"So is this something you can…" Before Chip could finish his question, Jeff had turned off the laptop and pushed it back to Chip.

"Done. Here is your new password," Jeff said, handing a piece of paper to Chip.

Amazing; almost a week of downtime only to wait for this three minute activity. This probably could have been done over the phone, Chip thought. Well, at least the problem was solved.

"Thanks. I appreciate your time. I'll probably see you guys at the next all staff meeting," Chip said.

Jeff and Darrell exchanged glances and chuckled.

"Probably not," Jeff said.

"You go to the "all staff" meeting, we have work to do," Darrell added.

"I take it you don't think highly of those meetings?" Chip inquired.

"If you think we're isolated down here, wait until you start dealing with HR. They're at the heart of the organization and they couldn't be more isolated from everyone else," Jeff said.

"They're completely insane and we have no use for them or their silly little plans. You want a cost cutting plan? Get rid of that entire department. They're completely worthless. Or better yet, get rid of that department and give us the money. We'll make this place hum," Darrell said.

Chip knew what they were getting at. Janice and her team seemed to be extremely busy with a lot of things. Things that seemed to Chip to have little to do with running a business, although he was confident that in the mind of Janice, the issues that she handled and the projects that she involved herself in were vital to the success of the organization. He assumed by Darrell and Jeff's comments that he would see much more of Janice's influence.

Germ Management (a.k.a. HR Run Amuck)

Another Monday morning. Chip poured a cup of coffee and added cream, no sugar. He felt like he was moving in slow motion. He felt lethargic. He had not wanted to get up this morning, hitting the snooze button twice. Despite this, he had still managed to get in by 7:20. A little later than the 7:00 standard he had set from the beginning, but respectable nevertheless.

Day one of week four and already Chip was bored. It seemed like he had been at GIT for an eternity. Stacy's words ran though his mind: give it time. I can't see how it will change, he thought. All he had worked on was preparing information for the SIMM meeting. Poring over numbers, doing everything he could to make sense of the data he was studying. Rajiv had been no help. In fact, most of his input had hindered any substantial forward progress. Chip never moved in one direction for more than half a day. One day Rajiv would provide a basic direction, define the final content the end presentation should contain and state that he was leaving how to get there completely in Chip's hands. The next day he would bring Chip a nearly illegible chart or graph, scribbled by hand and politely ask that the information be summarized in a very specific format. One minute Rajiv was sure he needed only this data, two days later he wanted that data instead. He would micromanage, all the while reiterating that Chip was in charge of the project and that Rajiv trusted his better judgment.

It occurred to Chip that he should be thankful he had a job. A lot of people were losing jobs nowadays. At least he had a salary, a fairly decent one at that. He could pay his bills and still save a little for later. In fact, if he and Stacy saved enough, they could afford for her to stay home when they had kids, at least for the first few years and maybe for longer. Yes, he was certainly lucky to have such a good salary and benefits. A part of him decided he should stop his complaining and make the best of the situation. He had a lot to be thankful for.

But still…so unchallenging. Give it time. So boring. Give it time. I could be doing so much more with my talent. You've only been at this for a month now, give it time, it will get better.

How? What will change? What would he be doing differently in 3 months, 6 months, or a year from now? Rajiv had outlined his responsibilities clearly and this was one of the primary functions. The other functions were similar. It wasn't like his previous job. Those responsibilities were outlined in a job description too, but it didn't matter. You just did what you had to do to get all the work done and take care of the customer. There were parameters, but they weren't rigid lines. Or maybe they were and it was just easier to ignore them or at the very least, redefine them.

Maybe that was it. Master this type of activity quickly and then talk to Rajiv about expanding the responsibility. Increase the challenge.

As Chip sipped his coffee and walked to his desk, he passed Dan and Kelly standing in front of the announcement board.

"Morning. What's the good word?" asked Chip.

"The bastards cut out our bonus this year," replied Dan. "Read," Dan said pointing to the memo as Kelly stood there looking disgusted and shaking her head.

E-MEMO
TO: All employees
FROM: CRDCM – BHC
SUBJECT: Germ Management

More than 520,000 person hours are lost each year due to health related issues. This translates into a $1,300,000 loss per year for the company. Much of this lost time can be avoided if we all follow some very simple rules:
- Wash your hands frequently
- Cover your mouth when you cough
- Cover your nose and mouth if you sneeze and wash your hands immediately
- Disinfect your phone before and after each use. An initial supply of antibacterial wipes and antibacterial hand gel can be found in the Employee Cafeteria. After that you will need to supply your own. Remember that the cost of the gel and wipes is small compared to the long run cost of work time missed.
- Don't share drinking cups or food utensils (i.e. spoons, forks, etc.) with coworkers
- If any bodily fluids are evident on the fax machine, your desk, someone else's desk, the vending machine, the cafeteria counters, etc., clean the area and disinfect your hands afterwards.

- If any bodily fluids are evident in the restrooms, clean the area and disinfect your hands afterward. Cleaning materials are located in the storage closet at the entrance of each restroom. The closets are locked for obvious security reasons, however, the key can be obtained from the Administrative Assistant located closest to the restroom.
- Bodily fluids can carry numerous germs and we should avoid the direct exchange of them with coworkers, especially during the cold and flu season! ☺
- Keep your DWA free from dirt, dust, and bodily fluids. A clean DWA is a happy DWA. A clean DWA promotes a positive, growth experience for all who enter. Remember, your DWA contributes to the group's overall healthy DWE.
- If you happen to feel ill, put forth your best effort to finish out the day. Often times a positive mental state can make us feel better and turn what seems like a mountain into a small bump in the road. Remember, Change Management Counselors are available if you need someone to talk to.
- In extreme cases, you may put your head on the desk for five minutes and close your eyes. Again, focus your energy on positive images and away from whatever is bothering you. You might just find that after five minutes you feel like a new person! ☺ But remember, when you are resting your head, don't drool on the desk. If you do, use an antibacterial wipe to clean the area. Additionally, this time should be deducted from any breaks or lunchtime, otherwise check with your supervisor to make up the time.

If we all follow these common sense guidelines, we can help reduce the losses incurred by the company every year. If we all work together, we can eliminate this $1,300,000 loss from last year and continue the bonus plan next year ☺.
Remember – T.E.A.M.

Kelly erupted first, whispering angrily. "How can they do this? You notice they don't have the balls to say it outright, they have to bury it in some freakin' health memo. You know what's funny, half these zombies won't even read that last sentence and will be all surprised when we don't get anything."

In another low whisper Dan said, "Does it mean that last year we lost money and that if we spend this year making up for it, maybe next year we'll make money and get a bonus. Which means we won't see that bonus for two years since the bonus is paid every March for the previous year."

"What?" asked Chip.

Kelly again erupted, "What are you talking about?"

Dan half-heartedly defended his position, "It just reads funny, that's all."

Chip and Kelly continued to read the memo, falling deeper into disbelief. Kelly spoke, laughing lightly out of frustration. "Don't drool on desk. The new DDOD rule is now in effect. What in God's name is this company coming to?"

As they pondered this question, Gracie walked by. "Another Monday morning announcement?" Gracie asked with a smile and cheerful tone.

"Yeah. Read," Dan said, pointing at the memo.

Gracie read silently then spoke, "Well it's about time someone said it."

Annoyed and puzzled expressions clouded the faces of Dan and Kelly. "Said what?" Chip asked politely.

"People are always sneezing and coughing around here. I never see anyone wash their hands after they sneeze…I was sick nonstop last year and I know I got it from this place. I'm glad to see someone's taking action," Gracie said.

Kelly's expression quickly changed to focused aggression. Adopting her game face, Kelly said in a very analytical, objective tone, "Don't you think they're spending a lot of time and money trying to dictate common sense. I mean, do we really need to spend money on a committee to remind us to wash our hands and not drool on each other?"

"Boy, somebody got up on the wrong side of the bed," Gracie replied walking away indignantly.

"Go back to the library," Kelly mumbled after she was out of earshot. "This is beyond stupid. How she got so much power so quickly is beyond me," she continued, refocusing her thoughts back to the topic.

"What do mean?" Chip questioned.

Kelly turned to look at Chip. "She's only been here for six months. I think she knew someone higher up. First thing she does when she gets in here is turn everything upside down. She has final say over everyone that gets hired in. Everyone, from the top of the food chain to the bottom. I'm surprised she let us hire you."

"She doesn't have final say," Dan said, shaking his head and walking away. "You and your politics."

"Oh, bullshit. She certainly does," Kelly shot back. But it was too late. Dan was disengaged, walking away, waving his hand over his shoulder. "You're jealous because you're not as connected as I am," she said in a raised voice, calling after him. And as an afterthought, to evidently make herself feel better, she muttered, "Loser".

Chip considered the memo before him. Germ Management. Certainly this had slipped by Janice. There's no way she had approved this. One of her people was confused and had come up with it on their own. No question, this did not reflect a real company communication, it was the work of one rogue employee who would no doubt be scolded for wasting their time on such nonsense. It was probably that Scott guy. This was the type of thing he would do, Chip decided.

Besides, even if it was legitimate, who cares? So some small faction of the company was a little off their rocker, big deal. It didn't affect Chip. If there wasn't going to be a bonus, they had to find some way to communicate it. This was just the medium and format of choice; it was as simple as that.

Still, if this was valid, then someone had spent time on it. Then someone had spent time approving it. Then someone had spent time posting it. Since it mentioned bonuses, it likely had the blessing from high up in the food chain, meaning high level managers had reviewed and likely discussed it. I wonder how that meeting went, Chip wondered. He envisioned a team of people sitting in room debating how best to suggest that people clean the FAX machine if bodily fluids were evident. First someone would suggest the concept. Then they likely discussed the optimal words to use. They could have discussed this for hours.

Chip's mind spun. No, it didn't happen that way. One person, with too much time on their hands and no sense of priorities, sat down at their desk and generated this silliness. Any thought to the contrary would certainly be too far fetched to even consider…

Wouldn't it?

SIMM Meeting

Chip took a seat at the back of the room around the periphery of the meeting table. This was known as the "outer circle". It was becoming quickly apparent that the internal battles were not something he wanted to be any part of. It was better to blend into the back of the room for now to avoid potential enemy fire. Besides, he was just a Business Analyst, sorry, "Marketing Manager," and most of the people who would be seated at the table in the "inner circle" were the higher ups: Directors, higher managers, and of course, Rajiv.

Individuals from a number of different areas began filing into the room, most notably Grant Richards from Finance and Hans Marx from Engineering. Grant was in his early forties and had been with the company for four years. He had joined GIT from a competitor and was considered one of the rising stars. He was well respected among subordinates and had developed somewhat of a reputation for being too hard on people, especially in these types of meetings. A popular story had been circulated that he had once had a closed door meeting with his counterpart from Germany, which ended in the German close to tears. Kelly had mentioned this story with complete disbelief. Kelly always referred to Grant as The Pussycat, believing that his reputation had been blown out of proportion.

Hans Marx, the Engineering Director, sat across from Grant. Little was known about Hans since he had just joined the group a month ago from their sister company in Germany. Rumor had it that he was the first wave of European managers to join the U.S. facility. His purpose, so it was said, was to get everything "back on course," despite the parent company being in Detroit.

Rajiv was the first to greet each as they entered the room. He viewed Grant and Hans as both competition and a threat to his position and as such, he was overly amiable.

The meeting quickly filled with over thirty people in a room meant for no more than twenty. Kelly came in and took a seat in the outer circle opposite Chip. She glanced at Chip and gave a quick smile and nod. A Financial Analyst from Grant's team, Angelina Moore, took a seat next to Chip. Angelina typically accompanied Grant to meetings and was considered his right hand. A black woman three years out of college, Angelina worked diligently behind the scenes making Grant look good. She was well liked (even by Kelly) and seemed like a person with whom it would be very pleasant to work with. Although not a dazzling performer, she was a solid, dependable worker that Grant counted on time and again. Given a few years experience in the trenches under Grant's guidance, she would likely become a well respected key player. Notably absent was Janice.

Once everyone was seated, Rajiv glided to the front of the room and using his most alluring smile, took control of the meeting immediately. Rajiv was comfortable in the spotlight and demanded an exclusive venue.

His first few words left one with the impression that he had orchestrated the entire meeting and everyone in attendance had come as a direct response to his invitation. The truth of the matter was that the meeting had been pushed on him by the "higher powers". Rajiv's superior had asked him to gather a rather large group of individuals from Finance and Engineering so Rajiv could update them on the activities of the Sales Department, allowing everyone to get on the same page. Rajiv considered these meetings a waste of time and an affront to his leadership skills. The meeting would turn into a stone throwing contest, with the stone's destination being the Sales Department. Although he never exposed his true feelings, he believed that he should not be forced to justify his actions or plans to his peers. Of course, when it came time for co-workers to explain themselves to him, no amount of detail seemed sufficient to quench his thirst for the burning questions, why or why not?

"I want to thank everyone for being able to make our second Strategic and Implementation Management Meeting. This communication format is vital to our future success and growth. We encourage an interactive exchange between the various groups in attendance. I assure you," he said chuckling lightly, "no idea will be taken off the table. We encourage you'all to think outside the box. Again, no discussion will be shot down. If we need to remain on course, we may opt to take a discussion off-line. If that's the case, Gracie will make note of the topic and it will be placed in the concept incubator," he said, pointing to a flip chart in the corner. "The goal of this meeting is to take a proactive approach in redefining the way we do business and generate a set of results driven, best practices so that at the end of the day everyone is empowered to implement a win-win game plan," Rajiv began.

He continued with a brief cheerleading speech, focusing on how, as a team, GIT could conquer any obstacle using every buzz phrase imaginable. He cited more than once the beautifully framed poster on the wall: TEAM: Together Everyone Achieves More. Chip remembered seeing this picture before and recalled the first thought that came to his mind: More what? More money? More bureaucracy? More freedom? More self-imposed barriers? From that point, whenever he saw the poster, he thought of a high school cheerleader, blurting out cheers that made you feel good but lacked substance.

As Chip pondered the significance of the feel good saying, Rajiv had already sat down and Dan had taken center stage to update the group on his projects.

Linda walked in about five minutes into Dan's presentation and took a seat in the outer circle. A number of people glanced at her entrance and quickly returned their attention to Dan. Chip noticed that Rajiv, however, was staring at her, breaking contact briefly to look at his watch.

After fifteen minutes, Dan concluded his presentation with a short discussion on his most recent project.

"...and the G1500 quote should be finalized and submitted to Purchasing by the end of next week," Dan said as he ended his portion of the discussion. Rajiv was on his feet and ready to introduce the next speaker when Grant raised his hand and without waiting to be acknowledged, began his questioning.

"I was of the understanding that this quote was already done. Wasn't it due last week, or did I misunderstand?" Grant said, looking directly at Rajiv. "In fact, when we discussed this two days ago, Rajiv, I thought you had made it clear that the quote was under control and had been handled in the appropriate timeline, which I was lead to believe was last week. Again, if I'm off base here, please redirect me."

Rajiv, always on his toes and always prepared to save himself, responded without missing a beat.

"I share your puzzlement, Grant." Rajiv said, turning his gaze to Kelly's direction. "Kelly, I thought this was handled?"

Chip could tell that Kelly had not been paying close attention to the discussion and was caught completely off guard. In fact, judging by Kelly's expression, it was likely that she had been on another planet for most of the discussion. To Kelly, it seemed like the entire meeting had come to a grinding halt and she had been thrust on center stage. She began what almost certainly would be an embarrassing response when Dan jumped into the fray. He saw the direction the discussion was going and somewhat resented the fact that Rajiv had turned to a third party for answers on what he considered "his baby".

Dan stated in a calm voice, "After careful review of the RFQ, we saw that more information was required from the customer. We requested this information two weeks ago and only received the information yesterday. From this point, it will take us one week to respond."

Grant persisted, as Rajiv became increasingly uncomfortable, "How long did we have the RFQ before we called the customer and requested additional information?"

Rajiv again looked accusingly in Kelly's direction. Kelly had now composed herself and was prepared for war. This time, she began what almost certainly would be a powerful, vigorous defense when Dan again jumped in and cut her short.

"I was on vacation for a week and a half, so we did lose some time there. However, keep in mind that the customer promised this RFQ over three months ago," answered Dan.

Relentlessly, Grant continued. "I'm not concerned when *they* promised it. What I am concerned with is *our* response time. From the time we received this RFQ to the time we will respond with a quote is going to be over five weeks. Is this correct? I think for an order of this magnitude we should be putting forth a little more effort. Have we explained to the customer that we are going to be late and have they agreed to grant us an extension?" he asked, staring at Rajiv.

Dan answered, "I spoke with both the buyer and the engineering team this week. They understand that we had a number of important questions that needed to be answered prior to issuing a quote. They granted us an extension until next week, which gives us ample time. They also informed me that only the incumbent supplier responded to the initial deadline. All the other suppliers asked for the same additional information we did and were all granted an extension. As far as not handling the quote when it came in, that was my fault. I should have laid out a better plan for when I was gone. However, be that as it may, based on the situation of our competitors, we still wouldn't have received the needed information until yesterday and would still have required an extension," Dan explained in a calm voice.

This sounded reasonable to Chip, but he noticed that Rajiv was preparing to talk, only to be cut short by Grant. It was becoming increasingly apparent who the real target of the conversation was. "I understand your situation, Dan. You were on vacation and didn't know the quote had come in, however, a system should be in place to alert someone else so the ball can keep rolling. I think it's management's responsibility to see to it that the system is put in place." Chip caught the implied accusation: why didn't Rajiv know that the RFQ was here and act on it in Dan's absence. Rajiv saw the attack and masterfully shifted responsibility.

"Absolutely. No question, Grant. We do have a system and again, I am in a bit of a quandary as to where the system broke down. In the interest of time, I suggest we take a system discussion off-line to a later meeting where we can devote our focused energy. Rest assured, a clearly defined system is in place," said Rajiv. Looking a final time at Kelly, he added, "Kelly, please arrange that meeting. I'd like you to be part of that discussion as well."

Kelly had turned slightly red and was now glaring at Rajiv.

Grant had not intended for the buck to be passed so quickly. Not one to let his prey escape, he continued, "I'd like it if the Division Managers and Account Managers could meet to discuss this, today if possible, tomorrow morning at the latest. Let's open a candid dialog on this issue and identify the best way to reduce our RFQ response time. Rajiv, I'd like you and the Account Team to lay out a roadmap outlining this process. We can use this as ground zero and progress from there. I think we as managers need to be responsible for the RFQ flow on orders of this size."

Rajiv turned to Gracie who had been taking notes and said, "Gracie, be sure to schedule a meeting for later today with all required parties," Gracie nodded.

The meeting continued for two hours more. Chip noticed a number of the slides he had created pop up a few times during the course of the presentation. All his hard work, finally coming to fruition. All the information was neatly organized and summarized in the exact format Rajiv had requested. He noticed on a few of the slides, ones that the team had put together without his assistance had a slightly different format; different line sizes, a similar but modified flow of information, a different logo, etc. At one point, a faceless voice pointed out the logo discrepancy jokingly, soliciting a few, brief chuckles as the meeting quickly moved on.

Chip tuned in and out of the discussion, occasionally looking in Kelly's direction and wondering if the same finger pointing he saw earlier was scheduled to come his direction anytime in the near future. He could see by Kelly's expression that she was thinking about the discussion and was extremely unhappy that it had taken place. What a terrible thing to do to one of your subordinates, Chip considered. A one-on-one discussion is one thing, but a public spanking? Maybe she had earned it from some previous transgression, he thought. Even still, that appeared a somewhat harsh reprimand, especially in light of Dan apparently trying to take responsibility while Rajiv strove to avoid it.

Chip made a mental note to review the event with Kelly later, deciding that he must be missing some information or underlying politics. After all, he finally concluded, no manager worth his weight would point a finger so quickly, so publicly, without at least asking the subordinate a few questions to discern all the facts. At that point, it occurred to Chip that maybe he was now beginning to see the real Rajiv. Maybe the distrusting sense he had at their initial meeting was a warning light that he chose to shelve, chose to ignore under the banner of forward progress. Time would tell, he decided. Until then, this first major deliverable had been tackled successfully; sail on course.

What We Have Here is a Failure to Communicate (a.k.a HR Clarifies Germ Management)

E-Memo
TO: All employees
FROM: Human Resources CRDCM
SUBJECT: Germ Management

We would like to invite all employees to a meeting in the cafeteria on Wednesday to discuss the recent memo concerning Germ Management. This is a mandatory meeting; please plan on attending.
Your cooperation is appreciated. TEAM

Everyone was seated, waiting for Janice to join the meeting. Chip sat between Kelly and Ted. He was finding it difficult to focus after the SIMM meeting that morning. Could he have done something differently, he wondered to himself? He had worked his tail off trying to balance his best judgment against the exact wishes of Rajiv. No, he decided. He had done his best. Besides, the information he had assembled was just detail stuff, no big picture discussion points like, are we responding to the customer properly? The information that he had provided was only summaries of actual data. The only dispute that could arise was over the format; the data was historical and could not change. Cut in different ways, maybe, but not changed.

"Why do they have these meetings? We know what the memo said. It was bad news. Do they really need to rub it in?" Kelly asked.

"They don't want you to just know what the memo said, she wants you to love what the memo said. She wants you to accept it with every fiber of your body," Ted said.

"Who's she?" Chip asked rhetorically, knowing Ted meant Janice.

"The Nazi bitch who thinks she runs the place," Ted answered.

"And Nazi bitch would be your name for…?" Chip asked, again pushing Ted to say her name.

"He's so colorful isn't he? He means Janice," Kelly said.

"I know. Just seeing if Ted was awake," Chip replied.

"And she does run the place. Ted's right. She wants you to fully embrace everything she says and you can only question her in the context of keeping her end goal or basic idea fully intact. Toss out a question or discussion that challenges her fundamental premise and you'll see her go right for the jugular," Kelly said.

"You two actually agree on something?" Chip asked lightly.

Ted laughed. "She's beginning to see the light."

Terry and Scott entered the room. Terry, one of Scott's teammates from Human Resources, looked somewhat pale and very nervous. Terry was a single white woman, twenty five years old, who had been at GIT for just under six months. Although friendly and easy to talk to, she found it difficult to make friends; her association with Janice seemed to follow her everywhere.

In contrast to Terry, Scott was overly confident. He glided into the room. He began handing out the Germ Management memo, smiling at everyone. Terry shuffled through some papers at the front of the room, keeping her eyes down, never once making eye contact with anyone.

Ted leaned over Chip and whispered to Kelly. "Who is that?" he asked, pointing to the young man.

"That's the guy who interviewed me. He is extremely arrogant," Chip answered.

"His name's Scott Snow, one of Janice's lackey interns. He worships her. She says jump and he says how high," Kelly added.

"How old is he?" Ted asked in shock.

"I think he's twenty. Twenty-one maybe," Kelly said.

"Is he off of breast milk yet?" Ted said laughing. Kelly chuckled. Chip stifled a laugh and shook his head. "If he's not, he has nothing of value to say to me. You watch, I'll bet the Nazi bitch sent him to answer questions on the bonus so she wouldn't have to," said Ted.

Kelly and Chip looked at him curiously. "You think?" Kelly asked.

"You watch. This is sickening," Ted said looking completely disgusted.

Terry finally looked up, appearing very uncomfortable. "Thank you for…"

Before she could finish, Scott jumped in. "Let's get started. I want to thank everyone for coming today. For those of you who don't know me, I'm Scott Snow and I'm in charge of the BHC."

Ted looked at Chip and Kelly with a "see, I told you so" glance.

Terry glared at Scott for a moment. Then, as if struck by some divine enlightenment, she smiled and slowly backed away to a wall, disappearing into the standing crowd, leaving Scott alone in the spotlight. Sometimes, it's best not to be the messenger.

"I just handed out a copy of the recently posted Germ Management memo," Scott continued. "There seems to have been a lot of conversations about this. We on the BHC of the CRDCMT have gotten some negative feedback on the contents of the memo. While we appreciate your feedback, we think many of you may have misunderstood the memo. We'd like to clarify things today and answer any questions you might have."

Ted raised his hand.

"Yes, a question in back?" Scott acknowledged, pointing to Ted. Scott leaned, half sitting on the table behind him with his arms folded, looking particularly smug and arrogant.

"What is the BHC?" Ted asked.

Scott smiled a condescending smile. "That would be the Better Health Committee, Ted. Nothing new, everyone knows that by now."

Ted gave a quick "oh" while a few scattered "oohs" could be heard around the room.

Ted quickly raised his hand again. "I have another question." Chip and Kelly exchanged quick smiles.

"Yes, Ted?" Scott said, irritated.

"Scotty? Can I call you Scotty?" Ted asked rhetorically while Scott rolled his eyes and refused to answer. "Scotty, why isn't Janice here talking to us?" he asked, looking and sounding completely puzzled.

"Well, she can't be in two places at once now can she, Ted?" Scott replied in a belittling tone, something he obviously picked up from Janice. "She had another meeting previously scheduled that took priority, so I'm in charge of the meeting."

Ted changed his expression completely and laughed out loud. "Oh! So you're the one in charge. I'd been wondering who was steering the ship all this time." The room exploded in laughter.

"If we can move on…" Scott said, turning red and losing his smile.

Ted persisted. "If you're in charge, maybe you can explain why we're being told that we're not getting a bonus in a Germ Management memo. Can you do that for us, Scott?"

"I can…just be a little patient, Ted, and we'll get to that. And I'm not sure that your comments are very constructive, Ted," Scott said.

"I'm sorry, I was just following the Open Dialog rules posted behind you, specifically the one that says to be open and honest and to challenge ideas."

"It also says to listen. Can you do that for a minute or two?" Scott said. Before Ted could reply, Scott was off and running, although, sensing the crowd was with Ted, he looked unsure of himself now, stuttering somewhat and refusing to make eye contact with the audience.

"We can…" he started, turning to the desk behind him and fumbling through some papers and producing a single sheet. "…we can keep this brief. I know everyone wants to get back to work." He giggled nervously, blushing slightly. The crowd remained unmoved, offering Scott no sign of support.

Ted smiled at Chip and Kelly, pleased with his ability to dethrone a representative of the source of corporate evil: Janice. He was proud that he rattled the young man's cage and completely derailed the now abandoned locomotive of arrogance. Kelly returned the smile, finding simple enjoyment in watching anyone squirm.

Chip just shook his head. Ted's going to get himself in trouble for sure, he thought. Irrespective of his accurate assessment of the situation or lack thereof, no reasonable manager would tolerate this type of sustained public questioning. This wasn't the first time Ted had challenged management openly over his decades at the company. That was likely why Ted hadn't risen to any level of prominence in the company, Chip thought. Rebels are such a double-edged sword, Chip considered. On the one hand, they can be the type of boat rocker good for challenging the status quo, for moving things forward, for making tough decisions when no one else will, and taking the blame without blinking under the spotlight of scrutiny. On the other hand, they don't follow orders very well, often spreading a poison of discontentment to everyone around them, and encouraging a mutinous attitude.

"Basically…um…well to start with…um…the bonus situation is…um…going to be reviewed this week. The reference to an actual bonus…or lack of a bonus I should say…um…in the Germ Management memo was…um…more of a…um… hypothetical…um…a…picture of what can happen when…um…people take a lot of sick time. It was more of…um…um…a guess of what the number…um…might look like in…um…an average year."

The audience just stared at Scott, offering no insight into their feelings or thoughts. "I actually feel guilty now," Ted whispered to Chip.

Chip nodded his acknowledgment and said, "You should." He glanced at Kelly who was still smiling and evidently still having fun with the situation.

Kelly caught Chip's eye. "What?" she whispered innocently, refusing to relinquish her smile.

Scott droned on for another two or three minutes culminating in one final message: the actual status of the bonus was to be determined. "Any questions?" Scott asked. And without waiting for a response added, "Thanks" and bolted out the door.

"Anti-climactic wouldn't you say?" Ted asked Chip, walking with him and Kelly out of the room and down a row of cubicles to their offices. "I feel kind of sorry for him now."

"He'll recover. He'll probably be doing something else next week anyway. I heard we're going to be restructuring," Chip said, looking for any insight into the rumors he had heard over the last few weeks.

"We're always restructuring," Ted responded, laughing. "The question is, are we consolidating to remove bottlenecks and improve synergy or are we decentralizing to foster ingenuity and flexibility while reducing bureaucracy."

Chip was at a loss.

"I've got to go. I have a meeting. When you two geniuses figure this out, let me know," Kelly said.

Ted ignored her sarcasm and continued talking to Chip. "I've been through this before, my friend. A couple times. It's like a big Merry-Go-Round."

"I think most of the changes are positive. Things change. When you move forward, things change," Chip said, trying desperately to play devil's advocate and convince himself that any change which required him to move out of Rajiv's group would be a good one.

Clearly his response was not well received. They reached Ted's office and Ted sat back in his chair, folding his arms. "Let me ask you a question, puppydog; how do you sleep at night?" Ted asked smiling.

"Pardon me?" Chip asked, not liking the direction the question was headed.

"How does any MBA sleep at night knowing that they have no heart, no soul?" Ted asked, smiling.

"I'm not even going to dignify that with an answer. We're talking about change and restructuring and off you go into the woods. You know, I don't know why I even listen to this crap from you."

"You're wise beyond your years. But back to having no heart…"

Chip stared at him, waiting for the remainder of the bait. This was stupid. Why did he even engage Ted in these discussions? Chip had work to do. "Ted, while I…"

"I know a way to show a little heart. You could devote some time to community service. There's a different sign-up sheet everyday on the bulletin board in the cafeteria. Lot's of opportunity to show you care. You know that community service is now part of your performance evaluation?" Ted asked with a devilish grin.

He just goes from one can of worms to another, Chip thought and wondered if he was being set up for a Ted conspiracy theory and proceeded cautiously and lightheartedly. "What do you mean? How can they make community service part of your performance evaluation? Who told you they were going to do that? They're not going to do that."

Ted showed a look of exaggerated surprise. "They most certainly are. They want to humanize our cold corporate culture. And how are they going to do that? By telling everyone that they should be out painting houses or devoting time at church: a church of their choosing by the way. And at the same time they're busy making us better people, they've got their boot poised and ready to kick out the people who've been loyal to the company for twenty years. Some humanization plan. It doesn't change a goddamn thing. I spent my life working here. I spent my work hours here and all my free time here. The time I should have spent with my wife and kids was spent working on whatever project that needed to be done immediately; whatever management entertainment exercise that desperately needed completion at the moment. They treat you like a fucking slave and then when they've had their way, they throw your ass out the door like you were a cheap prostitute."

"Well, Ted, you had the option of leaving. You could have left at any time and moved to greener pastures. It's nobody's fault you chose to stay. You knew they were working you like a dog and you knew that one day they could get rid of you if they chose to," Chip said.

Ted was now turning red. Clearly Chip's comments had hit a little close to the heart. Ted defended accordingly. "I believed that if I took care of the company, then they would take care of me. Not all of us want to spend our lives whoring ourselves out to the highest bidder, doing any job that happens to come along. I loved this work and I loved this company and what did I get in return? They let some damn MBA open his fly… sorry, her fly…she opened her fly, whipped out the dick she wished she had and pissed on me." Ted's words were now coming between breaths. Chip realized he had let the conversation get too far. He felt guilty since he knew this was a sensitive issue.

Ted continued, "And why? Because I'm a white man in my late fifties and I don't fit in to their diverse world anymore." He practically spit on the word 'diverse'. "That damn Brit said so himself. Except when he said old white males were the problem, he left out the word American. But you know that's what he's thinking since he doesn't seem to have any problems bringing in his old white male friends from Europe. And that's only part of it. I am still more valuable than eighty percent of these shits they bring in off the street, and that's after they've had five years of training. But I have a pension they have to pay out. That's just around the corner. I was out for four weeks last year with surgery that I'm sure they weren't happy to pay for. But most of all, I'm not multi-cultural and I'm old. I'm just one of the dumb saps who stayed around forever, building this fucking company."

Ted was completely flustered by this point. "You better be careful, my friend. You're going to be an old white man one day and you can see how they are going to treat you. I did what I was supposed to do for this company and my family and they abandoned me!"

Chip was struck speechless. Where did that come from, he thought? Ted stopped and for a moment there was an awkward silence. Chip felt embarrassed. He had received a little too much insight into Ted's world and wasn't sure where to go with it.

"You just think long and hard about that," Ted said, calming down. "Just think long and hard about how much devotion you want to give to a place that would do that to its people. Now if you'll excuse me, I have work to do," he finished, returning to his computer and his work.

This Situation is Crazy

6:30 am

Chip sipped his coffee, watching the familiar Windows logo pop up and advance into his desktop setting. Not a good week, he thought. He sensed that yesterday's presentation hadn't gone well: too many questions from Engineering and Finance that Sales and Marketing couldn't answer. The whole tone was accusatory; Grant accusing Rajiv, Rajiv accusing Kelly, Engineering accusing everyone who wasn't an engineer… In the end, the discussion seemed unproductive, despite everyone agreeing at the end of the meeting as to the usefulness of the discussion and all concurring that they needed to do this type of thing more often.

Rajiv had requested a meeting with Chip to discuss, no doubt, the SIMM meeting. Rajiv had said something on his way out of the office yesterday afternoon. "Chip, set a meeting for you and I for tomorrow morning. It's imperative we discuss a few things. Make it first out of the gate…" he seemed to search momentarily for a time, "…make it 6:30." Chip had responded with a "no problem", despite Rajiv's well known history of never arriving to the office prior to 8:00 a.m. and rarely before 8:45 a.m. Be that as it may, the meeting had been set. Chip had no problem showing up this early, assuming the meeting would take place. Since Chip had no experience with Rajiv standing him up, he thought it best to extend to him the benefit of the doubt. So Chip arrived at 6:20 a.m., gathered his notes, and waited. Kelly arrived five minutes after Chip, but still no Rajiv. Not surprising. Frustrating, but not surprising.

"You're in early," Kelly commented, unpacking her lap top.

"So are you. Early meeting?" Chip asked.

"With the office in Germany. The Fatherland is calling. How about you?" she asked in return.

"I had a meeting scheduled with Rajiv at 6:30."

Kelly laughed, "And you figured you would just show up and have a meeting. You know he's notorious for standing people up, especially for meetings this early."

"Yeah, I know."

"Don't take it personally. Besides, do you really want to talk to Gandhi this early?" Kelly asked, laughing. Chip didn't respond.

Kelly stared at Chip for a moment without speaking. " Have you read your e-mail yet this morning?" she asked seriously. Chip shook his head. "Take a look at it before you go talk to him," she said without looking at him. Chip detected complete annoyance in her voice. She looked like she was going to explode at any minute.

Chip quickly pulled up his e-mail. At the top of the list was a message from Rajiv, the little red exclamation point marking its urgency. The subject line read "SIMM Meeting". He opened it and began reading the message.

"I was very disappointed with the team's showing at the SIMM meeting yesterday. Frankly, I was embarrassed. I expect more out of our group. These internal meetings…"

He read each word, growing angrier with each passing sentence.

It was the last note, directed to him, that pushed him over the edge.

"Chip: I do not want a repeat of this performance next month. We hired you under the pretense…"

What the hell is this, he thought to himself? He glanced over at Kelly who looked at him.

"Now what do you think of your new boss?" she asked coldly, turning her attention back to her computer screen.

This is BULLSHIT! Chip shouted over and over in his mind. Rajiv hopes that hiring me would not be a poor decision, one which would require immediate reversal!? What kind of nonsense was this? None of the problems that had been raised had been Chip's fault. He hadn't let a quote sit a full week and not responded to the customer.

He stared at Kelly in disbelief. "What the hell is this?" he asked her.

"It's the same bullshit we've all come to expect from a prick like him," she answered, turning from her computer and looking over his shoulder at someone approaching.

Chip's stomach tightened into knots, thinking it was Rajiv. He turned to see Linda coming over. She was dressed as usual: a tight, virtually see-through blouse with a tight, very short, skirt.

"Good morning," she said, sliding her hand across Chip's shoulders as she passed behind him. She rested herself on his desk, half-sitting on it, immediately next to him; her legs an inch from his hand. After only a few weeks of knowing Linda, Chip knew that she was an extreme flirt. Every time he saw her with a guy, she was flirting, almost without exception. Although he liked Linda and part of him certainly liked her flirtations with him, he couldn't help but get a little uncomfortable when she came by. Not from necessarily anything she did, but more from a concern that people might think he was initiating the playfulness. He had seen and heard of more than a few guys who had had "conversations" with their superior about making unwanted or inappropriate advances to the females in the office. Chip had mentioned it to Kelly once, who swore that Linda had never complained to anyone. In fact, Kelly had mentioned that Linda told her in confidence that men were predictable and that she could get what she wanted whenever she wanted with just the right smile and toss of her hair. Chip believed that Linda had never filed a complaint; she certainly didn't seem like the type.

"Morning," both Chip and Kelly responded.

"Did you guys see what that bastard…" Linda started, being interrupted immediately by Chip.

"Yes! What's all this shit about line size and logos? Was that even discussed at the meeting? Did ANYONE EVER bring that up?" Chip asked raising his voice.

"Not once," Linda responded. "Did you see the swat he took at me for being a minute late? He's been relentless with me lately. I feel sick now just thinking about him. Every night I go to bed with this twisted, sick feeling in my stomach, knowing that I have to see him the next day. I have no motivation anymore. I dread coming into work."

Chip considered this and his own situation; it must be contagious.

"Did he ask you to come in early this morning so he can have an urgent discussion with you?" Kelly asked Linda.

"Yes. That asshole!" Linda answered. "That's the fourth time in three weeks that he's done that."

Kelly looked at Chip and gestured to Linda as if to say, see.

Linda continued. "Last week when he said he wanted a 7:00 meeting, I confronted him with it. I said I'd make the meeting later in the morning since I knew he didn't get in at 7:00. Then he looked pissed and insisted he wanted to get an early start and to make sure I was here. Prick."

"Did he show up?" Chip asked.

"Did he show up? NO!" Linda said, slapping his arm playfully. "He doesn't take me seriously, that's the problem. Well, I just wanted to see if you guys were in the same boat. I'm going to catch breakfast with one of my customers. I knew Gandhi wouldn't show up so I made other arrangements. See you guys. I'll see you for lunch?" She asked, looking at Kelly. "I've got other stuff to share." She slid off Chip's desk and patted his arm as she walked away.

"Later," Chip said, turning for a split second to watch her walk away; evidently enough to insight Kelly. Chip turned to her and saw she had a gigantic smile. Oh boy, here it comes, he thought.

"First her chest, now her ass," she said, giggling uncontrollably.

"That's enough out of you…shit disturber."

8:50 a.m.

"Good morning," Chip heard Rajiv say to Gracie as Rajiv entered his office

Simultaneously, Kelly and Chip glanced at Rajiv, the clock, then each other. Kelly smiled at Chip, "Showtime," she whispered.

Chip gathered his notes and planner, assuming the meeting would now take place. However, before Chip could get out of his seat, Rajiv was out of his office. Chip overheard him making his departure.

"Gracie, I'll be in a meeting for the next one and a half to two hours. Hold my calls," he said, passing Gracie's desk. She acknowledged with an affirmative and Rajiv was gone.

Kelly had heard the interaction as well. She turned to Chip and in a low voice said, "Forget Gandhi! I have a quote review meeting to go to, you want to go? It will give you a chance to see what else goes on around here. It'll also give you a chance to get your name and face out in front of other people. You know, lay a little ground work for the re-org."

Chip agreed with the plan. He was thirsty for even a small challenge and this would give him a chance to get his mind off the meeting with Rajiv. He grabbed his planner and followed Kelly out of their DWA. As they were passing, Gracie caught Chip's eye.

"Where are you going?" Gracie asked, looking directly at Chip.

"What?" Chip said, taken by surprise.

"Where are you going?" asked Gracie again, this time slower and louder.

Chip could feel his temperature rise. Who was Gracie to ask him where he was going, thought Chip. She wasn't his boss. Her very question reinforced Chip's belief that his current position didn't command a great deal of respect. He knew he would have to change that. He decided to draw a line in the sand. He sensed Kelly about to interject and decided he would handle the situation himself.

In a stern tone, Chip replied, "I'm going to the quote review meeting. If you need me I'll be back in about an hour and a half." Chip knew that Gracie would not need him for anything, nor would she even know that he was gone. Regardless, Gracie was going for a power play.

"Don't forget, you had a meeting scheduled with Mr. Chopra this morning to talk about your performance at the last SIMM meeting," Gracie said.

Now Chip was getting angry. Her statement was wrong on so many levels: the condescending tone, the fact that she knew Rajiv had no intention of keeping the meeting and most of all, the fact that she seemed to know what the meeting was about and was now holding that knowledge over his head. Although Chip's voice was calm and level, his eyes flashed a certain intensity as he responded.

"That won't be a problem Gracie, Rajiv will be gone for the next couple hours. In fact, he just told you that didn't he? I'll reschedule with him when he and I both get back," said Chip, beginning to walk away.

Gracie was not satisfied and continued, "Well, sometimes Mr. Chopra comes back early from his meetings. What should I tell him?" Her emphasis on "Mr." was meant to remind Chip that Rajiv was the boss and apparently, Gracie was now the boss's spokesperson.

Chip was amazed that she wanted to continue this discussion. What value was there? This was clearly nothing more than a maneuver on her part for some small amount of power. If she insisted on a fight, then Chip would oblige. He again responded in a calm but extremely assertive manner.

Chip turned around and walked back to her desk. He was now standing directly in front of her. "Tell him I'm in the quote review meeting. We went over this. Which part was unclear?" Chip said, keeping stern eye contact.

"Ooh, a little testy. You can tell you've been hanging out with some of the people around here too much," Gracie said, turning her eyes back down to her work.

Chip turned and walked away, catching up to Kelly. Under her breath Kelly muttered, "People around here? Damn librarian."

Chip worked the rest of the day stewing somewhat over the apparent lack of respect Rajiv had extended him. At one point during the day, Chip passed Rajiv in the hall and offered a nodding hello, the extent of the day's communication. As 5:00 approached, Chip was sure the meeting would wait until Monday.

"I think I'm gonna call it a week," Chip said, leaning back in his chair.

"Yeah me too," Kelly replied.

Chip and Kelly began to shut down their computers talking lightly about plans for the weekend. As Chip closed the last overhead cabinet, Gracie entered his office.

"Mr. Chopra will see you now," Gracie said, almost singing the words and not even attempting to hide her exuberance.

Chip was beginning to see why people found Gracie annoying. He had only known her for a few weeks and already found her painful to talk to. It annoyed Chip further that his schedule was evidently going to be completely dependent on the whim of Rajiv.

Chip glanced at Kelly who was staring disgustedly at Gracie's back as she walked away. "God, that bitch pisses me off," Kelly said. Then she turned her gaze to Chip, her expression changing completely. "Don't let him off the hook for standing you up this morning. He's very good at disarming people," Kelly said, very factually, with little hint of emotion.

"Thanks," Chip replied. He took his planner and entered Rajiv's office.

Rajiv was looking through papers on his desk as Chip walked in. "Have a seat, Chip," Rajiv said coolly, without looking up.

Chip sat directly opposite his manager. The chair he sat on seemed shorter this time. He felt like he was looking up at Rajiv. With yesterday's meeting playing in the background of his mind and the current scenario the way it was, he decided based on intuitive insight that it was possible, if not likely, that Rajiv was playing games with him. The thought of this bristled the hair on the back of his neck. He decided he would nip the game in the bud immediately. With defiant conviction he lifted himself slightly off the seat, reached underneath his chair and raised the seat to its highest level. At this vantage point, he peered down at the man across the desk. Chip felt much better.

Rajiv had watched Chip adjust his seat and now glared at him. Not wasting any more time, Rajiv started the discussion. "I am very disappointed in yesterday's showing. You need to be savvier with your presentation skills. Explore taking a PowerPoint class to build your competency," started Rajiv. "I expect you to be more creative."

This was not going too go well, Chip thought. This whole conversation was stupid. Chip had nothing to do with the problems discussed in yesterday's meeting and Rajiv knew it. Their conversation now was going to focus on nonsense details that had no real value. Chip knew that the "talk" would take this tone after reading Rajiv's memo. Rajiv's opening statement confirmed everything. No sense in trying to convince him that he wasn't part of the real issue yesterday. Rajiv already had it in his mind that he was. Try another approach. Chip was ready and defended quickly.

"I understand your point. However, please realize that I'm somewhat caught between a rock and a hard place." Chip's voice was firm and confident: aggressive without being confrontational. It was clear by Rajiv's new expression that he had never seen this side of Chip and wasn't sure if he was prepared to experience it now.

Chip continued. "On the one hand you were very specific with your requirements, even going so far as to complete some of the work yourself. On the other hand, you asked me to be creative and use my best judgment. I'm unclear as to which direction to proceed."

Rajiv made no attempt to hide his annoyance. His words appeared to compromise, his eyes and tone did not. "I guess I'll take that little ding. Just the same, you're my go-to guy. I need to count on you to present this material properly. Look into that class. And Chip, I want to make sure that in the future any information you collect or any analysis you do is only distributed through me." Rajiv turned his attention back to the paper spread out on his desk.

Was that it, Chip thought to himself? A formal meeting, all the build-up, mentioning it in an e-mail to everyone, all to recommend a Power Point class? This conversation was wrong on so many levels, he thought. Why should the work only be disseminated through Rajiv? So he can take full credit, Chip answered himself. Go-to guy? This was not Chip's idea of a fulfilling career, being Rajiv's go-to guy. In fact, he was hard-pressed to think of a bigger waste of time.

Chip knew the conversation was over, not only because of Rajiv's rude behavior but because of his own state of mind. Trying to argue over such a ridiculous point would be more worthless than the point itself. Chip opted for a strategic withdrawal. With a brief "No problem" he left the meeting and returned to his desk.

He passed Gracie returning to her desk. Her smile beamed brightly. "I have a schedule of upcoming Power Point classes. I've highlighted some of the ones that I think you should probably attend," she said, offering Chip a copy of the schedule.

Chip walked past her without responding, although he heard her last sling of mud in the background. "I'll e-mail you and Mr. Chopra a copy."

He felt a rush of emotions: anger, resentment, hopelessness, fear, but most of all, pride. It was this last emotion that fueled Chip's fire. He was better than this. He had spent years in higher education. Years sacrificing his time, his girlfriend, his hobbies all to lay claim to a knowledge base that would deliver him from being Rajiv's or anyone else's "go-to guy".

Or was it the money he had labored for? A little voice at the back of Chip's mind threw him this question. After all, if that was the goal, then these were the fruits of his decisive achievement. He became angered with himself. "Who cares!" he answered in his head. He was busting his butt so he could do something better, make better money, be something better. He was a MBA. Once you achieved this status you shouldn't be forced into conversations like the one he had just had with Rajiv. He shouldn't be forced to justify his time to a goddamn secretary, sorry, Administrative Assistant. Immediately upon thinking this, Chip realized how silly the thought was. A small light went on in Chip's head. The MBA guaranteed nothing, he had said so himself. It was a tool, a powerful tool, in the career-advancing arsenal, but it promised nothing. He knew this, however, the realization was now crystal clear at the forefront of his mind.

Together All Contribute to the Organizational Structure

"So what are the plans for the weekend?" Chip asked Kelly as they walked down the hall to their next meeting.

"It's only Tuesday," she responded.

"It's never too early to make plans."

"I don't know. I have to go grocery shopping tonight. Bob's been out of town this week and I said I'd make him dinner Friday night," Kelly said, looking completely disinterested in the conversation.

"That's nice. You're very domesticated," Chip said, as Kelly shot him a dirty look.

"What?" Chip said chuckling.

"Nothing. He's been a shit lately."

"He doesn't deserve you," Chip said provokingly.

Chip's comment got the desired result. Kelly erupted, "That's what I say! The little prick doesn't know how good he has it."

Chip smiled. It was always fun watching Kelly in action. "What are you going to make?"

"I have no idea. I'll think of something," she said, looking distracted. "What kind of idiot makes a meeting at 4:30 on a Tuesday afternoon? Can you tell me? Somebody with their head up their ass, that's who! I can never focus. I just want to call it a day," she added, changing the subject, from her boyfriend back to work.

"So let's blow this off. Will they really notice if we're not there?" Chip asked.

"Probably not. But there's going to be a couple directors there. Good face time. Your buddy Ted will be there too."

"Ted's not so bad," Chip defended.

"He's not worth anything anymore. They need to put him out to pasture. Don't get me wrong, personally I like him, even though he's still living in the 50's. He's very threatened by strong women. We just don't need an old fart like him around anymore," Kelly said.

Chip thought Kelly was wrong but didn't respond. Ted still had a lot to offer the company, especially to the new hires. He had a lot of good experience to share and could ensure the same mistakes weren't made over and over. Sure, Ted had his ideas and idiosyncrasies, but who didn't? As far as Chip was concerned, part of what frustrated Ted was that he found it unbelievable that no one wanted to tap into his experiences and learn from them. Unbelievable that these cold MBAs who didn't care what he had to say were the future of the company. Completely unbelievable.

They entered the room and seated themselves directly behind the Business Unit Manager. Chip gave a quick wave "hi" to Ted sitting directly across from Kelly and him. As the meeting began, Chip's thoughts drifted. Kelly was right; it was hard to concentrate in a meeting this late in the day. Chip drifted off into the weekend, thinking of Stacy, the wedding plans, finishing school; a flood of unrelated thoughts came to his mind, driving the Director's comments to the outermost edges of his attention.

"…critical to respond…" the Director was off and running.

If the meeting was important, it may be different. But Chip had seen the agenda and nothing on it seemed of any immediate value. The topics revolved around generating ideas to improve the process for responding to RFQ's on time. It was a vital topic to be discussed, no doubt, but there were no Account Managers in the room and no Business Planners. These were the key drivers of the process and they were nowhere to be found; another process meeting without the key people. What was the point? Completely unbelievable.

"…open a dialog and identify…"

In attendance were Engineering, Quality and a handful of people that neither Chip nor Kelly knew where they came from or what they did. Most likely, this group would define revisions and generate ideas for a process, which they did not lead and only saw a small part of. Inevitably, those with ownership of the process would reject most or all the ideas if for no other reason than they were not directly involved in the discussion.

"…capture these ideas and revisit the process…"

He could hear the comments now. "Who are they to start laying out what we should be doing" and "I noticed none of us were invited to meeting". "How can they define the process without the input of Account Managers or Business Planning or…" or whoever. The list could on and on.

"…create synergy to move forward…"

The bottom line was that the ideas set forth would likely be rejected. Possibly they would be embraced, but then likely would be bookshelved when the next fire came along that took priority. Either way the next hour would more than likely be completely useless. Chip started thinking about his plans for the weekend. He thought about his group project and how he could complete it the quickest way possible as the director continued.

The pep talk continued for some time when suddenly the momentum was abruptly broken by a faint voice.

"Tacos," the voice said. The voice was barely audible but loud enough for two or three people in the immediate vicinity to hear, including the Director. Chip realized the voice was right next him. He realized that the voice was Kelly's. Was she doing her grocery list? In the meeting? Chip laughed to himself and tried to suppress a smile.

Kelly wore a shocked expression, wondering to herself if she had really just said what she said. She now had the Director's attention. He turned around and looked at her while the room fell silent and waited with keen anticipation for Kelly to continue. Most had not heard her and wondered at the unusual pause.

After what seemed like an eternity to Kelly, the Director, looking directly at her, spoke. "Did you just say…tacos?" There were a few light chuckles and a couple 'somebody's hungry" comments from around the room.

Chip saw that Kelly's face had changed from a look of mild terror to a look of extreme confidence. Kelly replied, "That's right."

The Director continued, still interested in where this was going. "And what do you mean by that…tacos?"

Chip was again amused. There seemed to be no end to the entertainment that GIT afforded. As he glanced around the room, he saw that everyone was still focused on Kelly. The chuckles had disappeared and now the participants seemed truly interested in what she was going to say. Everyone except Ted, who sat with arms folded, shaking his head and looking completely disgusted. Chip attributed the group's interest to Kelly's look of supreme confidence, portraying that she was in complete control of the situation.

Kelly responded. "I mean…Together All Contribute to the Organizational Structure. I apologize. I was brainstorming off on my own and some of the ideas just came out. Everyone, not just the Account Managers or Business Planners, are vital to implementing customer response time. We're all working toward the same goal; we all need to be involved. I guess I was just mentally responding to the possible objection of Account Managers that they are not leading this process. Again, I apologize."

Nice recovery, Chip thought, keeping a straight face.

Her puppy dog eyes and soft words took their desired effect. The Director considered her comment for a moment, then turned to the rest of the group. "That's the kind of involvement I want to see. That's the kind of enthusiasm we need! I like the way you think, Hayman. Work on it a little. Too many "to's" and "the's". It's got potential though. Work on it and get back to me."

Kelly glanced at Chip and gave a quick smile and wink as the Director continued on. Chip was impressed. From across the room, Kelly spotted Ted staring at her with a look of complete resignation, shaking his head. Kelly smiled, puckered her lips ever so lightly, and blew Ted a kiss. Ted lightened a little, shaking his head more and smirking. Unbelievable.

It's Not Harassment! She Just Thinks It Is.

The office seemed somewhat subdued today, a good day for Chip to devote quality time to Rajiv's next presentation: another big internal discussion that was imperative to the future of the organization. A lot of work; a lot of nonsense. This meeting had come up a week after the SIMM meeting and he had been working on it non-stop since then, a full six days now. It seemed like an eternity. Rajiv had been gone four of the days on vacation, which had offered a minimal reprieve. However, once he was back, the suggestions, direction, and helpful thoughts had not stopped. It was the SIMM meeting all over again. I hate this, he thought to himself. I hate this job, this company, my boss. I should get out of here. God, this is boring!

Chip had started sending out resumes again with no bites. The time he spent on it was minimal, however. With school at night and the wedding plans, there didn't seem to be any time. And now Stacy was talking about buying a new house. More time. Still, for something that consumed so much of his time and made him so miserable, one would think he would devote maximum effort to change the situation.

Maybe it was laziness. No, he decided. Maybe he secretly hoped things would just change, just get better. Maybe Rajiv would stop being a prick one day and everything would work out. No, he knew that wasn't the case. Sure change might happen, but he couldn't count on it changing to benefit him. He knew he needed to manage the change. Maybe it was thinking that there was no more certainty at a new job at a new company than there was right where he was. Isn't the devil you know better than the devil you don't? No, he knew there was no future in that thinking; no future at all. Still, the sea can be a little intimidating.

Chip heard a knock on his partition. Ted entered his DWA and sat down.

"How'ya doing Ted?" Chip asked.

"Better than you and your little blonde friend are," Ted said laughing.

The Adventures of Chip Weatherbe, MBA

Chip held his guard up. "Really? How's that?"

"The CD149 quote is due today and I don't think anyone has started it," Ted answered laughing harder.

Chip felt a growing level of panic. "I thought we had another week or two?"

"Are you sure?"

"Let's call Kelly," Chip offered reaching for his speaker phone.

"She's not here. She's probably at an interview. You know how you MBAs are."

Chip refused to reply to Ted's provocation. "We can call her on her cell phone," Chip said, quickly dialing Kelly's number.

"Kelly Hayman speaking," Kelly answered.

"Hi, Kelly. Chip here. I've got you on the speaker phone with Ted," Chip said. Ted and Kelly each gave a quick "hi" while Chip continued.

"Ted and I were just talking about the CD149 project. When is the quote on that due?"

"We haven't received the RFQ yet. I expect that we won't get it for another one to two weeks. From that point, we should have four or five weeks to respond," Kelly answered.

"I heard it was due today?" Chip asked.

"That was an initial date that the customer gave us. But they kept pushing back the RFQ. We'll probably get it next Wednesday or Thursday. Dan knows about it; he talked to the customer this morning," Kelly said.

Chip and Ted sighed slightly. "Thanks Kelly, that's what we wanted to hear," Chip said.

Just as the conversation had come to an end, Ted jumped in. "Kelly? This is Ted. Where are you at?" he inquired.

Hesitating slightly, she said in a calm, cool and collected voice. "I'm on my way to a customer. Why?"

Ted smiled an evil smile. Chip had an idea of what was coming – another antagonizing comment, spoken for Ted's amusement and everyone else's misery. Chip didn't want any part of it, although as a spectator, he was sure it would be entertaining. Ted continued, "Well I was just thinking, shouldn't you be at home, baking cookies, taking care of the kids or your husband. You know, womanly things."

The heat from the other end of the line almost melted the speaker. Starting in a calm voice and ending in a yell, Kelly answered. "First, I'm not married. Second, I don't have kids. However, if I did, I would be at home raising them, not because it's 'my place' but because I'm the only one capable of doing the job. And…and I'm sure of this point…whatever I do or decide to do, irrespective of how small and meaningless, it's still a thousand times more important than whatever pissant, worthless chore you do everyday at your small, worthless D fucking WA!"

Ted was laughing at this point and obviously decided further provocation was necessary. "What are you wearing?"

"Oh you sick, vile, twisted old man. You can kiss my ass," she said.

Ted laughed harder. "Don't tease me." With that, Kelly hung up.

Chip could not help but to find this amusing – completely inappropriate and unprofessional, but amusing. Once again, his professional demeanor took hold and he kept his game face.

"Ted, do the terms sexual harassment or zero tolerance mean anything to you?" Chip asked rhetorically.

"You think that was sexual harassment? It wasn't. Getting a blow job from an intern in the Oval Office, an intern who is half your age and whose employment and reputation are completely in your hands…that's harassment. What I just said wasn't. And I'm not joking, you know," Ted said, his chuckle fading to a thoughtful tone. "She thinks I'm just tweaking her but I'm not."

"That's what's frightening, Ted. Why do you antagonize people like that? Are you looking for a reaction? I mean, do you want to get fired?" Chip asked, wanting to laugh.

"I'm looking for people to get off their asses and do the right thing," Ted said.

"The right thing? I see. And what would that be, O Blessedly Wise One?" Chip asked sarcastically.

Ted ignored the tone. "That's what's wrong with America today. Too many women trying to be men instead of raising a family. And too many men trying to be women. Women should be manufacturing good human beings while men manufacture other junk. If more women did what they were supposed to do and men did what they were supposed to do, we wouldn't have a lot of the problems we do today, like children…no babies, shooting each other. A woman's job is much more important in the long run than ours, you know."

Here we go, Chip thought. Ted's views were interesting but Chip had work to do and didn't want to take on a long philosophical discussion about the roles of men and women in society. This was a discussion best left for later, outside the walls of GIT.

Chip wanted to take the wind out of Ted's sails. "This kind of discussion is inappropriate for work, Ted. Let's talk about this later; I have some things that I need to get done," Chip said calmly, almost talking down to Ted as if he were a child.

Ted laughed loud and hard again, ignoring the condescending tone. "That's right! I almost forgot! You have to make some charts or something for your boss. Aren't you supposed to go to a chart making class soon? Now that's important!" Ted said, slamming his fist on his knee. "That's the same kind of shit work she does…" he said, pointing at the phone, "…only she just won't admit it. She wants

The Adventures of Chip Weatherbe, MBA

to elevate her work to some noble level. Maybe one day one of you will explain to me how making a chart with pretty colors and perfect lines or kissing some customer's ass is more important than the emotional and spiritual upbringing of a human being." With that, Ted rose and started walking out, still laughing.

Chip rolled his eyes and shook his head. "Oh for God's sake. Nobody said making charts was more important…never mind. I've got work to do."

"Go to it, Chart Boy."

Chip could hear Ted's laughter all the way down the aisle, echoing in Chip's head for years after Ted left his office.

Diversity and Zero Tolerance: The New PP Program

E-Memo
To: All employees
Subject: Diversity in the Workplace
From: CRDCMT – PMT and the CPPV

    The Career Resource Development And Change Management Team – Progressive Movement Team and the Committee for Promoting Progressive Values have united forces to create a new program to promote diversity and tolerance.
    We would like to invite all employees to a meeting in the cafeteria on Wednesday for a meeting on GIT's Zero Tolerance and Diversity In The Workplace policies as well as to review the new policy. GIT encourages diversity and believes that a diverse workforce is key to the survival of our organization.
TEAM.

    In his benevolence and wisdom, from the podium on high, he spoke. He spoke about tolerance. He spoke about diversity. He spoke about respect. He spoke about the environment, about giving back, about the importance of good corporate citizenship. Fausto appeared to be in pain. Pain caused by his powerful desire to work together, as a team. Pain caused by his desire for compassion, his desire to give, to care. He would help them see the vision. He was Fausto.
    "…we serve many diverse markets today. Markets whose customs are different than ours…"
    He held up a document in his left hand for all to see and, with his right, he pointed into the camera to the mass of lost workers he knew were out there, desperate for the vision.

As Moses once brought his people the Ten Commandments from the mountain, so had Fausto brought to his people the Corporate Core Values. Top among these values, he proceeded to explain, was diversity. Diversity in every possible form. Diverse people. Diverse cultures and languages. Diverse ideas and markets. If it was different, then it was valuable; it meant high quality, irrespective of its actual substance.

"...as our key customers are committed to embracing diversity in all areas of their business, so too, shall we. We are GIT."

He spoke for no more than fifteen minutes, concluding his sermon with: TEAM - Together, Everyone Achieves More.

Janice pushed STOP on the VCR and turned to her audience, her eyes misty. "I hope you all got as much out of that video as I did. I find it refreshing to see our management leading with a vision and thinking outside of the box. If we're going to grow, we need leadership that cares. Leadership that cares about tolerance and diversity. I think you can see from Fausto's comments that GIT is committed to its core values, which leads me into today's discussion."

The meeting room was filled with the usual staff. The room was at capacity with more than a few standing along the walls. Chip sat patiently next to Kelly in the back of the room. He again questioned to himself the value of these meetings. This seemed like an awful lot of people to take away from their desks for an hour or two every week, especially in light of GIT's current financial situation, he thought. After all, from what he understood, they had just lost two key orders and were in jeopardy of having a significant amount of current business put out to bid. Shouldn't GIT be focused on fixing problems and trying to win business, Chip wondered.

"As you know, there was a meeting last week of GLEE, the Gay and Lesbian Employee Empire. The meeting was not well attended. Only 2 people showed up. This was very disappointing to everyone involved."

"All both of you," giggled Kelly quietly.

Chip smiled and stifled a chuckle. Kelly never missed an opportunity to throw a punch. It was no longer a mystery why the likes of Janice never tangled with her.

Janice continued. "We want to again stress that diversity is key to our organizational survival. Without diversity, we cannot move forward globally. We would encourage more people to attend next month's meeting."

One of Ted's protégé's, Dennis, who was sitting in the front row, raised his hand.

"Yes? You have a question?" acknowledged Janice, although somewhat annoyed at the interruption.

"What if you're not gay and don't want to attend?" asked Dennis. "I mean, there's other things I like to do after work." A few smiles and light chuckles from small pockets around the room; dead silence and a face of stone from Janice. In an instant it was clear that this question was viewed as an attack on the diversity policy and as such, would not be tolerated. In a controlled voice, masking obvious anger, Janice responded.

"Again, for now, we can't force you to attend any functions after working hours. However, we want to encourage people to be open-minded to new ideas. Open-mindedness and thinking beyond the four walls is vital to moving forward in the 21st century. We won't tolerate bigotry or discrimination of any kind. Intolerance will not be tolerated. Also, keep in mind that part of your performance review is based on your ability to get along with other folks and your willingness to accept new ideas."

For now? Part of your performance review? thought Chip. Chip and Kelly looked at each other, each holding back their anger that Janice was clearly trying to make her pet project part of everyone's performance review. If she could do this, Chip thought, then she could tie it to a merit increase.

Then the unthinkable happened, Dennis tried to defend his position. "I don't think it's discrimination to not want to attend an after work club."

Chip and Kelly glanced at each other again with a mixture of awe, fear, admiration, humor, and a kind of sick fascination, similar to the feeling one gets when watching professional wrestling.

Janice's irritation quickly shifted to disciplined rage. Using the most condescending tone she could muster, Janice held firm. "Well, it's not just a "club" as you put it, Dennis. It's a group that represents diversity and tolerance. And we could all be a little more tolerant, couldn't we? You heard Fausto, diversity and tolerance are critical core values. I think he was very clear on these points."

Kelly leaned over to Chip and said playfully, "I think she secretly wants him."

Dennis wanted to continue the debate, but retreated under Janice's glare and cold segue-way into her next agenda item.

"…so I think it's pointless to re-review the points that have already been made. On to our second topic – the dress code. Many individuals in the organization use pocket protectors, predominantly in the Engineering Department." A quick glance and cutting smirk at Dennis was meant to remind him that she was in charge and would now prove it.

"A customer recently toured our facility and joked upon leaving that since everyone in engineering was wearing a pocket protector, it was hard to tell anyone apart." A low chuckle from Sales and Marketing; blank stares from Engineering. "Well, every joke has a grain of truth. That's what makes jokes funny."

"She wouldn't know funny if it bit her nipple off," whispered Kelly.

"Would you stop," Chip replied.

"However, we didn't think this particular joke was funny. We feel that this individual's comments have given our organization a black eye with respect to our diversity policy. It doesn't do us any good to adopt diversity as a core value and then have you'all look the same. So, for those of you that want to continue to use your pocket protectors, we will institute a new Pocket Protector Program."

The room had been shocked into a dead silence. The faint hum of a nearby computer was the only sound heard. All meeting participants leaned forward slightly trying to determine if they heard her correctly.

Janice had their attention and pressed forward. "We want to limit the number of people that use pocket protectors in the building to 8 people per day and no more than 2 people per division. A sign-up sheet will be posted weekly outside the cafeteria. If you want to carry a protector, you'll need to sign up. You can reserve as many days as you like, however, remember, sign-up is on a first come, first serve basis and the spaces available on any given day are limited. If you don't sign up, and wear a protector anyway, you'll be asked to remove it. Remember, the Pocket Protector Program is for everyone's benefit. It's vital to maintaining diversity."

Janice's blow hit her target with deadly accuracy. Dennis stared, looking like a lost puppy; his spirit clearly defeated. He would have to sign up early, make sure his name was on the list. But what if he took a day off? What if he was on vacation? What if the list was full before he got to it? Too much undue stress for one little engineer to bear.

Chip was stunned. His mind was a hollow void. He tried desperately to grasp anything even resembling reality. Was this a joke? Certainly, no one would sit around discussing pocket protector diversity. Clearly, this was insane. Could the company really be spending time, money, and talent on this garbage, Chip thought. Chip then noticed that a few people scattered throughout the room were nodding in approval. This proved more shocking than the discussion itself. How could anyone buy into this? A closer look at the other faces in the room suggested that most, although offended at the blatant silliness of the program, seemed to maintain their poker faces or indeed had resigned themselves to this new Wonderland.

Half laughing, Kelly whispered to Chip, "Look at Dennis. Look's like she just told him there's no Santa. You watch, Ted will hit the roof when he gets wind of the new PP Program." And with that simple statement from Kelly, the new diversity program was henceforth called the PP Program by all who were not involved in its creation.

As with all other programs the company instituted, once it was given a name and someone was assigned to it, it had a very slim chance of ever disappearing, assuming of course no reorganization. It could linger for years without being questioned or challenged. In fact, more than likely the PP Program would take on a life of its own, growing each month in its scope of responsibility and authority, consuming more and more resources, until one day when it might move from a simple program and become a Department with potentially dozens of people working in it. People who would do and say anything to justify the department's existence and thereby their own existence. People who would depend on the department to support themselves and their families. It was also likely that with any management change or organizational restructuring the department would be completely abolished. At this point of course, it would be difficult to find anyone who would remember how the PP Department started or what it did during its existence.

Janice concluded her bombing with a smile and bright cheery face, "Oh and before I forget, as always, Change Management Counselors will be available to discuss any difficulties anyone may be having with this transition. Remember, all conversations with your CMC are completely confidential and we encourage you all to use them as frequently as possible. Thank you for your time today. You can e-mail me if you have any questions." One final smile from Janice to Dennis ended the meeting.

With that, everyone began filing out. Chip looked at Kelly who was smiling at him.

"The lunatics have taken over the asylum," she whispered to Chip.

Chip followed Kelly out, wondering if it was too late to turn back to shore.

Cafeteria Talk

Dan and Chip picked up their trays as they walked into the dining area from the cafeteria.

"What did you think about that memo on diversity and the CIP?" asked Dan.

"GIT seems to be sparing no expense to let it be known that they are a diverse company," Chip responded cautiously. A number of topics kept coming up that Chip wasn't comfortable discussing: diversity and harassment. It always seemed that a discussion of this nature could easily get out of hand if one weren't careful.

"Yeah. They put a lot of effort into that," Dan replied dispassionately. He and Dan proceeded to a nearby table to be joined shortly by Kelly and Bruce, a black engineer from Nigeria who had recently joined GIT. Kelly was laughing and Bruce sat, shaking his head.

"What's going on?" Dan asked curiously.

Bruce jumped in. "Doesn't anyone in this place speak English anymore? I spent the last fifteen minutes trying to convey to the sandwich lady that I wanted yellow peppers, NOT green peppers on my sandwich, no tomatoes, and Italian dressing. This was all very confusing to her. I got tired of explaining it over and over so I walked away and got a salad. I am so disgusted with this place sometimes. Maybe they should offer English classes as part of the Career Enhancement Program."

Kelly glanced around the table chuckling at Bruce's frustration as he continued.

"It happens every time I come down here. She gets it wrong every single time. Is it too much to expect for people that they hire to have some very basic communication skills? I mean, I am from Nigeria. But when I came to the United States, I understood the necessity of communicating effectively. I took the time to learn the language and customs. Which is not to say that I relinquished the language or customs from my country. No, I simply learned and respected those of the people whose country I had come to. This is nothing more than being courteous.

Some of these people come with their hand out and they expect everyone else to do the work for them. I have never seen such tolerance for laziness. They act like they are doing you a favor by answering simple questions. They are doing no favors, that is their job. But they give you nothing but attitude. GIT should never have hired them."

Finally, Kelly jumped in. "Bruce? I think we contract all the food services. I don't think any of those people work directly for GIT."

"No?" asked Bruce.

"I don't think so. I could be wrong, but I don't think so," Kelly added.

"It doesn't matter," Bruce said. He continued. "In fact, that makes it all the worse. If they are contract, then I'm going to say something. Because in that case, we're paying for a service that is substandard and unacceptable. If these people want to work in the USA, then they should at least learn to speak English," Bruce concluded.

Dan looked at Chip. "Cultural Integration Plan proceeding nicely," he said, laughing sarcastically. Kelly and Bruce glanced at the other two. "I was just explaining to Chip about GIT's CIP and how they want people like Bruce to accept people who are different," Dan said with Kelly and Chip laughing.

Bruce looked questioningly at Dan. 'What is CIP?"

"The Cultural Integration Plan. It's HR's attempt to take people from different cultures and integrate them into a cohesive, well oiled machine. The plan is to make everyone tolerant and respectful of everyone else," Dan explained.

Bruce rolled his eyes. "I never will tolerate laziness or stupidity. And don't even get me started on HR or whatever they call themselves and their bullshit programs. If they took half the money they spent on their nonsense and gave it to Engineering, maybe we would have the resources to respond to customers like we should. We'd have the money to develop products we know we need and we'd have the money to hire the people we need to fix our current problems. Did you hear that talk on Pocket Protector Diversity?"

"The new PP Program," Kelly said, over Chip's laughing.

"That is exactly what it is, pee pee. What a disgrace! It is unbelievable that someone actually spent time and money on that. Every time I see Janice, I walk the other way. The woman makes me sick. That whole department makes me sick. What do they do other than waste our money?" Bruce asked in a low voice.

As Bruce said this, Kelly gave him a quick kick in the leg under the table while she and Dan glanced over Bruce's shoulder. Bruce and Chip looked behind them and noticed Terry from CRDCMT walking over with her lunch.

"Hi. Can I join you guys?" Terry asked nervously.

Everyone nodded approval with a round of 'sure' and 'no problem'. As Terry took a seat, a brief, awkward silence engulfed the table. Terry, looking close to tears, broke the silence. "You don't have to stop talking on my account," she said, making a desperate, uncomfortable attempt to be light hearted. Looks of embarrassment fell on everyone at the table with a resounding chorus of "no's" and "not at all".

Dan made a quick attempt to move the conversation in a different direction. "So, Kelly, are you still going up North this weekend?"

"I don't know. We were going to, then there was a change of plans and now it looks like things are back on again. The week's still early, anything can change," Kelly said, followed by another break in the conversation flow.

"What did you guys think of the Pocket Protector Program?" Terry asked, composing herself but still sounding tentative.

Surprised at the question and not quite sure where the discussion would lead, the table fell silent with all eyes on Terry. "I mean, did you think that the whole discussion was way out of control or what?"

The four glanced at each other, still not sure what to do with the comment, although all four leaned into the table, straining to hear Terry's low voice as she continued. "People think that these are my ideas and they're not. I mean, some of them are, until Janice gets a hold of them and twists them into these freakish… ideas or programs or whatever they are."

A sinister smile crept across the face of Kelly. "Really?" she asked inquisitively.

Terry continued. "I mean, look at the germ management memo. That came from a news story I saw on TV months ago about people getting sick and passing colds, flu and stuff in the workplace. I thought it might be a good idea to send out a memo and remind everyone that they can get a flu shot for free at the clinic we use to screen new hires. And I got this health memo from the clinic, which talks about colds and the flu and how to avoid them or deal with it if you get sick. I mean, this is something that came right from the health clinic that we could have posted in the cafeteria for people to read if they wanted, right?"

The four at the table nodded their understanding, intrigued by the story and hoping Terry would continue. Terry seemed to have no problem obliging them. "And I also thought we could put some complimentary antibacterial gel bottles out…we got a huge supply of these small little containers, like little plastic hand lotion bottles. I thought we could give these away to anyone that wanted them. And that was it. The next thing I know, I'm in a meeting with Janice and her devoted followers talking about man hours lost every year and putting your head on the desk for five minutes and talking about not drooling …it was disgraceful."

"The DDOD policy," Kelly added laughing. The others joined in.

Terry stared blankly at Kelly. "DDOD Policy?" Terry asked, looking somewhat terrified. As Kelly was beginning to say 'Don't…' Terry jumped in, looking disgusted. "Don't Drool On Desk Policy. I get it."

Michael F. Goyette

The four at the table couldn't contain their laughter. Even Terry began to join in. "You see, that's what I mean. Nobody takes her seriously. I don't think she knows what a joke this is to everybody. I mean, if you've got diarrhea, I can't really see how putting your head on the desk is going to improve your situation. 'Think positive thoughts' she said. I mean, what is all that about? If you're that sick, just go home so nobody else catches it. Isn't that common sense? Am I the only one who sees this?"

Again, the four around the table confirmed her statements with nods of approval.

"But everyone is too afraid to voice their opinion. They think they'll wind up on a hit list. I've tried to say things before, but I'm outnumbered up against her two little pets," Terry lamented.

"So, you are not involved in making these decisions about PP Programs and the like?" asked Bruce.

"Well, I'm involved with some of the discussions, like I said. But I usually come up with a good idea and it gets transformed into some monstrosity in our 'team discussions'. So don't think I'm pushing this garbage on you guys, cause I'm not. It was Scott, Tamika, and Janice that came up with the bullet points on that memo, not me. I'm tired of people completely avoiding me because of her."

Kelly put her arm around Terry. "Don't you worry, little camper, you come and tell Aunt Kelly everything. Kelly will help you take care of that mean old witch."

The mood at the table lightened dramatically. Chip excused himself after ten minutes of small talk; he knew with Rajiv in the office today, he would have one meaningless task after another thrown at him. The tasks had grown in their frequency and urgency lately. Chip suspected that Rajiv's management was putting pressure on him in light of the sales team recently losing a key order. Of course, at the end of the day, Chip had responded to all requests accurately and on time, not that it mattered. His response was just filed somewhere in oblivion and a new task sprang forth that was twice as urgent as the last one.

Chip approached his desk. Bingo. A note taped to his computer screen read: "Chip – Urgent! See me immediately. Rajiv."

Urgent. Always urgent.

Chip entered Rajiv's office. "Hi Rajiv. You wanted to see me?" Rajiv continued reading a piece of paper on his desk, not looking up as Chip entered.

"Hi Chip, come in, please," Rajiv said politely, still not taking his eyes from the paper. Finally, after a moment of silence, Rajiv looked at Chip and smiled. "Chip, I hate to ask this of you on such short notice, but one of the Business Unit Managers from Germany is flying in tomorrow morning. Something has come up and I won't be able to meet him at the airport or visit the customer with him. Is there any way that you could meet him, take him to the customer, and get him to his hotel?" Rajiv asked pleadingly.

This was the Rajiv Chip had met at the interview: suave, charismatic, and compassionate. His current tone and approach were in stark contrast to the Rajiv that Chip had come to know over the last few months.

"Sure, no problem, Rajiv. What time does he fly in? He's coming into Detroit Metro?" Chip asked.

"Check with Gracie for the details. She's got all the information, his name, flight times…" Rajiv said, rising and departing his office with Chip. He patted Chip on the back and with a brief 'thanks again', walked off to his next meeting. Chip proceeded straight to Gracie's desk to get the required information.

"Hey, Gracie. Rajiv mentioned that someone was coming in from Germany tomorrow? He wanted me to pick him up at the airport and said you would have the details," Chip said.

With a slight sigh, Gracie asked, "Do you know who?"

"Rajiv didn't give me his name. He just said that he was a Business Unit Manager from Germany and that he was coming in tomorrow. Again, he said you would be able to give me all the details," Chip explained, trying desperately not to get irritated.

"Do you know where he's flying into tomorrow?" Gracie asked, whining the words.

Chip got the distinct impression that Gracie was playing games and made a conscious effort to maintain a calm demeanor. Part of him wanted to confront her and demand the information he knew she had. Despite this impulse, he kept his composure. Perhaps a kind and gentle approach might yield the desired results, he thought. "Like I said, I don't have any information. Rajiv pointed me in your direction for help. Can you help me? Please?" he asked, being as polite as he could be.

"I don't know anyone flying in here tomorrow. Sorry," Gracie said, whining again.

Chip felt another surge of frustration. He knew she had the information and had seen her playing dumb like this with other people. He knew she had heard the conversation he had just had with Rajiv; she heard everything coming out of that office. Most people when dealing with her gave up in frustration and stormed away, only to come back later armed with more specific questions that forced her to reluctantly provide them what they required. Chip decided to take this route. He knew this would irritate her but so what? If she wanted to play then he would play.

"Maybe Rajiv got his dates wrong. Is there anyone from Germany flying into Detroit tomorrow?" Chip asked.

Gracie shook her head. "Not that I know of," she answered, singing the words and smiling a fabricated smile. Clearly the wrong question, Chip thought. Maybe it wasn't broad enough.

Michael F. Goyette

"Is there any Business Unit Manager from our German office flying into anywhere in the USA tomorrow?" Chip asked.

He could tell by Gracie's expressed look of annoyance that he had hit a home run. With a huff she reached over and pulled out a flight itinerary from her in-box.

"Well, Helmut Wittenbecher is flying into Chicago O'Hare tomorrow afternoon. Is that who you mean? Because no one is flying into Detroit tomorrow," Gracie said rudely.

Success. Chip had heard Helmut's name tossed around before. He knew he was one of the key Business Unit Managers who occasionally visited the US office. "That must be who Rajiv was talking about," he said, gloating.

"Well, when you said he was flying in here tomorrow, I thought you meant Detroit. You should really be more specific next time," she said, caustically.

It occurred to Chip that one of Gracie's biggest problems was her inability to choose battles wisely. Here she was, ready to nit pick and fight over a simple question; not very smart, Chip thought. Better to conserve the energy for a real battle. As this insight played in his mind, he felt some of his frustration diminish, making it easier to respond.

"Okay, I'll do that. In the meantime, can I get a copy of that itinerary?" Chip asked.

Gracie slapped a piece of paper on the counter and Chip reviewed it.

"So it looks like he flies into Chicago tomorrow, then into Detroit the following morning. Is he expecting someone to pick him up at O'Hare?" Chip asked.

"I don't know," Gracie cocked her head to one side. "Sorry," she said, singing the last word again.

The calming results of Chip's earlier exercise of trying to understand before being understood were fading quickly. He decided it was best to ask Rajiv directly. He had everything he needed from Gracie; best to just walk away. "Thanks for your help, Gracie," Chip said politely as he walked away, returning to his desk.

"Relax and breath," Kelly said lightly as she continued typing on the keyboard.

"Believe me, I'm trying. She's so annoying," Chip responded.

"It's no wonder he asked me to play delivery boy, he just doesn't want to fly to Chicago. This guy must not be that important," Chip said.

"He's important but the errand he's going on is not. He's supposed to stop by a small company that wants to buy one of our off the shelf products. It's a small volume and they'll never be a big customer. On the other hand, the product is a decent money maker…but it's not one of the hot glamour products so Rajiv doesn't really want to get involved. I can give you the file, directions to the customer, time of meeting, all the stuff you'll need."

"Wonderful. Thanks," Chip answered sarcastically.

Kelly finished her typing and swung her chair around playfully to face Chip. "Forget about all that," she whispered. "What are you doing tonight?"

"Some bullshit homework. Why?"

"You want to go to a soup kitchen tonight and help serve turkey dinners?" asked Kelly.

"Serve turkey dinners? To whom?" Chip responded.

"The poor, the homeless, the needy…They asked for volunteers at my church to devote an hour or two and I said I would do it. Bob canceled and I told the priest that I would bring another helper."

Chip looked at her skeptically.

"C'mon. It'll be fun. It's just for an hour or two. Besides, it's one more something you can put on your performance review," she said, hoping for a reaction.

There it was again, community service on your evaluation. "Now, we both know that that is nothing but a rumor. There is no way that a company like this would require community service as part of your evaluation."

"They don't require it, they encourage it…and you need to lighten up. Look, this is something for my church. It also might be nice to have someone else there to talk to who is under the age of two hundred and six."

"In that case, I'll join you," Chip finally agreed.

The Soup Kitchen, Jack the Knife, and Big Mike & His Love Posse

The kitchen was crowded with volunteers, fifteen total in the room. All eyes were on the priest as he reiterated his pep talk from the previous Sunday's mass, using words and phrases like 'crusade' and 'battle hunger' to inspire and motivate. Kelly and Chip were assigned to kitchen patrol: food on plate, plate on counter to be served. A simple enough task for two bright MBA's.

After the food had been appropriately distributed, Father Joe moved into phase two of the help initiative.

"I want to thank everyone again for coming today. Since most of the food has been served, I would encourage you to extend another giving hand and talk to some of these unfortunate souls. Sometimes a kind word or a listening heart can rejuvenate and lighten the soul. If any of you could take a minute to visit just one table, you might find that you bring a lot of happiness into someone's life. We cannot live on bread alone. We need to make a deposit, if you will, into their spiritual bank account."

Kelly looked at Chip. "Deposit into their spiritual bank account?" she muttered. Chip could only shrug.

The priest continued. "...and when you talk to them, say to yourself, 'There but for the grace of God, go I.' These people didn't win life's lottery like the rest of us. Let's join hands and pray for them."

After the prayer, Kelly patted Chip on the shoulder, nudging him gently out the door. "You first."

"Wimp," he responded and walked into the eating area. There were about twenty round tables dispersed throughout the room. People sat at each table eating their dinner. Chip spied a nearby table with a small sign in the middle, which read "Table 5" and began heading in that direction. Compared to most of the room, which appeared subdued and somewhat quiet, Table 5 seemed extremely boisterous; four men sat laughing loudly.

On his way to the group of four, Chip passed Table 1. A lone man sitting at the table grabbed his arm as he passed. "Tell them to be quiet. Please tell them to be quiet…they won't listen to me…nobody listens anymore…"

"Hey, Car Dude! Everything all right over there?" shouted one of the group at Table 5 while the others giggled insanely.

"Those guys over there?" Chip asked the lone man, pointing to Table 5.

The man nodded pathetically, close to tears. "Tell them to shut up. Tell them they're all worthless little bastards. They were never anything. Please…please…"

Taken back by the man's language and feeling awkward, he promised to do what he could to calm the table down. He glanced back to Kelly who was watching from the kitchen area. She could only offer a 'thumbs up' and a smile.

He shook his head and continued to the table. As he approached, he noticed the four were dressed in very old clothes, mostly torn and extremely filthy. The men had obviously not shaved or showered in weeks, maybe even months by the awful stench emanating from the general area. He noticed that a number of brown paper bags were lined under the table each containing a bottle of some unidentified drink. He saw one man pour the contents of one of the bags into an old, beaten-up Dixie cup, while keeping the bag under the table. The man gulped the drink back in one shot.

The man who had just taken a drink lifted the bag as Chip approached, offering its contents. "A little fire water, Mr. Yuppie Guy?"

"Would you put that down before the priest sees!" scolded his friend.

"What? I was just offering our friend here a little thank you for this great dinner."

"Just keep it out of sight, will ya?"

Chip wasn't sure how to begin the conversation. Keep it light and quick, he thought, then walk away.

"I just wanted to come out and say hi and see if there was anything else I could do for you guys."

The four stared at Chip for a second and then, as if the sun had risen for the first time in their lives, all smiled and started talking at once, each reaching somewhere on his person for some crumpled up pieces of paper.

"Yeah you can…"

"Here's my resume…"

"I'm looking for at least $90K a year and a car…"

"I'd like to be able to leave at 3:30…"

"Whoa, whoa…slow down guys. I don't think I can help you…" the four stopped their frantic search and stared questioningly at Chip. "…with your…

um…your a …career endeavors," Chip ended, feeling extremely uncomfortable and humbled.

"Why not? Where do you work?" asked one of the group.

The turn of the discussion took Chip by surprise. "Well…it's an automotive supplier…" The four leaned forward, listening attentively. Their expressions still asking the question 'Why can't you help us?'

"…and…I don't think we're hiring right now…" No change in the expressions. Chip found himself wanting to minimize his own success. "…and…and I'm going to quit soon and start my own business. You guys really don't want to work where I am now. It's very boring and my boss is kind of a snake. All I do is make charts all day…it's really not very good."

The men sat back and exchanged serious glances.

"You work in an air-conditioned building?"

Chip nodded as the members of the group began taking turns tossing out questions.

"You're on salary? You get a check every month?"

"You get paid vacations…?"

"Medical Insurance…?"

"Comfortable chair and a desk…?"

"A computer? Internet access…?"

"401k? Company matching…?

"Pension…

Chip nodded to all their questions, not sure where they were leading.

"What are ya belly aching for, man?" Asked one of the men.

Another grabbed Chip's arm. "Don't quit your job, buddy. Don't start your own business. Keep what you've got…Don't do it, man," he warned, with a look of terror.

"Yeah! He says that now!" said the man next to him, taking a shot from his Dixie cup.

The man who voiced the warning continued, squeezing Chip's arm ever tighter. "Dude, I'm telling ya, it's a bad way…Put that idea out of your head and keep your nice, comfortable, boring job."

The man's friend exploded. "Now you say that! Where the hell were you a year ago man!? I used to be a goddamn Assistant Director until I started listening to you!"

Another of the four chimed in. "Yeah! All we heard from you two was 'Let's start our own business' and 'I'm tired of working for the man'. Now look what happened," he said mockingly, accusing his two compatriots.

The accused sat silently. One man covered his eyes with his hands, another rested his forehead on the table staring at the floor. The other two just stared and drank more from their paper cups.

The group abruptly became solemn. "We used to make smart investments," said one of the quartet, breaking the silence.

"If we had made smart investments, we wouldn't be here! Dumb Ass!" said another.

"We all used to have great jobs, great benefits, great lives…I used to be an Assistant Director at a big company…I was respected…had it all…then we started our own investment club. That went good and we made some decent money…but then we listened to these two and we decided to quit our jobs and go into investing full time. When that went belly up…our wives all left…they took our children…

"…they took everything…" one of the other four chimed in.

"…all cause you two wanted to be your own bosses! I was an attorney once! That fucking Greenspan! God damn it…"

"Okay! Okay! I got it! We screwed up! Do we really need to relive this again and again!?" exploded one of the accused men. Chip couldn't help but silently question the authenticity of the claims. These guys couldn't have done anything with their lives. Look at them, they're bums. Chip's thoughts were broken by a nearby shout.

"Stop whining!" shouted the man from Table 1. "You people are losers! Stop telling that stupid story! You never made investments! I made investments! You were never anything. You were just little people…little worker bees, flying around making honey for me. You were nothing compared to me…nothing…" The man fell silent rocking slowly in his chair. The four looked at each other and the depressed mood was suddenly replaced by hysterical laughter.

Time to leave, Chip thought, and he slowly slid back to the kitchen. As he walked away he could hear the quartet jeering at the lone man at Table 1.

"Hey, Car Dude…your quality sucks!"

"You know the last SUV I bought was a Toyota…and guess what…it never rolled over, I'm still alive!" The group continued to laugh.

"That must have been a long drop from that high up in the food chain, Knife Man."

Chip returned to Kelly. "What were you talking about for so long? Did they give you their life' histories?"

"They had a lot to say, a little too much maybe. They're drunk, every one of them," he said. "And the smell! Oh my God. I don't think any of them have showered in weeks. I think they're having a field day with that guy at Table 1. It seems to piss him off just knowing that they're there."

"Oh. Well maybe I'll go talk to him. Maybe he needs a little comforting."

"Go to it but be careful of Table 5," Chip said.

Kelly left the kitchen area and began walking to Table 1, noticing as she went that a man at Table 5 was staring at her and waiving a $10 bill while the other three at the table laughed uncontrollably. Kelly was caught off guard by the action, but continued walking. Still staring at the $10 bill and pondering its significance, she was unaware that she had reached her destination and was standing two feet away from the man at Table 1.

"You're so beautiful," said a voice. Startled, she looked down at the source of the voice. Kelly noticed the lone man wore what, at one point, might have been a nice suit with a tie. Now however, the clothes were covered with the remnants of recent meals and dirt and had clearly not been cleaned in some time. Rips and tears covered the suit. She was also immediately struck by his smell - a repulsive combination of alcohol and urine.

Still unsure of her new environment, she looked puzzled at the man. "What?"

"I said you're beautiful."

"Yeah baby, you're beautiful. C'mon over and have some fun with Big Mike and His Love Posse here at Table 5," said one of the men over the giggling of his cohorts.

A light went on in Kelly's mind and her expression changed from one clouded with confusion to one of anger. "You sick little bastards," she said quietly, but loud enough to get a round of "ooohs" from the group.

"Shut up you losers! You're all pigs! You're fired! We have a zero tolerance policy here! Do you understand what 'no sexual harassment means'? You're fired, all of you! Get out!" Said the lone man. Then, turning his attention back to Kelly he said in a whisper, "Forget them lovely lady. Would you be so kind as to get me a coffee?" Kelly shifted her glare back to the lone man. "Sure," she said going to the kitchen and fulfilling his request.

As she returned, she set the coffee on the table and tried to ignore the group at Table 5. She made an attempt at initiating a light conversation with the lone man. "Is that okay?" she asked politely.

"I was the CEO of a huge auto company once," was his only response, inciting a chorus of taunts from Table 5.

"Yeah, I was a CEO too, baby…

"Come on over here, sweet pants, and I'll show you the presidential salute."

"Me too…CEO Ric they used to call me…

"I was a CEO too…"

Kelly glared at them, but reminded herself that these were unfortunate souls who needed love, understanding, and compassion. They just needed someone to say, 'Tell me, I care', and their burden would be lifted. The lone man was not so generous and forgiving.

"You were not, you lying bastards! Now shut up!" screamed the man at Table 1 and quickly turned to again whisper to Kelly. "…but they couldn't see the vision. It's all about cost and diversity…but that Little Billy bastard just refused to see… don't they understand…cost and diversity, diversity and cost…" he said, rocking slowly in his chair, trying to be heard over the insistent murmur from the nearby table.

"...cost don't mean nothing at this table, baby, bring your cute little ass over here."

"...we got some money, baby," said one of the men. The two men to his right each slammed a $10 bill on the table. The man to his left rolled up a $1 bill, put part of it in his mouth and laid his head on the table, staring at the ceiling with the bill protruding straight out of his mouth. His friends laughed hysterically and chanted, dancing in their seats while pushing their friend forward.

"Go, President Brian...Go, President Brian..." then, "...go, Stock boy, it's your birthday...go, Stock boy..."

The man at Table 1 turned to the rebellious group, overtaken with a consuming rage. "Shut up! Just shut up! Do you know what that means! Shut up! You're all losers! You were never like me..." he said as his gaze shifted back to a blank stare off in the distance. "I was king of all I surveyed, feared around the world...they trembled when they heard my name...Jack the Knife they used to call me...I was a king..."

"Hey, baby, leave Jacques alone and come over and see King Eric...I wanna show you my royal scepter," one man said loudly as the group laughed.

Kelly stood looking horrified at Table 5. Having heard enough of their onslaught, she addressed them directly. "Okay... now listen, everybody just keep their scepters in their pants. This is NOT a brothel. I'm not here to serve anything but a very old, very disgusting turkey dinner to your sorry asses. This is not a strip club! In fact, you should all get off your dead, worthless, lazy butts and go get jobs!"

"Touché, lovely lady! And for the love of God...Shut Up!" added the lone man.

Before they could respond, she turned and stormed back to the kitchen, hearing only a crazed laughter behind her.

Chip greeted her as she returned. "Everything go okay?" he asked, smiling facetiously.

Kelly exploded. "They are complete pigs."

"Table 5?"

"Yes!" Kelly could barely contain her anger. "Freaks! I wasn't out there two minutes and they started pulling out $10's and $1's. They don't have any money for food, but they have money for booze and to put on the table when I come by! Bills just start showing up."

"I told you to watch them. You should feel flattered, $10 is probably a lot of money for them..."

Michael F. Goyette

Kelly gave Chip a dirty look. "I'm teasing. Just a joke...They're a rowdy bunch all right. I guess they started an investment group or something that took a dive. Their wives left them..."

"Wives! I find it hard to believe that anyone would marry any one of them!" retorted Kelly.

Father Joe happened to be walking by as Chip and Kelly were reviewing their experiences. "Are the natives restless tonight Kelly?" he asked gently.

"Big Mike and his Love Posse at Table 5 are having a difficult time containing their love juices. The testosterone is way out of control, Father." Kelly said. The priest seemed at a loss for words.

She's talking about testosterone and love posses to a priest, Chip thought in utter amazement. It's no wonder no one messes with her at work.

"I'm serious, Father, we have some sin going down in the trenches as we speak. I think we need some preemptive absolution at Table 5," Kelly said.

"Sin...?" Father Joe started as Kelly jumped in and finished his sentence. "...unfolding before our very eyes. I think you should go out there right now and do something about that guy and his hormonally exuberant friends."

"O...Okay." The stunned priest said as he slowly entered the eating area with Kelly close on his heels, pushing him forward.

As the four saw the priest headed their way, their fiery behavior was quickly extinguished. The cups and paper bags quickly fell out of sight under the table. Kelly saw one of the four mouth the words, 'Oh shit'.

"That's right, buddy. I brought the power of God with me this time. Your ass belongs to Kelly now, bad boy," Kelly yelled over the shoulder of Father Joe.

The priest stopped and turned to Kelly. "I'll tell you what. Why don't you go and talk to that nice man at Table 1 and let me handle Table 5. Okay?"

"Yeah, okay." Never losing eye contact with the quartet, she pointed her index and middle fingers directly at her eyes and then pointed at the group, mouthing the words 'I'm watching you'.

She arrived at Table 1, catching the lone man apparently in the middle of a conversation with himself. "...and then my wife left..." he said, jerking his head to the left and spitting out the word "bitch" under his breath. "...she just didn't understand..."

Kelly became distracted from the four and refocused on the lone man. She hesitated, then decided to ask, "Understand what?"

"All I wanted her to do was get three quotes before she bought anything. It works for General Motors, why couldn't it work for us..."

Kelly was verbally paralyzed. "...three quotes?"

"It was all very simple. If she was going to buy something, I just wanted her to get three quotes on the item to compare costs and allow us to source the lowest cost supplier. It's all about cost...couldn't she see that? Cost and diversity..." the man said almost in tears.

"What exactly did you want her to get three quotes on?" Kelly probed.

"Everything! Cars, houses, milk, eggs, toilet paper, everything! We have to minimize cost and maximize diversity. I told her to get different types of paper towel but she insisted on buying the same ones every time...every time, the same ones...no diversity...then she said she couldn't take it anymore...Bitch!" he said, jerking his head again. "She said she wanted a normal man, one of the worker bees... like one of them." He and Kelly looked at Table 5. All heads at the table were bowed and each held the hand of the man next to him, forming a circle, as the priest led them in prayer.

"Look at them pretending to pray...Hypocrites! I see through your little charade! You can't fool Jack the Knife! If this were my company, I'd have all your heads!" he shouted at the men. One of the four glanced up at him, gave a wink, and quickly looked back down while the priest wasn't looking.

"You see! Father, did you see that! They're all hypocrites!" He shouted again and turned his attention back to Kelly. "She left me...bitch...but I know if I had a woman like you by my side, I could climb my way out of here...I just need the right person...not someone like her...bitch..." he said, jerking his head.

"I understand things must be hard for you...but...but um..." she started as he stared at her with pleading eyes.

"Kelly?" Kelly felt a hand on her shoulder, turned and saw it was Chip. "Are you about ready to go? I have an early flight tomorrow," he said.

Father Joe had also walked over at the same time. "Thank you two for helping these unfortunate people today. I know they appreciate it, although they may not always show it," he said, glancing over his shoulder at Table 5. All heads were still bowed and all hands were still held. "They shouldn't bother you for a while, I gave them a firm scolding and told Big Mike to lead his posse in 50 Hail Mary's and 50 Our Father's each. They are really very good people deep down, Kelly."

Chip and Kelly watched as the Priest proceeded to the door.

"...if only you would be mine lovely lady..." The lone man said tugging at Kelly's sleeve. "...we could rule again, as husband and wife, king and queen..."

Kelly looked at Chip. "I think you're right, it's time to..." she began, being abruptly interrupted by a trumpeting voice at Table 5.

"God has left the building, I repeat God has left the building..." said one of the group using his hands as a mock blow horn." The group started laughing again, each reaching for his brown paper bag and paper cup.

"Hey! Car Dude! You shouldn't bother us while we're praying, it's not polite."

"You weren't praying, you worthless piece of shit!"

Michael F. Goyette

"The Rabbi left honey, you can come visit us now…" said one of the four. The other three fell momentarily silent, then burst out laughing.

"That wasn't a Rabbi, man…"

"It wasn't?" he asked, looking puzzled. The others only continued their insane laughter.

"Did he have a Yarmulke?"

"A Yar…?"

"Oh Jesus! It's no wonder…it's no freakin wonder…" The group only laughed as Chip and Kelly headed for the door.

"Remember, Kelly, there but for the grace of God go I." Chip said.

Kelly glared at Chip. "Yeah, right."

Out of the Box Thinking

"It's important to have everyone cross-trained by the end of second quarter. Fausto has made it clear that every individual in the organization needs to develop multiple skill sets allowing them to be interchangeable between departments. He believes, and I agree, that this will do a couple things," Janice said.

The team huddled in Janice's office, brainstorming white board ready to go, concept incubator awaiting its first arrival. Scott and Tamika leaned forward, waiting with keen anticipation for Janice's next syllable. Terry sat back with arms folded and bit her tongue. She wondered if her annoyance with these conversations was apparent.

"First, it will enhance people's appreciation of the work their coworkers do, thus breaking down some of the walls that we tend to build between groups. It's not as easy to just toss a project over the wall and forget about it, if you know the ramifications it will cause on the other side. Second, it will enable GIT to shift resources as necessary with greater ease. If, for example, we have a design engineer skilled in business planning or finance and one area gets slow, we can move the person to the other area that may need resources, instead of letting people go. I would hope people would see this as the benevolent plan that it is intended to be."

Scott and Tamika sat back with synchronized "Ahh's", in complete awe of what they had heard. Never had they seen someone so far reaching in their vision, so precise in their execution, so articulate in their explanation.

"So I'd like to hear some of your thoughts on the matter. I thought we could brainstorm and open a dialog on these issues. I'd like to come up with a set of action items that we could present next week to Fausto and the Steering Committee," Janice asked. And with a tilt of her head and a fabricated smile she added, "Any thoughts?"

"So everyone will be an interchangeable resource?" Scott asked.

Showing herself the experienced mentor, Janice responded. "In a sense, Scott. The term resource is somewhat broad though. We should really be more specific and say something like...oh, I don't know, maybe Interchangeable Labor Resource."

"Do you think people will buy into this idea," asked Tamika cautiously.

"We'd like everyone to buy in up front of course, but there are always those naysayers out there that may take some convincing."

"What if to promote this idea, we started kind of a grass roots movements to sell it. We could put up bulletins like I did with the Germ Management memo. That got a heck of a response. And once a person was cross-trained, we could have them wear a name badge that identified them as an Interchangeable Labor Resource. Like getting your wings. Once a few people got them, I have to believe that everyone would be pushing to get theirs," Scott shared.

Terry stared dumbfounded. The discussion irritated her on many levels. Germ Management was his idea? A heck of a response? What a joke! That dirty little prick, she thought. But beyond Scott trying to steal her thunder, what bothered her most was the very foundation of the discussion. No one would care about this. This would be one more insane program that people would make fun of when Janice wasn't listening, just like the PP Program. Knowing she was outnumbered but desperate not to be associated with another HR fiasco, she delicately threw her two cents into the pot.

"I'm wondering if it will mean enough to someone for them to want to wear a badge everyday that says they're interchangeable between departments. It's hard enough to get people to wear the little sticker that says "I gave blood" for a whole day to promote a blood drive. It seems that people might be likely to wear it for a day or two then forget about it," Terry said.

Janice shot Terry a stern look. "Well, thanks for contributing, Terry, but remember the Healthy Open Dialog Guidelines," she said, pointing to the guidelines on the wall. "We don't challenge people or pass judgment. I think Scott's on to something. Let's hear him out."

Terry withdrew, becoming more agitated.

"What if we warmed the name tag up a bit. The word "Resource" is, like you said, Janice, somewhat broad. Everyone is really an individual labor unit," Tamika suggested.

"And valuable ones at that," Scott added.

"What if we put on the nametag, Valuable Interchangeable Individual Labor Unit?"

"It seems kind of long," Scott observed.

"We could take out the Individual part. I mean, doesn't everyone know that they're an individual? Doesn't that go without saying? And besides if everyone is interchangeable, why is it useful to be identified as an individual," asked Tamika.

"Good point," said Janice. "I'm happy with this dialog we've established. I think we've addressed a lot of good issues here today."

"What about a Labor Unit number…" suggested Scott.

"No, no. No numbers. That promotes individualism."

"What about actually getting people trained?" asked Terry. The group sighed collectively and turned to Terry with intolerant stares. "It seems like we're low on resources as it is. I hear people talking about not having enough time to do their everyday work, let alone take on new roles and responsibilities. How can we pull someone away long enough for them to become proficient in a new job? Who will do their job while they're off being trained? Will they be able to do it at the same level or will we see a decline in productivity? Additionally, I'm skeptical that you can just put any hat on anyone and have them perform. Like putting a design engineer in finance. I wonder if that really works in the long run. Maybe we should focus on some of these key issues first, before we worry about what goes on somebody's name badge," Terry said.

The scowls of the faces of her coworkers made it clear that her views were not of the majority opinion.

"I think you may be falling prey to some of the pessimism and tunnel vision out there, Terry. We've heard a lot of that from you lately. I'd personally like to see you take a much more optimistic and positive approach to your work. Start thinking outside the four walls, look outside the box, and I think you'll see a whole world of opportunities," lectured Janice.

Scott and Tamika nodded and spoke in unison, "A world of opportunities."

"Let's take one step at a time and I think you'll see that we really do make some progress. Scott, I want you to lead this grass roots effort. We also might be able to incorporate some of these new, diverse ideas in our upcoming out-placement program."

As a punishment, the team avoided any further eye contact with the boat rocker, Terry, leaving her to reflect on her divisive, unorthodox ideas in solitude.

Germans and Airports

Chip arrived at the airport a little over an hour prior to take-off. With constant delays and long lines, it was best to start out early in case alternate plans needed to be exercised. Since he had no luggage, he proceeded directly to the gate. There was no line as he approached the check in counter. He noticed a large sign hanging above and behind the desk attendant which read: "We fly both ways."

Kelly had provided him with the necessary information: description of Helmut, customer contact information, map to customer facility, and other pertinent information. The plan was fairly simple. Meet Helmut in Chicago, go straight to the customer, meet for two or three hours, grab lunch (maybe with the customer), head back to the airport, and fly back to Detroit.

The attendant greeted him in a chipper voice and a brilliant smile. She was about 5'3", petite, with short highlighted hair. She wore two pins, one espousing the slogan hanging behind the desk and another with the phrase "Tell Me I Care". The latter phrase required a second glance. Although Chip couldn't explain it, he had nagging feeling that something just didn't look right. He made a mental note to consider it later.

"Well, good morning and welcome to Pizaza Airlines. How are you today?" asked the girl behind the counter.

"Good. How are you?"

"Wonderful! If I was any better, I'd need two of me to enjoy it all!" she proclaimed proudly. At 5:50 in the morning, it was difficult to believe that anyone could be this enthusiastic about anything. Yet here she was, energized just by starting a new day. Her exuberance and overly positive demeanor were more than what was needed at this time of the morning Chip decided. Pizaza must be a great place to work.

"You'll be boarding though gate twelve," she said, pointing to a gate no more than twenty feet away. "If you get lost, come back and I can draw you a map," she said giggling.

Chip smiled politely. Why all these lame attempts at being funny this early, he wondered. Upon thinking this, he remembered a recent commercial for Pizaza Airlines; it was sort of funny. It looked like they were trying to model themselves after Southwest; an extreme model it looked like. Tell Me I Care...

As Chip boarded the plane, he was greeted by the flight attendant.

"Welcome aboard." He wore the same pins as the girl at the desk and maintained a like demeanor. Maybe this was a requirement to work at Pizaza. "Do you know how to fly a plane?" he asked without smiling.

"What?" Chip said, taken off guard.

"Just curious. Nevermind. Nothing to see here. Move along," said the flight attendant.

The jokes just didn't seem that funny to Chip, especially not this early. Chip found his seat and sat next to another apparent business traveler.

"What do think of their attempt at humor?" the man asked Chip.

Chip rolled his eyes. "A little too much this early. Later in the day might be okay, but I haven't had my coffee yet. He asked if I could fly a plane."

"Yeah, a little inappropriate. Did you see their badge? The one that says Tell Me I Care?" the man asked. "The dummies forgot the comma," he said, chuckling.

"The comma..?" Chip asked, puzzled.

"Yeah, the comma. It should say: Tell Me, I Care. You know, tell me about all your problems because I care."

Chip now understood what had bothered him about the tag.

The man continued his explanation. "Instead, they left the comma out and now it sounds sarcastic. Like they're challenging you to make them care. There was a write-up about it in the Detroit News last weekend. These guys are a joke all right. What a bunch of dummies. Although a comma is the last of their worries. They're going down fast. Their dream team isn't working out as planned. They'll probably be bankrupt in a few months," the man finished, returning to his paper.

"Welcome aboard Flight Edmund Fitzgerald with service to Atlanta," said the voice over the intercom. "We'll make a quick stop in Chicago to get gas and directions and will continue on with non-stop service to Atlanta. In the event of a water landing, your seat cushions can be used as a flotation device. Remember however, these *are* the property of Pizaza Airlines and should be returned promptly upon arriving to shore. For those of you that can't swim, thank you in advance for flying Pizaza Airlines," the flight attendant ended his attempt at humor.

"I don'ta get it," Chip heard a voice in the background over the speaker. The flight attendant had obviously forgotten to turn off the intercom.

Michael F. Goyette

"Look, Geseppi, it's not easy coming up with a perfect jewel every day. They just put a comedic hat on me one day and said go to it. They gave me no training other than a four hour session lecturing me on the importance of being funny."

"I told you my name. It's a not Geseppi, it's a Bob."

"Ok, A Bob. What ever! Roberto! If you think you can do a better job, it's all yours!" At that point the intercom went dead and the flight attendant appeared from behind curtains at the front of the plane, smiling a plastic smile. The passengers collectively looked down as he appeared, leaving only a puzzled look on his face.

After Chip had settled in, he dozed off, only to be awaken some time later by the flight attendant's voice over the speaker.

Chip looked at the passenger next to him. The man was shaking his head watching the cockpit door. "You were sleeping, but that guy has been making wise cracks the entire flight. And he keeps leaving the intercom on, so every time he tries to make a joke, we hear the other guy say he doesn't get it and then they start arguing. Pretty messed up if you ask me," he said to Chip, only glancing at him.

Chip nodded, still not fully comprehending the input.

Upon landing, Chip proceeded to the gate Helmut was scheduled to arrive at. The arrival board indicated that Helmut's flight had landed over an hour ago as scheduled. Chip held up a small GIT sign he had brought with him, hoping Helmut was in the vicinity to see.

Immediately, a rather big bellied, slightly balding man carrying a large briefcase in one hand and pulling a huge, aluminum colored hard shell suitcase in the other approached Chip. Chip spotted him walking over. He was in his early fifties and dressed professionally in a tie and older sport coat. He wore glasses and was slightly shorter than Chip.

"Hi. Are you Helmut?" Chip asked, extending his hand.

"Yes, I am Herr Wittenbecher," he said with the emphasis on Herr. "You must be Herr Vezerbe," the German said shaking hands with Chip. His voice was loud and assertive.

"I see your flight was on time. Small miracle," Chip said lightheartedly.

"Of course! Zis is no miracle Herr Veazerbe," Helmut said, acting completely surprised that Chip would state something so obvious. "We always choose Lufthansa and zerefore zee flight is always on time, unlike zee American airlines, in vhich case you are never sure vhen you vill arrive or vhere you vill be once you get zhere," Helmut said, booming with laughter.

Chip laughed off the little dig politely and attempted to move the conversation forward. "Should we go get our car? I think we are scheduled to meet the customer in about an hour. That gives us enough time to…"

"Yes, you see Herr Veazerbe," Helmut interrupted, "I do not sink zhere is a need to visit zis customer zhat you speak of. I sink vee should be on zee next flight to Detroit, which I have booked us on. Zee flight shall leave in approximately one point five hours from now."

"Oh? Our meeting was canceled?" Chip asked, somewhat taken by surprise.

"Yes, I believe vee vill cancel this meeting," Helmut said, beginning his apparent walk to the next terminal.

Chip walked after him, unsure how to interpret what was just said. "Will cancel the meeting? It hasn't been canceled yet?"

Helmut became slightly irritated. "Yes Herr Veazerbe, as I said, I have canceled zis meeting," he said, continuing to walk.

"Does the customer know the meeting is canceled?" Chip asked, cautiously.

"Vee vill call zis customer and give him zis information."

Still uncertain of the situation, Chip pushed the questioning forward. "I don't understand. If the customer is still expecting us, why are we canceling the meeting on this short notice? What am I missing? That doesn't seem like a good thing to do. Can you share with me the reason for this?" Chip inquired politely.

"Yes. You see, Herr Veazerbe, zis is a small customer and zhere are many unanswered items zhat need clarification before vee can have an informed discussion."

The line of reasoning perplexed Chip. The size of the customer seemed an irrelevant point; shouldn't they be served irrespective? And weren't they supposed to have a meeting in order to clarify the open issues? Besides, he and Helmut were already in the neighborhood. Although Helmut was at least two levels above Chip, Chip couldn't resist questioning the wisdom of the decision.

"With all due respect, Herr Wittenbecher, isn't it poor customer service to cancel on the customer with this short of notice? The meeting shouldn't take that long; we'll still be back in Detroit this evening. I think…"

Helmut stopped, put both pieces of luggage on the ground and turned to Chip. "I understand you, Herr Veazerbe, however, I find zat you are wrong."

Chip looked at him indignantly. "Really? How's that?"

"You see. Zee customer does not know vhat he vants and zerefore, vee vill not waste our time driving here, zhere, everywhere, hoping to find an answer," Helmut said, gesturing dramatically waiving his arms in the air. "No answer vill fall from zee sky, Herr Veazerbe. You see, zee customers here in zee USA are cowboys. Zhey ride off as fast as zhey can visout sinking vhere zhey are going. Zhey do not understand quality. Zhey only make decisions on vhat is cheapest and easiest und vee vill not waste our time vis such nonsense. Vee vill return to your office in Detroit, call zee customer, and tell him in very clear terms vhat he needs. Eventually, he vill see our point of view and at zhat time vee vill invite him to visit our facility in Detroit. In zhe meantime, if he does not understand our view, zhen by our own choosing, ve vill not continue to do business with him. Zis is zee best vay, zis is zee vay vee vill proceed. Zhere vill be no further discussion on ze point. Ja? Gut." With that, Helmut picked up his luggage and continued his march forward.

"Well, okay then." Arrogant dictator were the only words that came to Chip's mind. However, seeing the futility of the discussion, Chip started with Helmut for the gate back to Detroit.

"I have booked us on Pizzaz Airlines," Helmut said without looking at Chip, staying completely focused on his destination. "You are familiar vis zis airline, Herr Veazerbe?"

"Yes. I used them to fly from Detroit. Have you flown with them before?" Chip asked, hesitating slightly. He sensed additional verbal mud slinging on deck. Much to his surprise, Helmut took a completely different route.

"No, I have not. However, I have heard many good sings. I understand they have a gut sense of humor making zee flying experience very enjoyable. Zhey are very funny. You see, Herr Veazerbe, I also have a gut sense of humor," Helmut said, booming a laugh as they approached the security scanners.

"That's good to know," Chip said. An arrogant dictator with a sense of humor, lucky me, thought Chip.

"If I remember correctly, zhere was a another such airline zhat was very lighthearted. Do you know zhis airline?" Helmut asked.

"Southwest used to package themselves along the same vein. I think they thought better of it after September 11. They backed off a little from that approach."

Chip put his planner on the scanner and walked through the security gate. At the end of the conveyor, he picked up his planner and turned around in time to see a security guard approach Helmut's briefcase.

"Sir, can you open your briefcase for me?" a male security guard asked in a cold, matter of fact way.

"Of course," Helmut responded exuberantly opening the top.

The guard began rifling through the contents and found nothing but papers and GIT documents: Business Plans, SIMM meeting summaries, a couple reviews; typical business material. The review of the briefcase was almost complete. He was almost at the end of his search. Chip could almost hear the words 'thank you' coming out of the guard's mouth. He could almost see himself walking to the gate to wait for his flight. However, Chip saw his vision disappear when Helmut spoke. "Nothing in zhere except for dangerous explosives," he said, laughing loudly.

Chip's heart felt like it came to a dead stop. For a brief moment, Chip thought the entire airport was silent, everyone staring at Helmut.

The guard stared seriously at Helmut, unmoving, hands on the briefcase. Helmut stood smiling, evidently happy with his contribution to the conversation and proud to participate in the perceived new joviality of the airlines. It did not appear that anyone else had heard his comments.

"Excuse me?" the guard asked.

Helmut paused for a moment, still smiling. "Yes. You see, I am traveling on business and I am going to our facility in Detroit. Zhe briefcase only contains all zhe company paperwork and on and on."

The guard didn't budge, obviously contemplating his next move. One look at Helmut - middle-aged German, glasses, soup stained tie, mostly balding and power belly – it would have been difficult to envision him as anything even resembling a threat. Be that as it was, Chip decided that the comment alone could cause some severe ramifications. Time for a Hail Mary throw and hope for the best.

"I'm sorry. My coworker is a little confused. He's heard about Pizzaz's particular humorous approach and he thinks he's just joining in," Chip said quietly, pleading his case.

As he finished his statement, another guard walked up and put his hand on the shoulder on the first. "Tom says you should take your break now. If you don't take it now, he says he ain't gonna give you another one. He says things are getting busy and the lines are getting too long so you gotta make sure you're back in fifteen minutes." The second guard glanced quickly through the briefcase and looked at Helmut. "Okay, go ahead." The line behind them was growing as a large number of people pushed their way past. The first guard had not taken his eyes off Helmut.

The second guard seemed to become agitated and whispered to the first, all the while watching the line. "C'mon. You gotta start listening to Tom. Just do what he says and he'll leave you alone. Go on break and come back in fifteen minutes like he said."

The first guard remained motionless, staring at Helmut, who was wearing a silly grin. After a moment he turned to Chip. "Pizaza?"

"Pizaza," Chip replied.

"C'mon, man. I can't keep covering for you. Get going," the second guard said.

The first guard looked at him and then Helmut, sighed, and slowly turned and walked away.

Chip and Helmut began walking away. "You know they'll put you in jail for a joke like that just to make an example of you."

"You Americans are too serious; you need to lighten up and enjoy zhe day a little more. It is clear, from one look at me zhat I am not a terrorist. Zhis should be clear."

"It's clear to me…it might not be clear to security. Just the same, no more jokes. Please?" Chip pleaded.

"Of course, of course," responded Helmut, looking particularly annoyed that no one appreciated his sense of humor.

After waiting an hour, it was time to board. Chip had been flipping through a newspaper while Helmut made a number of phone calls back to the office and his family in Germany. Chip wondered for a moment if he should check his voice mail at work. Why, he asked himself. If he had any messages, which was highly unlikely, it would just be from Rajiv with some bullshit assignment that needed to get done as soon as he returned. In fact, he thought, there was likely a message from Rajiv. That's exactly the type of thing he would pull; wait until he knew Chip was out of the office and leave an urgent voice mail or send an e-mail with high priority. Then when Chip returned from wherever he was, Rajiv would ask why he hadn't responded sooner.

The game had gotten very old, very quickly.

Chip heard the boarding announcement for his flight and guided Helmut, who was now on a cell phone talking to someone locally, to his seat.

Don't worry, he said to himself. Fix the situation. Push hard and find something new; either internally or at another company. It can always be worse, he reminded himself; just look at Linda. That poor girl was almost in tears the other day at lunch he remembered.

Rajiv had called her at least four times over the previous week and a half, demanding she meet with him immediately to review the status of some customer activity. Each time he called, it was at 4:55 p.m. She had left at 4:30 one of the days and Rajiv had been relentlessly calling her cell phone until she finally returned the call at around 7:00 p.m.

He had grilled her on where she was and requested that she come back to the office. When she finally became frustrated and absolutely refused to discuss it anymore, he did a typical Rajiv about face.

"Look it's been a long day. Let's revisit this tomorrow morning. Stop by and see me at your convenience. Maybe we can even discuss it over lunch. My treat. It's the least I can do. Your hard work is not going unnoticed, believe me. You're one of GIT's key "go-to" Account Managers," he said in a warm, sympathetic voice.

Chip had overheard Linda telling Kelly the whole story.

"God, I hate him," she said, almost crying. "I never know where I stand with the guy. One day he's all sweet and telling me how I'm going to get a promotion and the next minute he's lambasting me in front of the entire team for some stupid little detail that I overlooked. I want to get out of here. I think I'd rather work at McDonalds than do this anymore. And after I deal with him, I get to go get bitched out by the customer because our quality rating slid. I get it from everywhere. Aren't I lucky."

Chip remembered her saying all this while sitting on Kelly's desk. He had gotten used to her coming by to talk to Kelly every few hours and as such, had tried to desensitize himself to her continually revealing attire. This time, however, the combination of her very tight, short skirt combined with the fact she was sitting on the desk, made for a compelling distraction. The vision of her crossing and uncrossing her legs was the last thought Chip had before he fell into a light slumber.

"Attention, attention. Dis isa you captain speaking." Chip woke with a start at the Captain's voice. "Wesa approaching Detroit Metro airport. Da good news isa they have a gate waiting for us and theres a no terroists on board," the captain said laughing nervously.

Chip looked at Helmut who was elbowing him and laughing loud. Apparently, the airline was living up to Helmut's expectations.

"Da bad news isa we lost a wheel on the landing gear when wesa took off from a Midway," the captain said.

Helmut sighed and shook his head. "You see, Herr Veazerbe, zhis is American craftsmanship. Of course in Germany, we do not have zhis problem," he said, laughing to himself. Chip looked around, still trying to wake up and questioning if he had heard correctly. He looked questioningly at the guy next to him.

"I heard them whispering something earlier about losing the wheel, so I called my partner who is waiting for another flight at Midway…" the man explained to Chip in a whispered voice. "Apparently, a wheel flew off the plane when we took off and flew through a concrete wall."

Chip looked at him, stunned. "You're kidding."

"No, I'm not. I wish I was. I guess it hit a car on the road after it busted through the wall. Nobody was hurt but we're stuck up here with no freakin' wheel," the man said.

"Buta not to worry." The captain continued. "Itsa only one wheel and wesa got 3 left and a lotsa altidudes left before we hit the ground. Theres a no reason to panic. Wesa gonna circle the airport a couple a times to burn off some fuel on da side with da missing wheel, to lighten the load and make a landing a little bit easy," the captain concluded. "Oh and a tank you in advance for flying Pizaza Airlines where we fly a both ways and a tell me I care."

What a mess, Chip thought. We lost a wheel and could possibly have a catastrophe because of it, and here the captain is making jokes and trying to clumsily regurgitate company slogans

Helmut leaned over to Chip as if to whisper but never lowering his booming voice. "Yes, you see, Herr Veazerbe, zis is very good strategy on zer part," Helmut chuckled lightly.

"Why is that?" Chip said, almost afraid to ask.

"Vis less fuel, zer is less of a fire to extinguish," he said and laughed loudly at his own joke, elbowing Chip in the arm.

This is not the death I envisioned, Chip thought.

"Ok. Wesa gonna try to land now," the captain said. The flight attendant who had been making jokes on the earlier flight, was ghost white and no longer even pretending to be happy.

Michael F. Goyette

Chip peered out the window. As the plane approached, he could see the runway…and fire trucks and ambulances lining either side. Oh boy. Here we go.

"There's a nothing to worry about. Theys a waiting for us wisa a big welcome party," the captain offered.

At this, Helmut laughed loud again, causing everyone in the vicinity to turn and stare at he and Chip. "Yes! A party! You see, Herr Veazerbe, even in zhe face of certain doom, zhe captain still maintains zhe company policy and tells us jokes, never once deviating from zhe plan."

"What plan?" Chip asked cautiously.

"Zhe plan of Pizaza Airlines to make zhere customers comfortable by telling jokes. Only a true professional could continue vis zhis plan in light of zhis impending and inevitable disaster. His ancestors must be German," Helmut explained.

Chip stared at him, stunned. "I never thought of it that way."

"I am glad I could assist you in sinking beyond zhe four walls."

Chip continued to watch out the window, wanting to see whatever was coming his way. He could see the strip getting closer and he mentally braced himself for the worst. He saw the emergency vehicles flashing by the window and felt the landing gear touch the ground. He held his breath until the plane came a stop. A normal landing.

"You see, Herr Veazerbe, nothing to be concerned about: true professionals," Helmut said, unbuckling his belt and preparing his notes and items to exit the plane.

The plane pulled to the gate without incident. A lady in a Pizaza uniform waited at the end of the exit ramp and greeted Chip and Helmut with a bright smile. "Sorry for the inconvenience. We hope this makes up for it. Please fly with us again," she said while beaming and sliding a six-minute calling card into each of their hands.

After all that, a six-minute calling card? "Wonderful. Thank you," Chip said to her.

"You're very welcome!" she responded, missing Chip's sarcasm.

Crazy. That guy on the plane was right, Chip thought. A few months and this airline will be out of business. I wonder if the people who run the company know what they're in for? I wonder if they realize what's happening to their business.

Radical Entrepreneurial Ideas: I Don't Know if You've Ever Really Considered the Benefits of Being an Alpaca Farmer

"You sound distraught my friend," Ted said without looking at Chip. Ted sat at his desk typing furiously, appearing preoccupied with his thoughts.

"He's got me running in every direction," Chip said.

"Who?" Ted asked, staying focused on his computer screen.

"Rajiv. He's driving me crazy. None of my work seems to live up to his expectations. Not that I know what the expectations are; he never seems to be clear as to what he's looking for. And I know most of the time he's just dicking me around. Sending me chasing my tail just to show he's the man. And the work…I am so bored. I've tried talking to him about doing something a little more challenging but he just blows me off. I even put it in writing and outlined a growth plan; a path I can follow over the next few weeks and months. I thought it would be useful to him and me but he just ignored it and sent me off with a list of new charts and business summaries he wanted to see done by the next morning. I know I can do better than this. It's very frustrating."

Ted had no response other than to stop typing, pull something out of his desk drawer, and turn to Chip.

"I don't want my six month old granddaughter having this because it's a weak little habit we teach babies so they can hide from the world when they grow up. But it sounds like something you can put to good use," Ted said with a smile and presented Chip with a baby's pacifier.

Chip felt embarrassed for having even brought this subject up to Ted. He rose and began to leave the office.

"Thanks," said Chip snidely, not accepting the gift.

"If you're looking for sympathy, my friend, you can find it in the dictionary somewhere between shit and syphilis. Problems don't happen, they're chosen and cultivated in times of human stupidity. If you're an adult, you live with the consequences. If you're a smart adult, you put your energy into solving the problems and making sure they don't happen again...instead of standing around whining and lamenting your fate," Ted said laughing.

One nasty response after another came to Chip's mind. Who was Ted to lecture him? Ted wasn't exactly the icon of the perfect life. After all, wasn't it Ted who felt he had been screwed by company and never lifted a finger to change the situation?

"Maybe you should be looking in a mirror when you say that," Chip shot back.

"Maybe," Ted said, still laughing. "But then again, maybe I have some wisdom that you would be smart to consider, lest you go down the same path. Besides, I'm not sure you really appreciate how good you have it. For a guy your age, you're making good money. There are a lot of people out there that would die for your job and the money that goes with it. You should stop whining all the time; your life isn't that bad." Ted's phone rang. "Excuse me. I have work to do and you have to go wipe your tears away," he said, turning his back to Chip.

Chip left Ted's office and walked back to his. 4:50. Time to think about leaving anyway. He had agreed to meet Kelly for an after work drink at 5:30, but decided it was time to get a head start. Deep down, he knew Ted was right; this was a lot of unproductive whining. He knew what had to be done: find something else to do, either at GIT or outside. He knew he was responsible for the current situation and had the power to change it if he really wanted. Still, he had found himself not doing a lot and instead just complaining. And to hear someone point this out...especially Ted...was somewhat annoying.

The room was dimly lit. The after work crowd was gradually starting to flow in. The waitress slid a Killians across the bar to Chip. He looked around for any sign of Kelly. His decision to leave ten minutes early would no doubt be completely unacceptable to Rajiv, had he seen the actual departure. Fortunately, he was at an off-site today and would likely, hopefully, if he was doing *his* job, be too preoccupied to notice.

"Thank God It's Friday. TGIF," said the man sitting next to Chip at the bar.

"I'm sorry?" Chip said turning his attention to him.

"I said, Thank God It's Friday. TGIF."

"I don't want to burst your bubble, but it's only Thursday," Chip replied lightheartedly.

The man became glum, slumping his shoulders and head. "Oh. Well in that case...Sure Happy It's Thursday," the man said finishing his statement by laughing loudly.

Chip nodded and smiled politely, not knowing why the man was so entertained by his statement, "Yeah right."

While Chip glanced around the bar again, he could see the man still staring at him. What the hell is he staring at me for? A light went off in Chip's head and he turned back to the man. "Sure Happy It's Thursday. I get it," Chip said.

The man laughed again, beaming with pride. "You finally got it. You must be an MBA."

Ouch, what a presumptuous jab from a complete stranger. "As a matter of fact…"

"I knew it," the man said, cutting Chip off and laughing. "I can spot'em a mile away." The man was shorter, about 5'9", and thin. Chip estimated that he was in his early fifties. He wore a plain white shirt, a tie, and an old yellowish color sport coat. The coat looked almost as old as the man. His hair was dark and slicked back. Used car salesman came to Chip's mind. The man's demeanor and expressions reminded Chip of a cartoon character or maybe a leprechaun. Yeah, that was it. Put a green hat on the guy and he would the poster boy for any St. Patrick's Day festivity.

"John Taft," he said, extending his hand to Chip.

"Chip Weatherbe. Nice to meet you."

"Chip Weatherbe the MBA. So what do you do Mr. MBA?" John asked.

"Marketing Manager over at GIT," Chip replied, half-heartedly.

John stopped smiling. "GIT's going through some rough times now."

"You're telling me."

"I hear they're on the chopping block."

"In different pieces as I understand. Although I'm not privy to that type of information. I'm like a mushroom…" Chip said.

"They keep you in the dark and feed you shit," John finished Chip's statement, laughing again.

"You got it," Chip said, taking a drink of his beer.

"For what it's worth, I'd be getting out of that situation. I know I don't have to tell you that. You already know that. You're a smart guy, I can see that." Chip could hear a sales pitch coming on. A leprechaun *and* a used car salesman, what an amazing combination.

"I bring it up because I know what it's like to be in that situation. I'm in that situation now," John said. "But I was talking to a friend of mine, a guy I've known for twenty years. He's an honest guy, a hard worker and he got me involved in a great opportunity."

"You don't say," said Chip, completely disinterested, still looking for Kelly.

"You can hear the pitch coming, right?" John was laughing. And as quickly as he started laughing, he stopped and took a more serious tone. "Don't worry, this isn't network marketing or some pyramid scheme. You don't have to get everyone you know to buy a bunch of crap from you. Hear me out, you should always keep your options open."

"Uh huh," Chip responded, only half listening.

"I've got a little money tucked away that I'm going to invest in this opportunity and I'm looking for a smart, aggressive guy like you to team up with. Other people who have invested have an annual return between 27% to 64%," he said, immediately putting his hands up as if submitting to a forthcoming objection. "Of course, that all depends. There's a lot of variables that play into something like this. You probably can't expect 64% right out of the gate. It's possible, but…well, you know what I'm saying. The best thing is, you're your own boss. Nobody standing over your shoulder telling you how to run things. No set work hours. You're in command of your destiny. You're steering the ship."

Command of your own destiny? Steering the ship? Chip was now paying slightly closer attention. How did this guy know to push those buttons? A very old trick of carnival psychics he quickly answered himself. Guess at some likely common denominator, some feeling or thought that most people feel or think at one time or another, throw it out on the table like it was meant for them alone, and wait for a reaction. Repeat process until you get the reaction you're looking for. Despite knowing this was likely a gimmick, a scam or something he just wouldn't be interested in, he couldn't help being attracted to the idea. Worth a quick listen until Kelly gets here. Worst case, I tell the guy to take a hike.

John continued. "Have you ever heard of Alpacas?"

"Alp…?" Chip began to ask, unsure of what he had just heard.

"Alpacas. They're like llamas, only smaller. Gentle animals. You know how some animals will butt each other? These animals don't do that. And they don't bite. Anyway, these are farm animals that you can raise."

Chip stared at the man in disbelief. Alpacas? "Why would you want to raise an al…alpac…?"

"Alpaca," John finished for Chip. "The fleece is like cashmere and stronger than wool. You can sell it."

Quit the job in automotive and be an alpaca farmer. Chip wasn't sure how to respond. This seemed too stupid to even question further. He picked up his beer and began to leave. "I don't think I'm interested…"

John lifted his hands slightly, again offering a sign of submission. "I know. I was skeptical when I first heard about it. But this is a ground floor opportunity. They used alpacas in the Inca Empire in Peru. They're still big in South America, a few in Australia, but they're just now taking off in this market," John said seriously.

"All the way back to the Incas? World's second oldest profession I'll bet. That's a hell of a product life cycle," Chip said facetiously, wondering why he was still having the conversation.

John laughed and continued to press forward. "The investment to start one of these alpaca farms is about $55-$60 K. You need a barn, a large fenced in area, the standard farm stuff. The nice thing is, they live about twenty years. You can sell the fleece or you can breed them out. Like I said, the return is excellent. Now I've got the up front money, but I need somebody to manage the farm and the business side. The animals would starve in a week if a dumb sales guy like me took care of them. But a smart MBA like you could run things. It'd be a way into your own business without sinking a lot of money into it."

"Are you serious?" Chip said, unable to contain his amusement of the situation.

"Yeah. Are you interested in a partnership?" John said laughing, looking more like a leprechaun with each drink of beer.

"Well, John, I don't know. I never really considered alpacas as a way of life. It doesn't seem like that's something you should just jump into. I'll have to give it some thought," Chip answered sarcastically.

John was still laughing and patted Chip on the back. "It's an honest life being an alpaca farmer."

Chip spotted Kelly and waved to her. "I'm going to join my friend now, but I'll keep your offer in mind."

"Give it some thought and get back to me," John said, slipping Chip his business card.

"Thanks," Chip said, leaving John alone at the bar and making his way to Kelly.

"Did you want to sit at the bar?" she said as Chip approached.

"No. Here is fine."

"How is everything?" Kelly asked.

"Par for the course," Chip answered. "I have made up my mind that I don't want to work anymore…for anyone…ever…I'm tired of doing this shit work day in and day out. And after I work all day, I go home and do more shit work for school. I'm tired of the work force."

"I think you're looking too deep in this. This crap we're doing is not representative of what people with real jobs do, it's only representative of what people who work for Gandhi do," Kelly said.

"I've heard that from a couple people. I wonder though. I talk to other people and they all have the same complaints. Most of them just handle it differently than I do. They grin and bear it a lot better. Some of them don't even care that they're going to spend the rest of their lives working for the man. They're happy with their job and that's that."

"No. All wrong," Kelly said. "Forget this working for the man shit. Look at yourself as a temporary contractor. GIT, or any other company, is paying you to provide a service: a service that you're good at, find challenging and in general, enjoy providing. Now, it's possible and maybe even likely that at some point you'll get bored with providing the service. Or maybe you'll decide there's another service you want to provide to someone else. At that point, you move on. What you don't do is turn your back on the entire job market and assume all the jobs are the same and you won't like any of them. There are thousands of career paths out there that you could do and I'll bet at least hundreds that you might even enjoy doing. I know there's got to be at least one. Don't pass judgment based on this one experience. Besides, not every step along the way is glorious; there are a few pot holes. Pick up your cross and bear it."

"I hear the Alpaca industry is booming," Chip said facetiously.

"The what?" Kelly looked confused.

"Nevermind. Anyway, you're probably right. In any event, someone responded to a resume I sent out and I was asked to come in for an interview tomorrow," Chip said.

Kelly brightened and asked excitedly. "With who?"

"A retail store, selling corporate computer training classes. I didn't call the guy back yet. I probably will tomorrow morning," he answered.

Kelly looked surprised, but had no comment other than "oh".

"It doesn't sound very good does it?" Chip asked.

"I didn't say that. It just seems like you could do a lot more than that with your experience and education," Kelly responded.

"I'm just so sick of Rajiv, I'm willing to listen to just about anyone else. It can't hurt to see what they have to say."

"No, it can't hurt. Just be careful you don't go out of the frying pan and into the fire just because you're pissed off now. There are worse jobs out there, believe it or not. And you don't want to jump around too much; you'll look unstable. You don't want to leave in six months because you don't like an individual you're working for. Never quit a job because of a personality conflict with one person," Kelly said, taking another drink.

"You're right. What I'd really like to do is to start my own business," Chip said.

"What kind of business?" Kelly asked.

"I have no idea."

Kelly seemed somewhat disappointed that no revelation was forthcoming. "Well, when you figure it out and start making millions, let me know…you can hire me."

For the next hour, they talked about work and the gossip moving from department to department. Despite her defense of the job market earlier, moving into her third gin and tonic, Kelly was providing advanced insight into her truer feelings. "If we disappeared tomorrow…if we just didn't show up tomorrow, would anyone notice? Would it make one goddamn bit on difference? Somebody else could do the job in a minute and if nobody did, would anyone really know? Would anyone know that the work you do was gone?" Chip heard a subtle change from "we" to "you" and knew that the conversation had shifted from a philosophical discussion on the overall importance of various jobs to a sparring contest.

Sure enough, Chip had seen it coming just in time to mentally brace himself. "How do you do that job everyday without wanting to jump off the roof? All those years of schooling pissed away on work that some college intern should be doing," Kelly said with an evil grin and taking another drink of her gin and tonic.

Chip felt his face flush. Damn! She's seen a weakness and now she's moving in for the kill. If not for the dimmed lighting, Kelly would have noticed Chip turn a pretty shade of red. Masking the gnawing in his gut, Chip laughed and fired back. "It must just grind you that you'll never be an Account Manager. All these other idiots out there got the job, people with half your talent. I mean, even Linda is in Sales. But here you are…not an Account Manager."

Kelly pretended not to hear. "I mean, you're an MBA for Christ's sake! And here you sit making charts for *the man*. That must drive you insane. It would drive me crazy. I give you a lot of credit for sticking with the job. Thank God I'm not in that position."

Chip continued with a rigorous offense. "You know they gotta be just stringing you along with all that talk about moving into Sales. We promise…tomorrow, we promise…"

While Chip was talking, Kelly broke into the refrain from *Swing Low, Sweet Chariot*, singing into her drink. "The man's keeping me down," she added in her best Chip impersonation, giggling at the end.

Ouch, that hurt, Chip thought.

Kelly moved in for the kill. "But you never say anything. You just sit, quietly making your charts. You're every slave owner's dream. Hell, maybe I'll own you one day." Kelly ended her attack with another verse of *Swing Low*.

Ignoring the intense mental pain and her poor singing, Chip persisted. "Do you know how sad and pathetic it looks every time you **beg** one of the account reps to take you with them to entertain a customer?" Then Chip added mockingly, in a whining voice, "I wanna go to the game too, can I go to dinner, I can be a salesman too, I promise I won't embarrass anyone, please can I go?…uh?…please?" Chip laughed loudly.

Kelly glared at Chip. "Shut up." And after a short pause threw in, "bastard" just for good measure.

Chip sat back and laughed. Victory. Painful, but a victory nonetheless.

As is common when imbibing too many adult beverages, Chip's judgment became slightly impaired. His bath in the limelight of triumph was short lived and he decided to continue on with the same topic.

"Which brings up another question. Why did you tell Rajiv to hire me for this job if you knew it was a shit job and I was overqualified?" Chip asked, raising his voice slightly and creating a second chance for Kelly to assert herself.

"Because you asked for it, dumb-ass. And as God gives you what you want, so does Kelly," Kelly said, beginning to slur her words ever so slightly.

Chip laughed. "Did you just compare yourself to God and refer to yourself in the third person?"

Kelly giggled uncontrollably and nodded.

"That's how most serial killers start out ya know. I think you belong at GIT with the other loonies. Especially the ones in HR," Chip said laughing.

"Now there is one twisted group," Kelly agreed. "Compared to the rest of us crazies, Janice and her crew are on another planet. She's mean too. I would stay out of her way or you're likely to find your ass booted out the door."

Cheerful Good-byes: The New Outplacement Program

It was 7:40 a.m. when Chip arrived at his desk. It seemed so much harder nowadays to get in early. All motivation was completely gone. He saw the red light flashing on his phone and he felt a knot in his stomach. He knew who it was from before ever listening. This is bullshit. What is that bastard's problem? He picked up the receiver and dialed his pass code. One new message, from Rajiv. He played the message. "Chip, this is Rajiv. I called you last night at 4:55 and wasn't able to reach you and I'm somewhat confused as to why. Call me immediately upon receipt of this message. We really need to have a discussion. I have a number of priority issues you need to be working on. I look forward to hearing from you as soon as possible."

Chip deleted the message, hung up the phone, and immediately left a reply on Rajiv's voice mail. "Hi Rajiv, Chip here. I received your message from yesterday. I'll make contact with you this morning at your earliest convenience to discuss the priority issues you mentioned. Thanks."

Chip could feel his entire body tense. Why does he play games like this? It was exactly 4:51 when Chip had left the night before. Then it occurred to Chip how silly it was that he had to commit the exact minute of his departure to memory. What a complete waste of time! He knew Rajiv wouldn't be here until late. He wondered how long this priority issue would take. Would it be another 7:00 night? He suspected that there was no real issue, only some detail task that Rajiv created to punish Chip for leaving early. I have to get out of here, he thought.

At 8:00 a.m. Chip heard Kelly walking quickly down the hall. She was almost sweating as she entered her and Chip's DWA.

"Did you see this?" she asked, placing a copy of an e-mail in front of Chip.

"See what?" he responded, looking at the print-out of the message. It read:

Michael F. Goyette

E-MEMO
TO: Valuable Interchangeable Labor Unit
FROM: CRDCMT – PMT
SUBJECT: Outplacement Program for VILU's

Congratulations, you have been selected for GIT's new Outplacement Program! You have been a valuable interchangeable resource to GIT over the last (insert number of years or months here). In recognition of your contribution we would like to award you with a check equal to 2 weeks salary! Additionally, you were to receive a merit increase of 6% of your base salary in return for your service ☺! Unfortunately, due to current economic conditions, we find it necessary to terminate our relationship with you, Valuable Interchangeable Labor Unit, in order to continue our forward progress. Consequently, no additional pay will be forthcoming.

Since, Valuable Interchangeable Labor Unit, GIT has placed such a high value on your services over the past (insert number of years or months here) years, we would like to provide you with this care package to assist you in your future endeavors outside GIT. Included in this care package is: a book of coupons for your local grocery store worth well over $25, a $5 gift certificate to the Honey Baked Ham Company, and a new GIT pen. See your designated Change Management Counselor as soon as possible to pick up this gift package. Good Luck! ☺
TEAM

"No. Where did you get this?" Chip asked, feeling more sick by the moment.

"One of the guys in Finance. He was just let go this morning. That's a hell of a thing to wake up to," Kelly said.

This place is falling apart. The lunatics have taken over the asylum. Chip felt the knot in his stomach growing, while a desperate desire to run overwhelmed him. I have to get out of here, he thought in a panic. He immediately dialed his home phone and picked up the number left on his answering machine. Okay Mr. Robert Schimel, I'm going to give you the chance to hire one of the best and brightest.

"Who are you calling?" Kelly asked curiously.

Chip picked up the phone and dialed the number. "I'm gonna call on that training position I was telling you about. I gotta get out of here. I got another message from Gandhi this morning. I think he's going to punish me for leaving nine minutes early last night. If you need me later this morning at about 9:00 when he waltzes in, I'll be at the whipping post. If you need me at about 5:30 today, I'll be at an interview."

Kelly shook her head. "Just remember...out of the frying pan and into the fire," she said, calmly returning to her desk and her work.

"Hi Robert, this is Chip…" Chip left a message, obsessed with one thought and one thought only: I have to get out of here.

Desperate Interviews: The Sea is Getting Rough

Chip entered the store at 5:25 p.m. and asked a passing clerk where the Corporate Training Center was. She directed him to the back of the store where a large open entranceway was marked by a sign identifying it as the targeted area. A small reception desk sat empty and Chip looked around for someone to guide him to his contact. Two hallways extended in front of him on the left and right of the reception desk.

"Hello?" Chip called out lightly. "Hello, anyone here?" The area appeared to be empty. Great, he thought, another employer that can't manage his time, not a good omen.

Chip waited until 5:30 and decided to find his contact. He walked down the hallway on the left, checking each room for an occupant as he passed. The first two rooms he came to were offices. The remaining three were large training rooms, each containing tables and computers that could accommodate what looked to be about twenty people. All the rooms were empty with the doors closed and locked. Everyone must take off at 5:00, he thought to himself.

He made a right at the end of the hall and passed two additional rooms before making another right and heading back in the direction he had just come from. Passing more training rooms and a few offices, all of which were empty of inhabitants, he quickly returned to the reception desk. A tall man in a suit was leaning up against the desk reading a training brochure. He looked at Chip with a raised eyebrow and a crazed look in his eye.

"Can I help you?" asked the man without taking his accusing eyes off Chip.

"Hi, I'm Chip Weatherbe. I'm looking for Robert Schimel. I have an interview with him at 5:30." Chip said, shaking the man's hand.

The man stared at Chip, remaining silent and not changing his insane expression.

"Would you know where I could find him?" Chip asked, feeling very uncomfortable.

"What were you doing down that hallway?" the man asked.

"There wasn't anyone available at this reception desk, so I thought I'd look for..."

"...look for Robert," the man said slowly and quietly, nodding his head and softening his wild expression. "A real take charge kind of guy." And then, after a long moment of silence, "Good. We need that." His comment was followed by further silence as he stood staring at Chip.

Chip's first reaction was to leave. This was a bad idea. Why am I even here? Because I hate my job and anything has to be better than dealing with Rajiv, he answered himself. No, Kelly was right. I should be chasing the jobs I'm really enthused about instead of jerking around with this nonsense, he thought. Chip had a desperate urge to tell the man that there had been a mistake and that he was no longer interested. No, that would be unprofessional. Have a short, to the point conversation, then leave. Twenty minutes, tops.

After what seemed like an eternity, the man spoke. "I'm Robert. Let's go into my office."

"Okay. Sounds good," Chip said and followed Robert to one of the closed offices. Robert unlocked the door and entered, taking a seat behind his desk. The office was small, no more than a ten by ten cube. Chip sat opposite him.

Robert stared at Chip without speaking. The man's far off, vacant expression suggested that the man was looking through him, focused on some unidentified point in space located directly behind the center of Chip's head. Chip contained an urge to snap his fingers in the man's face and ask if anyone was home, but instead, waited patiently for Robert to take the lead. The wait was unbearable. The man just sat staring at Chip, nodding his head slowly.

"Where would you like to start?" Chip said, unable to contain himself any longer.

After a brief silence Robert responded. "Tell me about what you bring to the table. Why should I hire Chip Weatherbe? Convince me."

Convince him? Chip thought. He felt his blood pressure rise at the mere thought of having to establish his credibility and justify his talent to someone like this. I could do his job and here I sit having to kiss his ass and explain why I think I'm worthy enough to join his little team. Chip knew at that moment that he wanted nothing to do with the job. Once this realization happened, a calm overtook him and he felt completely in control of the interview. He remembered Dave's advice and proceeded to describe his abilities to Robert, not in a tone to convince, but to educate. He proceeded in a confident, matter-of-fact manner. He talked for close to ten minutes, at the end of which he concluded with a quick "any questions?"

Robert's gaze now shifted from Chip to somewhere high on the wall behind Chip. Robert rocked gently in his chair, staring blankly. Chip couldn't resist and took a quick glance behind him to where he thought Robert's eyes might be fixated. Nothing but wall. Robert remained expressionless, gazing into the unknown.

"Let me answer that by asking another question…do you have any questions for me?"

Robert answered, raising a questioning eyebrow.

Chip immediately pictured Robert in a public service announcement. Robert sitting and staring into oblivion with the caption: You on drugs…just say no. Chip almost laughed out loud.

Torn between wanting to end the interview quickly and not wanting to appear rude and unprofessional, Chip again remembered his conversation months ago with Dave and came up with a question. "What does a bad day in this office look like? Can you describe a bad day?"

Robert considered the question carefully. So carefully in fact, that Chip wondered if he was still alive. He finally answered shifting his gaze slowly back to Chip. A piercing, menacing gaze with the same wild eyed look he had had only moments ago. "If you didn't show up for work one day…" and after a dramatic pause added, "…that would be a bad day for you."

Medication. He must be on medication and therefore the bizarre behavior should be overlooked. This was the wrong question, Chip decided. Too late to turn back now without looking stupid, he thought. Of course, how could he or anyone else possibly look stupid when in the same room with Robert? "Maybe I misstated the question…"

"If you continually show up late for work…those would be bad days for you," Robert furthered his answer, apparently feeling the need to clarify with an additional example.

"Oh…okay. What I meant to ask was…"

"If you lost a customer…that would be a bad day for you," he continued.

That's the last time I ever listen to Dave, Chip thought. Robert's clearly not getting it. "What I meant was, within the context of any job, there are events that likely arise, because of the nature of the job, that may make the job difficult or painful for the person doing the job. Can you describe these events?" he attempted to explain.

"If you're caught stealing coffee packets from the cafeteria, that would be a bad day for you. Or if you come in drunk…weaving stories of government conspiracies and alien abductions…that would be a bad day for you."

I wonder if this guy and Bern drink together, Chip pondered. Focus. Stay focused on the point. Be Robert's lifeline to reality. Reel him back in. Chip pushed the question forward. "For example, the instructor doesn't show up for class and we don't have a substitute and I have to explain to the customer why class is canceled, I would consider that a bad day," Chip persisted.

Robert paused, finally appearing to hear Chip's comment. The pace of his nod quickened but he continued to stare blankly at Chip for again, what seemed like an eternity. "That would be a bad day…"

Where do I go from here? Chip asked himself.

"If we catch you in the women's restroom, wearing ladies undergarments… that would be a bad day for you."

The door, he quickly answered himself.

Standing, Chip offered his hand to Robert. "Robert, I appreciate you taking time out of your schedule to meet with me to discuss this opportunity, but I'm not sure I'm suitable for the position. Thanks again for your time."

Robert remained expressionless, frozen at some point in time and space. Then slowly he began nodding his head again. "If we catch you taking a peak down the secretary's blouse, that…

Chip never heard the rest of the statement as he was already half way to the parking lot.

Why Am I Doing This?

"You're going to end up spending the rest of your life chasing after that almighty dollar, jumping from company to company, and you're going to end up losing your soul," Ted said emphatically, turning slightly red.

Here we go again, Chip thought to himself. Doesn't Ted ever give up? Chip leaned back in his chair, rubbing his eyes.

"I guess I could spend the rest of my life dedicated to some long dead sense of company loyalty, only to have the company pull the rug out from under me one day because I don't fit their financial model or because I don't fit in with their New and Improved Company Culture anymore," Chip retorted.

The deep redness of Ted's cheeks stood in stark contrast to his white beard.

"Look, Ted, all I'm saying is that there is nothing wrong with watching out for your own interest and the interest of your family. I'm not cheating the company, I'm giving them everything I've got while I'm here, 110% effort. I'm not a slacker. I come in early, I stay late, I don't call in sick…"

"But you're only committed in the short run. Inevitably your decisions will have a short term focus. You won't have to live with the long term consequences. It's like two people shacking-up for a couple years and not getting married. There is no real long term commitment. It's short term thinking. And the consequences of many decisions aren't always felt in the short term. Sometimes it can take decades to see the fruits of your labor or decades to experience the problems with making bad decisions," Ted said.

"That's my point. This is not a marriage. A marriage is a marriage and a job is a job. This is a job. And you should look at yourself as a temporary contractor and not a life long partner. And besides, you'll never be able to apply the same type of long term thinking to your job or company as you can to your spouse or family. When you're ninety and can't remember you own name, laying in a home somewhere, drooling all over yourself and pissing your pants, GIT isn't going to remember

Ted. If GIT is even around, the best you can hope to be is maybe, maybe…" Chip emphasized the second maybe, holding a finger up, "…a faint memory of one or two individuals who won't know or won't care where you are now."

"Then why are you doing this? Why devote so much of your life to something that you're not passionate about, something that doesn't have any long term meaning," Ted asked.

"First, I didn't say it doesn't have long term meaning; it's just that it's not the same type of meaning that you can apply to a marriage or family. Second, the answer is very simple. I need to do something to make money. You know? Earn a living, pay bills, buy food, pay my mortgage…And as long as I have to spend fifty hours a week doing something to support myself and my family to be, I might as well make as much money as I can during that fifty hours."

"You're going to spend your entire life working forty to sixty hours a week just to pay the bills? What a sad waste of a life," Ted said.

"It's only part of your life, Ted. That's my point! There's a whole lot of other things to life. There's a whole lot of other stuff out there that has meaning and value; a lot of good stuff. That stuff is different for every person, but don't discount or diminish the importance of it. It's all that good stuff that makes the hard work and longs hours all worth while. The work is just a part of your life," Chip said, raising his voice slightly.

"A major part that you are completely reducing to a trivial pursuit of cash. And don't forget the time you're spending at school, which, according to your own words, is just to get a better job to pay the bills. That's an awful lot of your life to surrender, my friend. A lot of time doing something you're not happy with. Not a lot of time left for any of the good stuff."

Chip was getting frustrated. "Working to make money is not a trivial pursuit. It is a major part of your existence…working, I mean. But that's life. People go to work to pay bills. There's maybe a handful of people out there that get up every morning and go to work because they really want to, because they love it so much there's nothing else they would rather be doing. The fact is, they're going to make money and the particular job they're at fits their needs at the moment."

"I think you're wrong my friend. There are plenty of people I know who love what they do, will do it for the rest of their working days, and wouldn't do anything else, regardless of the money," Ted said.

"That's what they say," Chip responded.

"That's what they say because that's what's true," Ted said, sensing Chip's frustration and taking a sadistic pleasure in watching it blossom. This produced a calming affect on Ted, making him grin antagonistically while fueling Chip's fire.

"Really? Next time you talk to one of these people, apply the lotto test," Chip said.

"The lotto test?" Ted asked curiously.

"If they won the lotto tomorrow, what would they be doing next month or next year at this time? Take the need to make a living or make money out of the equation. Would they still want to go and do whatever it is they are currently doing, day in and day out? Would they still want to come into work and answer to their boss? Or would they move off and do something completely different? A few may not change what they're doing, but I'll bet most would."

Ted paused, considering Chip's point. "You think about that," Chip pushed. He rose from his chair. "What would you be doing if you had, say…ten million in the bank. What would you do with your time if you didn't have to work for money? Would you really still be coming here everyday if you had a choice?"

"Maybe…" Ted said, scratching his beard. Chip was taken back momentarily. Ted looked as if this were the first time he had ever really considered what he would be doing if he wasn't coming into GIT every day, wasn't working and keeping his nose to the grind wheel every waking hour. He looked somewhat confused, after all, what else could there possibly be outside GIT? What else could possibly exist outside these four walls? And for the first time, Ted appeared tired.

Bern. Again

The computer monitor was motionless for what seemed like an eternity. Everyday now seemed like an eternity, every moment. One more day of a life sentence. With a click of the mouse, Chip switched to his spreadsheet, then back to the presentation file, making no changes to either. He repeated this meaningless exercise at least a dozen times, occasionally switching to the intranet homepage for a little variety.

God, I'm bored. I don't want to be here; I don't want to be doing this.

The pessimistic, diseased thinking began to creep further into his soul, slowly eating away at its strength, like a cancer. The prophecy was self-fulfilling; the more bored he felt himself to be, the less constructive things he could think of doing. The more he considered his current environment, the less useful alternatives he could consider. He was trapped in his own thinking, trapped in a self-created box from which he was completely unable to think outside of.

I need to get out of here. Taking this job was a mistake. And the real kicker is, I knew all of that coming in here and I came here anyway. And now, all I have to choose from is this hell hole or those interviews for worthless jobs that I'm not going to be happy at.

I need a change, I need to do something, he thought as the phone rang, waking him from his paralyzing trance. That is so creepy. He stared at the phone, hesitating and letting it ring twice before answering.

"GIT, Chip Weatherbe speaking."

"Chip Weatherbe," said a familiar gruff voice sounded on the other end. All Chip could think was, not today.

Knowing it was a mistake, Chip answered, "Speaking."

"Chip, this is Bernard Jones of Bernard Jones and Associates. You can call me Bern, Chip. I got the resume you sent for the Sales and Marketing position," Bern said.

"Hi Ber…" Chip started.

"Chip, listen. I've got a sales position with your name written all over it. This is definitely up your alley. I shot eighteen yesterday with the CEO of the company and all we did was talk about you. He wants to meet ya. He can't wait. I've got you set up for tomorrow morning at 9:00 a.m. This is a great opportunity, Chip," Bern said.

"Bern, how did you get this number?" A complete sentence, less than one minute into the conversation. Chip felt he was making great progress with his communication skills.

"Chip, listen, stay with me, you're off in the woods again. Try to stay focused on what we're talking about. You're never gonna make it in Sales if you can't stay focused. You gotta listen," Bern lectured. "You know anything about Six Sigma? Chip, listen, this job has all the bells and whistles. Six figure base, bonus, international travel, car, big expense account…" Bern continued.

As tempting as Bern's description sounded and as much as he wanted to get away from his current situation, after his experience with the training interview, he had no desire for another fiasco. In all likelihood, Chip thought, anything Bern was involved with was highly suspect. Remembering Kelly's words "…out of the frying pan and into the fire…" he tried to push Bern off. "Bern, I'm not really interested. I just started this position a couple months ago and…"

"Yeah. Chip, don't talk, listen. This is the opportunity of a lifetime…" Bern interrupted.

"I am not interested," Chip interrupted back, taking a very assertive tone.

"C'mon, ya can't tell me your happy doing what your doing, can ya? I know GIT; they're on the chopping block, at least your division is. Not doing good these days. You're on a sinking ship, kid."

For someone who seemed one can short of a six pack, at least Bern had done a little homework, Chip thought.

"Chip, I know at your age you think you know everything about everything and you don't need advice from nobody. Well this gray hair I got didn't come for free, ya know! I've been around the block, a few times. I've seen a thing or two," Bern said with conviction, although this wasn't too much of a surprise since Bern said everything with conviction.

"Bern, I have to…" Chip said, making a fruitless attempt to end the exchange.

"I even saw an Unidentified Flying Object once," Bern said.

"An Unidentified Flying Object…? Well there we have it," Chip said in amazement.

"Yes sir. I was driving through Ohio in the middle of nowhere and there it was floating about ten feet off the ground. Let's just say it didn't look like it was from around here. No shop I've ever been in could make something like that. Not many people can say they've seen what I've seen!" Bern said.

Now we've gone to UFO's, Chip thought. Pirates, Al Jolson, UFO's... The insanity which seemed to consume the abyss known as Bern's mind apparently had no limits.

"You're *from* Ohio aren't you, Bern? Look, we all enjoyed the X-Files but it's time to move on..." Chip started again.

"Chip, listen. You gotta stop wasting people's time. You keep leading people on. You need to shit or get off the pot, my young friend."

"Wasting *people's* time, Bern? And how exactly am I wasting your time?" Chip asked, getting angry.

"You're not a player, kid. And what's worse is... you don't wanna be. Some guys and gals love this game of job jumping for the best deal. Getting in there, working for the man, proving yourself, moving on... It's a passion with some people, but not you. You send out these resumes hoping a fulfilling, lifelong career filled with happiness will land in your lap. I know. I've seen people like you before. Well, I'll tell ya, it ain't ever gonna happen," Bern said.

"I appreciate your advice Bern, but you really don't know me..." Chip retorted.

Bern ignored him and continued, "You're not serious about these jobs. They're not what you really want. They're just a paycheck to you. They're a place to go so you can tell people you work at a big company. Mr. MBA working for a big company, so you can hear your friends tell ya you're the man. So you can buy a SUV for fifty grand or a fifty-two inch TV. You're not following your heart, kid. And if you keep looking for a paycheck instead of following your heart, you're gonna be miserable forever. And you're gonna make people like me miserable with ya! Cause we're fighting to get ya something you really don't want. Happiness just don't fall out of the sky, kid. You gotta go get it! Fight for it. Have the courage to make it happen. Like that picture of the ship on the water says, you'll only find new lands if ya got the guts to leave the shore," Bern said, paraphrasing clumsily.

A vivid picture of the ship on the sea floated through Chip's mind. Fairly insightful, Chip thought, giving Bern some minimal credit.

"The problem is you're not really leaving the shore, kid. You're just walking up and down the beach looking for a better spot in the sand and you're thinking that's progress. Well it ain't! There's lots of happy people at big companies, small companies, and every size in between. The problem ain't with the jobs or the companies, it's with you. Nobody's holding you back! Not the company, not your manager, not your coworkers...You're the one responsible for your destiny and you're the one putting the chains on. Find something you're passionate about, have a powerful desire to succeed and just go do it! Now that would be progress. That would be leaving the shore! Stop strolling up and down the beach, leave the shore, and stop wasting the time of busy, helpful, kind hearted people like me!"

Chip paused and considered Bern's words. This was the first thing that Bern had ever said that made any sense.

Maybe Bern was saner than Chip gave him credit for.

"Chip, listen. I gotta go. They're thinking about sending me to China to help build their job hunting system and business infrastructure. President Bush called me personally and wants me to go. Big Al Jolson fans over there. I gotta go, Chip," Bern said, hanging up abruptly.

Then again, maybe not.

Incoming!
(The Revised Evaluation Form)

Friday afternoon at 2:00.

Chip entered the room and took his usual seat at the back next to Kelly and Ted. Another HR meeting. His blatant defiance of Rajiv's "suggestion" to sit at the front would not go unnoticed, he was sure. Be that as it may, Chip didn't care at this point. He was disappointed and bored with his work, tired of playing games with Rajiv, and tired of dreading coming into work everyday. The despair that had gripped him over the last few weeks had now been replaced with a powerful determination, a determination to fix the current situation, to move on. There would be no middle ground. He was better than this. He knew he could do more, he could be happier. A challenging life that he was passionate about was within his grasp, he was certain of it. He just needed to make it happen. Acknowledgment of this single fact alone seemed to lift a tremendous burden off his shoulders, offering a new, enlightening perspective.

Yet here he sat in another Janice meeting. He was hard pressed to think of a bigger waste of time. Discussions about PP Programs, recaps of Germ Management memos, diversity pep talks were all beginning to wear thin even though his stay at GIT had been short. The meetings were predictable. Janice would start talking and do everything she could to move the organization further into Wonderland, while everyone sat quietly not wanting to rock the boat and potentially jeopardize their jobs, or worse yet, become like Ted, labeled a shit disturber and stuffed in a corner somewhere. Where of course, you would stay with no pay increases until they built a case to fire you or until you became so discouraged you quit.

On cue, Janice began in one of her typically Mountain Top tones. "First, I want to thank you'all for coming. As you know by now, we completed Phase 1 of our reorganization earlier this week with the implementation of our cost cutting measures and the Outplacement Program. Phase 2 will be implemented in the upcoming week or two. In preparation for this event, I wanted to spend a little time today to discuss reviews. Specifically, I wanted to address rumors that have been circulating around the organization and clarify a number of questions that have subsequently risen. Many of you have been wondering why your reviews are somewhat late this year. Well, I'm here to assure you that there is a very good reason. We in CRDCMT, and specifically the CPPV group, have been working very hard over the past year to create a review process that was fair and incorporated all our policies on diversity into a new format. Reviews will be completed next week and we will use the new review form, the one that Terry is now handing out." Terry began distributing a handout while Janice continued talking.

Ted, Chip, and Kelly exchanged glances of disgust.

"We won't spend time reviewing the entire form today, however, you can look it over at your own convenience and then if you have any questions, you can e-mail or call your assigned CMC. I want to make clear that this revised evaluation moves away from the former evaluation that was interpreted by a very vocal minority as being biased against the elderly," Janice said, snarling the final sentence. "Although I think these claims were groundless and frankly, there were a lot of sour grapes involved. Be that as it may, our new, improved form should quell any such discussions," she finished, returning to her political game face.

Ted's face flushed and he glared at Janice.

"I would also like to point out one new section that we are particularly proud of. As you all know, we at GIT encourage you folks to maintain a healthy balance between your work environment and home environment. By balancing these two environments, we believe that everyone wins. You win because you can incorporate rewarding, diverse activities into your day, making you a happier, more well-rounded person. And when you are happier, you bring to the table a rich, diversified experience base. GIT wins because a happy employee is a more productive employee. Additionally, we know how important it is to give back to the community. We all take so much from our environment and the people around us that it's only fair to give a little back. So, working closely with our Committee for Promoting Progressive Values group, we've combined these two guiding principles into a new subsection to the Diversity Evaluation section entitled 'Life Balance'. The "Life Balance" section will be weighted 25% toward your overall evaluation."

Rumblings of shock and disapproval could be heard throughout the room. Chip glanced quickly at the evaluation form he now held in his hands. More social experimentation, he thought to himself. More forms on how to create a perfectly "fair" company, that fit only a small group's vision of fair and in the end only resulted in very unfair work and consequences for those not privy to establishing the rules of fairness in the first place. Moreover, these policies on diversity and fairness seemed to be like building a castle in the sand. More effort was being put into the appearance of the structure than on making sure the structure itself was built on stable ground. What about the basics? What about making a high quality product that somebody would want to buy? What about the search for quality employees, establishing a trust and loyalty with the employees, and sharing a vision and direction in order to compete in an aggressive market? These all seemed to take a back seat to appearing fair and diverse. And now someone's vision of fairness and diversity included guiding Chip's life outside GIT, if not indeed controlling it. How presumptuous, he thought. Absolute nonsense, he repeated to himself, feeling his frustration level mounting. One more trendy, fake, condescending, southern wannabe "you'all" or "you folks" out of Janice's articulate, MBA mouth and he felt he would explode.

Janice heard the negative reaction from around the room and retorted. "I would remind everyone of a few things. First, this new evaluation has the full support of Fausto. Second, GIT prides itself on being an upstanding citizen of the community. Community renewal is one of our core values. Anyone whose personal values are not in line with those of GIT is welcome to find an employer who better meets your value system. No one is forcing you to stay. If you wish to enter our employee outplacement program, just let me know."

The room fell silent.

Chip and his two compatriots glared at Janice. So much power in one person's hands.

"Now, you will notice that we have outlined some of the activities that constitute a contribution to the Life Balance section. Although this is not a complete list, we feel that it is fairly representative of the types of activities we would like to see in this section. Of course, we would love to hear any ideas and suggestions that you'all may have on activities that should be included. This is a progressive process and we want it to be inclusive of all the diverse ideas that we know you'all will want to contribute. Remember, we need to think outside of the box."

Chip glanced down at the paper in his hands. The list read as follows:

Acceptable activities which count on your evaluation
    Volunteer work or continued involvement at any of the following:
- Approved local area orphanages (see attached list)
- Approved senior citizen homes (see attached list)
- Approved local area food banks (see attached list)
- Habitat For Humanity
- Church volunteer work (limited to specific inner city churches – see attached list)
- United Way
- PETA
- Green Peace

- Parks For Our Children (limited to specific inner city parks – see attached list)
- GIT Health Resource Center

Participation in any of the following diversity rich organizations:
- GLEE
- AADC
- CADA
- CPPV
- Any diversity training classes

    A minimum of 3 hours a week is recommended to receive a Satisfactory rating on your evaluation

    A minimum of 5 hours a week is recommended to receive a Great Job rating on your evaluation

Activities which DO NOT count in the Life Balance section of your review
- Spending time with your children
- Spending time with your spouse
- Spending time with your "extended" family
- House maintenance/work on your own home or the home of a family member, friend or neighbor
- Participation at your church (unless the church is one of the specified churches on the attached list)
- Participation in non-inclusive, close minded social clubs which do not value diversity (example: the Boy Scouts)

Although we are sure that a few people at GIT choose to engage in these confining activities, they are activities which are conducted as a part of a traditionally narrow lifestyle and are not considered diversity rich. Therefore, these activities will not be counted toward the "Life Balance" section of your review.

Chip noticed that GLEE was one of the acceptable groups in which to participate. She had finally done it, he thought. She had made a link between her personal pet organization, her own social agenda, and his merit increase. Chip couldn't take it any longer. The very thought of a company trying to strong arm him into spending his time outside of work as they saw fit, regardless of the organization or activity, repulsed him.

"The soup kitchen we went to isn't on her approved list," Kelly whispered.

Chip didn't appear to hear and glanced at Ted who looked like he was ready for war. Chip beat him to the punch.

"Excuse me. I have a question," Chip said.

Ted looked at Chip with surprise. Chip noticed out of the corner of his eye that Ted was subtly shaking his head as if to say "don't do it". At the same time,

Kelly, who was still staring down at the form, whispered the sentiments at a barely audible level. Janice acknowledged him with a look of curiosity. "Yes, Chip."

"I just want to make sure I'm clear on the new evaluation section. You say GIT encourages me to do two things: balance my life and give back to the community. At first glance this sounds fine and certainly espouses some noble intentions. I mean, who can argue having a balanced life? Who can argue with feeding the hungry, spending time with orphans, or helping someone out who can't afford to fix a leaky roof. But you take it a step further and you define for me how my life should be balanced and how I should give back by making my merit increase, to a large extent, dependent on your definition of fair, diverse and balanced. According to your definition, spending time repairing my house or the house of a family member or friend doesn't count but working to repair someone's home that I don't even know does count. Spending time with my kids doesn't count, but spending time with other people's kids does count. Who is with my kids when I'm with someone else's?"

"He has kids?" Kelly whispered to Ted. A shrug was his only reply.

Janice stood, hands folded, almost as if she was praying. The condescending smile and raised eyebrows suggesting pity fueled Chip's passion.

"Well, Chip..." Janice attempted to answer.

Chip continued without breaking stride or changing his tone. "That was a rhetorical question, let me finish. It seems to me one of the biggest contributions you can make to 'the community' is to take care of your own children, extended family or house so that no one else has to. I'm sure there's a number of people at GIT with elderly parents who devote time helping them with their daily lives or help neighbors that may need assistance or devote time at their church. You go on with this list and say that spending time with my wife to ensure a healthy relationship and stable home or taking my son to Boy Scouts doesn't count. But going to a GLEE get together and talking about how traditional values are oppressing "progressive, open minded" folks does count. It seems to me that you have this list backwards."

Janice's expression changed. She was no longer smiling and appeared to a have a slightly red tint to her cheeks. "Well, I'm sure most people do not share your point of view, Chip. Again, we can't force you to accept new ideas and be open-minded. Nor can we force you to find the kindness in your heart to help others. But what we can say is that these are the values that GIT embraces and we expect that as long as you're working here, you respect those values and adhere to them. Remember, at any point if you find that your values aren't in line with those of GIT, it might behoove you to find an organization with values closer to yours."

Ignoring her veiled threat, he continued. "Janice, I think it's unfair to suggest that I'm questioning the premise of being kind, helping others or accepting new ideas. I am not. I am, however, questioning GIT's place to define fairness, implement social equity, or define how its employees should spend their time outside of work. Shouldn't GIT management focus on some fundamental practices, like making a decent product that our customers want to buy? I mean, let's be honest, this has less to do with helping someone in need than it does with making GIT appear to be a good citizen. If we focus on being the best in what we make or do, we'll continue to keep people employed, improve shareholder wealth, and ideally share the fruits of the labor with the workers that made it happen through bonuses, profit sharing, and merit increases. Isn't that really the best that we can offer a community? Creating a stable, profitable business."

Kelly groaned slightly. Chip was coming very close to seeing the full wrath of Janice.

Janice looked furious. "Well, I'm sorry you feel that way, Chip, but the majority of folks here embrace the idea of diversity and kindness. I think you're in the minority view and I wonder at the value of further listening to the extreme, radical ideas of a select few. Let's move on."

Chip began a response and received a kick from Kelly while Ted bumped him with his arm. Chip opted for a strategic withdrawal and fell silent while Janice continued spelling out her new plan.

After the meeting concluded, Chip left, making no eye contact with anyone. He decided it was time to cool off a bit. For the next forty-five minutes, he wandered the building attempting to look busy. He returned to his DWA just in time for his 3:00 meeting with Rajiv. His cooling off period hadn't accomplished much and he found himself still on fire. He had no desire to now deal with his boss.

He gathered his notes for the Director's Strategy Meeting. Chip had stayed until 8:00 p.m. the previous night to finalize the details. Rajiv had commended Chip for staying late yesterday, even as he himself was leaving at 5:00 and didn't appear too concerned about any last minute details.

All charts, graphs, spreadsheets, and summaries were complete and up-to date. After weeks of preparation, Chip was sure that all was exactly as Rajiv wanted it. Everything met his precise specifications. The multiple summaries of identical information had the correct font and format, all graphs and tables had the appropriate line size, and all slides had the right color and logo. Chip should have felt a sense of accomplishment upon this completion, a feeling of a job well done, and maybe even a hint of relief. Instead, he had a nagging sensation in his gut. He had been down this road before and had an intuitive feeling that this endeavor for the perfect presentation was far from over. He knew that Rajiv would almost certainly throw him a curve ball and point out some imperfection or problem that needed to be addressed immediately, lest Monday's entire presentation and discussion be put in jeopardy of completely failing. Or maybe the presentation would take a completely new direction and new information would need to be gathered.

The Adventures of Chip Weatherbe, MBA

Of course, addressing these issues would require that Chip stay late on yet another Friday night and in all likelihood put in time tomorrow and perhaps even Sunday. Chip had a burning desire to drop the presentation package on Rajiv's desk, piss on it, and walk out.

But what bothered Chip more than the time and relentless attention paid to every little detail was his recollections of conversations with Kelly and Ted. Did anyone really care that each font and line point size had been meticulously critiqued? Would anyone know if the information was only cut and summarized in two ways as opposed to the five ways Chip had been asked to do? Would it have been a catastrophe if directional figures had been used for this high level discussion, instead of the overwhelmingly detailed data Chip had collected? Would anyone even notice if this didn't get done at all? It seemed to Chip that the answers to these questions were inevitably, no.

Certainly some of the key financial information needed to be reviewed. Of course, the strategic marketing information that would help to define the direction of the company needed to be discussed. Obviously engineering and manufacturing plans needed to be defined. But these were all issues that would be covered regardless of Chip's portion of the presentation. His part was predominantly information that Rajiv may or may not use as backup, *if* he was brought into the conversation at all. It seemed to Chip that the level of detail Rajiv had asked for was completely inappropriate for the high level audience. Where was the added value? These Directors weren't going to care about every little number and every little bullet point on every little slide. They were big picture people. They cared about the overall direction and strategy. And besides, Chip thought, if a detail did catch anyone's eye, Rajiv would no doubt take complete credit for including the information in the first place.

It also seemed that for the amount of time spent collecting and summarizing this data, the subsequent payoff would be minimal. In Chip's mind, they were well past the point of diminishing return and indeed were experiencing opportunity losses, since Chip firmly believed his talent and time could have been spent on more valuable projects with larger payoffs.

However, being the consummate professional, Chip buried all these thoughts and entered Rajiv's office with a positive outward appearance.

"Hi, Rajiv. Is this still a good time to meet?" Chip asked.

Rajiv smiled when he saw Chip. "Hi, Chip. No problem, come on in."

Warning bells went off in Chip's mind - the nice Rajiv. Chip thought for sure that more work would now be required before Monday.

Chip wanted to avoid any changes to the final draft and took the helm as quickly as possible, beginning the conversation. He wanted to say his piece, hand off the presentation, and walk out as quickly as possible before Rajiv had a chance to start modifications. "I've got a final of Monday's presentation. I'm confident everything is in order. I think you'll see it follows your comments and suggestions that we've discussed. I've also e-mailed you a copy of the presentation and of all the supporting spreadsheets."

"Great," Rajiv said in a lighthearted way, quickly glancing at the work and setting it aside. "This is great. Great work. Chip, I appreciate all the work you've done on this. I know you've been pushing yourself hard to put all this together. You really stepped up to the plate."

Stepped up to the plate? Pushing myself? thought Chip. Forced enslavement more like it, but it sounded good when Rajiv said it. Rajiv continued. "The information isn't always easy to come by, as I'm sure you know. But now we've got a good base that we can turn to if ever we're asked questions. It should be easy to update now that we have the foundation built. Why don't you take the rest of the afternoon off. I think you've earned a well-deserved break. Enjoy the weekend. They're calling for a gorgeous couple of days. We'll see you Monday." Rajiv smiled, clearly taking pride in his benevolent suggestion.

Chip paused. So many thoughts ran through his mind. No changes? No minor modifications? No different ways of cutting the information? If ever we're asked questions…if ever? He must mean, if we're asked the questions at any point on Monday, Chip thought. And what a gift, I get to leave a half hour before everyone else starts leaving. Although Chip wondered what Rajiv was up to, he didn't want to look a gift horse in the mouth. He rose from his seat. "Thanks Rajiv, I appreciate that. I know the meeting starts at 8:00 am on Monday morning so I'll be here at 7:00 if you have any questions or last minute changes," Chip said, starting to leave.

"Not necessary. The meeting has been postponed," Rajiv said looking down at some document on his desk.

Chip felt his face flush for a second time today. He felt his heart begin to race. Clearing his mind, he quickly asked, "Until when?"

Rajiv looked up at Chip. "At this point, indefinitely. Gracie didn't tell you yesterday? I'm surprised, I thought she would have. Because of the reorganization, some of these meetings have been put on hold. But again, rest assured that the work you have done will not go to waste. At some point, someone will ask these questions and we will have to answer them. Thanks again for all the great work." It was clear that the conversation was over and that he was being dismissed.

Chip stared at Rajiv, not knowing what to say. Rajiv had apparently known yesterday when he was leaving and saw Chip staying late that the meeting was postponed. It had obviously slipped his mind to mention it. You bastard, Chip thought. Instinctively, he took the high ground. With a brief "okay" he began to leave. After all, what good would it really do to argue with the prick at this point, Chip thought. The meeting was canceled, there was nothing anyone could do about it. Meetings get canceled. Chip had done an exceptional job on the presentation.

The Adventures of Chip Weatherbe, MBA

Best to just walk away now. No need to rock the boat. Take Rajiv's gift and just walk away.

As Chip reached the door, a vision of the future flashed through his mind. A future spent staring at the smallest details because Rajiv wanted it that way. A future playing out as this scenario was playing out, over and over again. Where was the added value to anyone: to GIT, to the Directors, to Chip's career, and to his paycheck? This final thought stopped Chip at the door. It occurred to Chip that in all likelihood, when it came to merit increases, when it came to promotions, to advancements in the company, this activity would not be viewed as valuable. Certainly if Chip saw much of the activity as a waste of time, wouldn't others? And if others saw this and Chip was competing for another, higher position in the company, wouldn't his current activities be taken into account and put him at a disadvantage? He decided to begin changing the situation now.

He turned to Rajiv. "Rajiv, one last thing." Rajiv looked up and sighed, showing his complete annoyance that the conversation might continue. He stared at Chip. Rajiv's attitude strengthened Chip's resolve.

Tactfully, Chip proceeded. "I was just thinking about the amount of time we put into this presentation. I wanted to make sure everything was perfect but I'm starting to think that I may have put a little to much time into it. Perhaps some of that time and attention to detail could have been used on other activities, activities that might bring more value to the table. For example, identifying the market potential for some of the products that the Advanced Product Group has been working on or working closer with the Account Managers could have been more beneficial. I'd like to move in that direction in the future if you agree."

Without missing a beat, Rajiv responded. "That may be a frontier we explore in the distant future, but right now I need you to focus on maintaining and keeping up to date the information we've gathered so far. Spend next week reexamining your figures. I noticed one or two of them appeared to be a little off."

Chip was now angry. "Really? Which ones?"

"Best to check them all. Let's make sure we're bullet proof. You may want to schedule a meeting with Finance and the Account Managers to double-check everything. Provide me a status report before you leave today, outlining your plan for next week," Rajiv said in his typical condescending tone.

Chip now knew without question where he stood. Of course, he had known this since the beginning. Rajiv could care less what Chip wanted. Nor did Rajiv care if Chip wasted the next ten years of his life working on this kind of nonsense – no skin off Rajiv's back. Rajiv would continue on his career path of growth without ever looking back. How many of these discussions would it take before he did something about the situation, Chip wondered? Zero, he answered himself. There would be no more of these discussions or projects, or nonsense from Rajiv. It was time to move forward.

With his path clear there was nothing further to say. Between clenched teeth he made his exit. "No problem, I'll do that. And be sure to let me know when the meeting gets rescheduled. I'll make sure everything is in order." With that, Chip turned and departed the office, not waiting for a response.

Chip returned to his desk and began closing up for the weekend.

"Leaving early? Did Gandhi say that was okay?" Kelly asked sarcastically without taking her eyes off her computer monitor.

Chip didn't respond.

Kelly turned and looked at Chip. "You still upset about the whole volunteer work thing with Janice?" she asked lightheartedly. "You should really find more kindness in your heart."

"The meeting was canceled," Chip said quietly and harshly.

"Monday's meeting?" she said with surprise.

"Yep."

"No way! That's all you've been working on! Why was it canceled? Was it canceled or postponed? Did they reschedule? " Kelly said, becoming more analytical.

"It's been postponed indefinitely. And despite that fact, I should, and I quote, '…spend next week reexamining my figures'."

"Oh, my God," Kelly said, sympathetically.

"That, by the way, was my punishment for suggesting that I begin working on other things. You know what really pisses me off?" Chip inquired.

"Something pisses you off more than spending another week on that shit? I can't imagine," Kelly answered, smiling hesitantly.

"You know I stayed last night? I was here until 8:00. That bastard knew I was staying and didn't say a goddamn word when he left. He knew it was postponed and let me work my ass off. He threw me a bone though. He told me I could go home 'early' today. After, of course, I outline a plan as to how I will spend next week. If I didn't know better, I'd say he was rubbing my face in it. Isn't he a swell guy?" Chip replied.

"What an asshole. Did you let him have it?" Kelly asked, laughing and trying to lighten the mood.

"I tried to point out that maybe my time could be better spent on other activities, but he wouldn't hear of it. It was right after that comment that he suggested I reevaluate everything in the presentation, clearly putting me in my place. So I figured I made enough friends for one day and made my exit," Chip said.

Kelly became somewhat serious. "Yeah. You made the right move. He's a snake. If you would have said anything, he would have come back to bite you. On the other hand, since you didn't fight him, now he knows he can bully you."

"It doesn't matter. I'm out of here. I'm tired of him. I'm tired of Germ Management and PP Policies. I have to find something else to do with my time or I'm going to go nuts," Chip said.

Ever the voice of reason, Kelly responded. "You should never quit a job because of a person, even a prick like him; we discussed this. The company's too big to do that. This reorg they've been talking about could happen next week and you could be working for someone else, just like that," Kelly said, snapping her fingers. "And besides, if you quit based on a personality conflict with one person, you're going to end up job-hopping every six months. There's always going to be somebody you don't get along with. There's always going to be that daily bump and grind, wherever you go. You can't let that little stuff get you down. Don't sweat the small stuff, right?"

Chip knew she was right but stared at her skeptically. "You don't have to deal with him every day."

"You know, as we're talking, it occurred to me that Janice may be right," Kelly said, bringing Chip to a complete halt in his packing.

"What does that mean?" he asked.

"It means that there's a lot of shit like this that goes on everywhere. It's part of *this* game, this automotive industry game, regardless of the company size. And I'll bet other industries are no different. I'll bet we're not the only company with a Janice. And maybe, if your values are different than the values here, you'd probably be a lot happier doing something else, somewhere else. But keep in mind, there's a lot of shit in other games too, just a different kind of shit. I think it's a question of choosing the poison you can tolerate the most."

He was at a loss. Too much had gone on today to focus on her argument. He promised himself he would consider it later.

"You know I'm right. C'mon! Buck up, little camper. Lighten up a little. Take the weekend and relax. Take your extra hour and a half bone, go home, and forget about this place," Kelly said laughing.

Chip resumed packing his laptop when his phone rang. He looked at Kelly and smiled. "How could it get worse, right?"

"Tell'em you're leaving and if they have a problem with that they can kiss off," Kelly laughed.

In a professional tone, Chip answered, "GIT, Chip Weatherbe."

"You're still here," said Ted.

"As a matter of fact, I was just leaving," Chip said.

"That wasn't a question, it was a statement. Stop by and see me before you leave," Ted requested.

"Okay," Chip agreed and hung up the phone.

"Was that Ted?" Kelly asked.

"Yeah. How did you know?" Chip said.

"I was going to tell you to call him. After you told everyone how you wouldn't help the poor and down-trodden..." she said, smiling and looking for a reaction. Chip just frowned as she continued. "...she and Ted had a little heart to heart meeting. She's blaming your bad attitude on him and I think he's encouraging her. They've been talking for the last hour while you've been dancing with Rajiv. I casually walked by her office and heard a piece of the conversation. When I walked by, he was taking credit for everything you said. I think the old fool is trying to get himself fired. He probably wants to give you a high five or something," Kelly said.

Chip finished packing, said goodbye to Kelly, and headed off to Ted's office.

Ted and Janice

"What are you doing?" Chip asked, entering Ted's office. The office looked extremely neat: neat and empty. The few pictures Ted had of his children and grandchildren were gone and a large pile of paper and folders sat on top of the garbage can. Ted was adding to this pile as Chip entered the office.

"Cleaning," Ted replied, continuing to shuffle through papers. He looked tired, defeated. "And you may not want to stay in this office too long; there's no reason for you to get in trouble too."

"Did they let you go," Chip asked.

"They let me go a long time ago, my friend. I just didn't want to believe it and they didn't want to put it in writing," Ted said, finally looking up at Chip from his papers. "Don't look so distraught. They're giving me a nice package and like I said, you're still here."

"That's comforting," Chip answered sarcastically.

"Yes, it is," Ted replied, looking very serious. "I would feel very bad if I knew you got reprimanded or fired because of me. You're just starting out, you have a wife to be and future kids to think about. And despite our previous discussions, you're right, you have to make money. This isn't a battle you want to take on right now. And besides, this is a great place to work despite the Rajivs and Janices of the company. But I've been here long enough, my friend, and it's time for me to leave. This is all I've ever done. But everything comes to an end. Time to sail into the unknown."

A knock sounded behind Chip, causing him to turn. Janice's Administrative Assistant stood in the doorway of Ted's office. "Hi, Chip. Kelly said you would be over here. Janice would like to meet with you if you have a minute," she said, seeming to know what was going on and being overly sweet to Chip to compensate for it.

"Okay. I'll be right over," Chip said.

"No problem. She has to leave in about twenty minutes, so don't wait too long," she said, leaving the office.

"You're too young to get fired or a bad reputation over something stupid like this. Keep your mouth closed and keep your job. I know it's going to kill you to do it, but you have bills to pay and it's easier to find a job when you've already got one."

Chip started to leave Ted's office. "Oh and Chip..." Ted said.

Chip turned around to see Ted wearing one of his evil grins. "You may want to avoid the whole topic of working moms, she may be a little sensitive right now," Ted said laughing.

Ted was right, he thought walking to Janice's office. Getting fired over something silly like this was not worth it. It was time to move on anyway; no reason to burn the bridge while doing it. Be strong and confident, but in the end, let her have it her way, whatever that may mean.

Chip knocked on Janice's office door, taking a step or two in.

"Hi Janice, you wanted to see me," Chip said politely, professionally.

"Hi, Chip, come on in and shut the door," Janice said. Her tone and expression were aggressive and professional but showed no sign of hostility or anger. Chip took a seat across from her.

"Thanks for stopping by. I know you were getting ready to take off for the weekend and I don't want to hold you up," Janice said sincerely. "But I did want to touch base and wrap up any lose ends from today's discussion."

"Okay," Chip said.

"Chip, I know you look up to Ted as an informal mentor," Janice said.

How insulting, Chip thought. Here was a woman maybe three or four years older than him lecturing him in such a belittling tone. Ted wasn't his mentor. A friend and coworker he happened to get along with, but he was certainly not a mentor. It wasn't surprising, however, that she put the conversation in this context, painting Chip as some very green, blind follower, thirsty for guidance.

"But you have to realize, Ted is at odds with this company and its management and has been for a long time. I know Ted's thoughts on...on...well let's just say I think his views are somewhat antiquated to say the least. They are not representative of the cultural direction that we want to take this company in," Janice said.

Chip nodded. "I see."

"Diversity of all kinds is key to moving this company forward. And women play a vital role in the work force. Just so you have a balanced view of women's place in our company...women play a tremendous role in an organization. I mean...you just don't see women nowadays...serious career women who are moving forward with their lives...you won't find me wasting away at home baking cookies and changing diapers. I'm worth more than that. I need more than that," she said turning red and raising her voice.

Chip heard Ted's warning flash through his mind and actually felt somewhat sorry for Janice. He also found her level of frustration slightly amusing. Ted must have really got into a heated discussion with Janice. He could hear Ted now, endlessly provoking Janice until she was so mad, she wouldn't be able to complete a coherent sentence, like now.

As quickly as her temper seemed to rise, she regained control and continued her conversation with Chip. "But we don't need to go over that ground again; I've had enough of that nonsense for one day."

"Okay," Chip said agreeably, not wanting to go anywhere near that discussion.

"Look, despite my vehement disagreements with Ted, no one has ever been fired for having a different opinion about morality or society than I have. It's stupid to even think that. Like I said, the issues with Ted are long standing and don't have anything to do with his social views," Janice said.

Although she sounded genuine, Chip found her statement difficult to believe. How could his opinions and beliefs not be impacting the situation, especially since he was so vocal about where he stood, and indeed tried to make his views a focal point for many work discussions.

"Which brings us to you," Janice continued. "I don't blame you for Ted's situation or his views. And I certainly don't want to continue our discussion from earlier. But I would suggest you take a closer look at where you want to be in this organization. And no, that's not a threat, it's just friendly advice. The Management Team has decided to move the organization in a particular direction. The people here should get on board with the plan or, at a minimum, not introduce obstacles to progress. Lead, follow, or get out of the way," Janice explained.

"Aren't you interested if people see a problem with the plan or if they have a better plan. Wouldn't you want people to speak up?" Chip countered.

"Yes. That's what I mean by leading; at least contributing to a leadership role. And offering an alternate solution or plan is much different than just sitting back and throwing stones; which is where your friend Ted is now. He's not offering anything constructive," Janice said, raising her voice again.

"Forget about Ted. I meant what I said. If you're not going to be happy here, for whatever reason, then find somewhere where you will be happy, otherwise you'll never live up to your potential," she said.

Chip wasn't sure where to take the discussion. There seemed to be a threatening overtone, however, Janice still didn't appear like she was after Chip in any way. Before he could say anything, she jumped in.

"And I think you have a tremendous future and potential here at GIT. We hired you for a reason; we don't just hire anyone. From what I understand, you're a very hard worker and very good at the work you do. You're an MBA, right?" Janice asked.

"Just finishing up," Chip answered.

"I suspect that you're overqualified for the work you're doing and are somewhat bored?" she said, raising a confident eyebrow, confident she was completely on target.

"You hit the nail on the head," Chip said.

"I thought so," she said, smiling. "You see, I think when people are underutilized like you are, they tend to be very negative," Chip bristled. This was more than just a simple case having a bad attitude he thought. Janice saw his response and responded before he could say anything. "I'm not suggesting that you're just being negative. I'm sure you were sincere during today's discussion. Somewhat misguided, but sincere," she said forcing a smile. "But we're not talking about that right now. The point is, if we as an employer were challenging you, you would likely have a more positive disposition and would likely be more productive. Even if you did disagree with some direction, you would likely offer constructive input. Not that it's GIT's sole responsibility to challenge you. Everyone here is a professional and I think it is incumbent on the individual to play the primary role in defining their own path and challenging themselves. But we need to do a better job of matching skill sets to specific positions. I'm not convinced we did a good job of that in this instance."

Chip found it difficult to disagree with anything she was saying. And although he did find her suggestions about accepting constructive input valid, he had yet to see this happen. Usually, anyone who disagreed with her was shot down instantly. Be that as it may, she seemed to be having a constructive conversation with him now, willing to now accept his input.

She quickly glanced at her watch. "Chip, I have to apologize, I have to get going. I'd like to continue this discussion next week. Check with my Administrative Assistant and arrange a time next week that fits both our schedules. In the meantime, think about what I've said; I think you could have a brilliant future here at GIT," she said.

Chip thanked her and left her office. A brilliant future at GIT? He thought to himself, envisioning the possibilities and feeling a small amount of the initial enthusiasm he had felt when he had first heard of the job. It was something to consider, but most likely he would end up leaving. This just wasn't for him. The work, the company, Rajiv, Janice, and everything else had left him soured to GIT. Better to leave and start fresh, with something he enjoyed, something he was passionate about. But where would he find that passion? Maybe it was better to stay here for awhile, ride out these temporary storms, get some more experience and then move on. He decided he would think about it over the weekend, maybe talk to Stacy about it. Decisions, decisions…life is full of so many tough decisions.

Decisions, Decisions...Rajiv and Linda

It was 6:00 p.m., Friday night, and Linda had just ended a meeting at the customer. The meeting had started at 4:00 and was scheduled to last no more than forty-five minutes. Of course, unexpected questions had arose, pushing the meeting to just under two hours. She had exited the customer building and was making her way to her car. The original plan was to go straight home from there to begin a relaxing weekend.

However, it appeared that the pager she carried in her purse had other plans. It had been going off while she was in the meeting, every ten minutes for the last two hours. She got into her car and began to drive. Without looking at the display, Linda knew who it was – Rajiv. She immediately felt herself tense up. Since she had shut her phone off for the duration of the meeting, the pager was her last electronic tether. Her first instinct was to ignore the pages, leave the phone off, drive home, and forget about Rajiv and GIT for two days. She knew this would only postpone the inevitable. Come Monday morning at 8:30 (if not sooner), the page bombardment would begin again and not let up until the source of the onslaught was recognized.

After ten minutes of staring at the pager and watching it buzz two more times, she decided it was time to respond. Her stress, mounting with each moment, was reaching a critical level. She had an intense headache, which seemed to have just come on since she left the customer. It occurred to her that it was sad that a dialog with her boss was constantly more stressful than dealing with the customer. She was beginning to feel queasy. She wanted to run and hide. She wondered how much more of Rajiv's scrutiny and games she could take before she walked away from GIT for good. In fact, her whole attitude about working for anyone was souring. She found it difficult to envision herself living at someone's beck and call for the rest of her life. What perhaps frustrated her most was that she knew Rajiv wouldn't have anything of substance to discuss. The topic would most likely be one of Rajiv's self generated fires that needed everyone's attention immediately. In reality, she knew that the problem could probably wait until Monday to be addressed. In fact, she suspected that no real issue existed at all and that after an hour or so discussion tonight, the topic would mysteriously disappear by next week.

Another buzz. It was time. Linda turned on her cell phone and as she did it rang. Taking a deep breath and trying to relax herself, she answered, "Linda Carlile speaking."

The voice on the other end made her cringe. The combination of condescension and accusation nauseated her. "Linda, this is Rajiv. I've been trying to contact you for over four hours now. I'm wondering why you haven't responded."

Linda knew the time of the first page she received since the beginning of her meeting two hours ago, it was 4:10 pm. He's such an asshole, she thought to herself. He knew full well when her meeting was and where it would be. She had done an exceptional job keeping her Outlook Calendar current. He also knew the particular customer contact she was meeting with and his tendency to ramble on; espousing his thoughts on this or that, long after the meeting was scheduled to conclude. She knew Rajiv had waited to just after the start of the meeting to page her, just so they could have the discussion they were having now. God, what an asshole! Again, she tried to calm herself. I won't let him run my life like this, she thought. Despite the anger she felt, she knew how to play the game and answered him calmly.

"Sorry, Rajiv. I was at a customer meeting and it ran a little over. I was just about ready to call you," Linda said.

"Linda, are you planning on returning to the office?" Rajiv said. She noticed that his entire tone had changed. In one simple sentence, in less than a minute, he had changed from black to white and she saw the charming, witty, likeable Rajiv coming through. His voice was sweet and alluring. A wolf in sheep's clothing if ever one existed.

"I hadn't planned on it," Linda said, annoyed.

"Linda, I know it's late and I know it's Friday, but I really need your help. I have a presentation first thing Monday morning in front of the SBU directors and I know I'm going to be here all weekend working on this. If I could have just a few minutes of your time, it could save me hours. Can you stop by the office on your way home? I'll only need you for a minute or two," Rajiv said, pleadingly.

Her first thought was, why isn't Chip handling this? Isn't he Rajiv's piss boy? Although she couldn't put her finger on the exact source, Rajiv's words made her shudder. After getting to know him the past year, the sweet, sincere Rajiv had become scarier than the slave driving Rajiv. She felt now like she was being manipulated and set up for something she inevitably would not like.

"I'm really in a hurry, I'm already late for…" she started.

Before she could finish, Rajiv interrupted. "Please. It would only be for a few minutes." Again, the soft Rajiv, again, her nervous feeling.

"Okay. I'll be there in about ten minutes. But I can't stay long," she finally conceded.

"Thanks, Linda. I'll be in Conference Room 2. I'll see you then," Rajiv said, hanging up.

Fifteen minutes later, Linda pulled into the familiar parking lot. Flashing her badge at the automatic door lock, she entered GIT and walked straight to the conference room. She wondered why he was in Conference Room 2. It was the smallest meeting room, off in a remote corner of the building. It was hardly ever used since it could only accommodate three to four people comfortably. It had no whiteboard for brainstorming, no phone line, no network drop for computer access, no windows and no glass on the door. Until recently, a number of people had come to use the room as somewhat of a storage closet. A month ago, however, Rajiv had personally seen to it that the room was thoroughly cleaned and transformed into a meeting place. It was also the farthest conference room from his office. She became more nervous.

The door to the meeting room was open. Linda could see Rajiv sitting at the table thumbing through some papers. She noticed that he didn't have much paper at the table and no laptop, odd for someone working on such a big presentation. As Linda approached the doorway, Rajiv stood up from his seat and greeted Linda at the door with a warm smile. He extended his right hand to shake hers and put his left arm around her gently pulling her body close to his.

"Linda, thanks for coming. I can't tell you how much this means to me," Rajiv said as he escorted her to the chair opposite his. As she sat with her back to the meeting room entrance, she heard Rajiv close the door.

"Now we can have some privacy," said Rajiv as he slowly began walking back to his seat.

Linda was now extremely uncomfortable. She asked herself why she was here. Why did they need privacy at 6:30 p.m. on Friday night? No one was around. Was this going to be another turn at the whipping post? Upon closer examination of the few notes he had on the table, it was clear to her that he had not been working on any presentation nor did it appear that he would be any time soon. The nauseating feeling intensified.

Trying to move the discussion along, Linda asked, "So what's up?"

How ironic a query. Before the question was fully uttered, she saw in a blinding flash of awareness what her environment had become and indeed what was up. She saw in an instant the evil smile on Rajiv's face. She saw a secluded room with a closed door in an empty building. She saw herself alone faced with a predator. Her instincts had not failed her, she felt for sure she was being positioned for something very unpleasant.

Rajiv now sat across from her, obviously preparing for his little game to begin.

Michael F. Goyette

"I hope you don't mind, but I took the liberty of putting together a summary at a glance of your programs," Rajiv said, passing a copy of a spreadsheet to Linda. "I know you've been busy and I thought my small contribution might alleviate some undue stress. I wanted you to take a look at it before I incorporate it into the main presentation. That's really all I needed, just a quick review of the numbers. You know how these Directors can be. You feel like you're constantly under a microscope. I thought if you and I could have one final sanity check, we, well really I...I might rest a little easier this weekend."

His charm and grace caused her to pause momentarily. Had she misjudged? She looked down at the paper and saw that it was indeed a summary of her programs, and a very good one at that.

"There was one number in particular that I wasn't sure of. Look at the line for the GT 184 program. Is that revenue projection really right? It seems excessively high," Rajiv questioned, appearing extremely concerned.

As she looked down at the summary, she noticed that Rajiv had gotten up and was moving to her side of the table. She could feel her heart race and felt stupid for almost second-guessing herself. He continued talking about the summary as he positioned himself behind her. She was so intent on his movement she had completely tuned out his speech. He settled in behind her. He gently placed one hand on her shoulder, leaned into her back and began using his free hand as a pointer on the spreadsheet, his mouth, inches from her face. He was talking softly now, almost in a whisper. After pointing to the paper in front of her, he rested his other hand on her shoulder. His face had not moved.

She could feel his hot breath in her ear and his weight on her shoulders. She was repulsed by his closeness and overwhelmingly frustrated that he was putting her in this position. He knew exactly what he was doing, she thought to herself. What an arrogant prick! She felt for a moment that she would vomit.

With her gaze fixated on the spreadsheet, she stared at the fork in the road, weighing her potential options. It was a life defining moment. The kind of moment you might look back on with tremendous pride thirty years down the road saying to yourself, "God, I was awesome! When it looked like catastrophe, I was strong. I stood tall." Or then again it might be one of those moments that faintly nags at you from the dark little corners of your mind for the rest of your life. A little voice that forces you to occasionally think to yourself, "If not for that decision..." After what seemed like an eternity, she made her decision – what must be done, must be done.

She breathed in deeply, arched her back, and ever so slightly turned her face closer to his. Taking her voice to his level of whisper she said, "Well the program is so...big. But I understand your question. I know I'm not the most experienced Account Manager but I think I can handle something this big if you give me a chance," she said in a subtly seductive way.

She could hear him breathing harder now. "I'm glad to hear you say that, Linda." Rajiv said moving both hands down her chest. At the same time he moved his lips to hers and kissed her roughly, trying desperately to push his tongue into her mouth.

Linda managed to stand and turn around, pushing the chair and Rajiv away as she did. She was now partially sitting on the table, legs somewhat spread with her feet still on the floor, hands behind her with palms on the table, and chest out. "Rajiv, I don't know what to say."

Rajiv pushed forward, forcing Linda completely on the table and onto her back. He was now on top of her and close to panting. His lips grazed Linda's as he spoke. "I've waited so long for this. I know you've been waiting too. I can see it every time you look at me. Do you feel that?" Rajiv said with a slight thrust of his hips. "I want to start our relationship over with a proper introduction."

His entire weight was now on her and he was pushing her hard into the wood table. As Rajiv finished speaking, he again plunged his face into Linda's. She resisted and managed to move her head to one side.

"Stop it! Get off me now!" she screamed thrashing wildly and poking him in the eye. Rajiv yelled out in pain and loosened his grip. With all the force she could muster, she pushed him off and ran out of the room and to her car. She got in, locked the door and realized that she was crying. She glanced at the entrance she had just run out of, no sign of Rajiv following. The hard part was over she thought trying to calm down. Time to make a phone call. Time to put an end to Rajiv at GIT.

Come Monday, It'll Be Alright…

Chip turned on his laptop. As was customary, he searched his e-mail for a message from Rajiv. He found one since Friday at 5:00. His stomach tightened. Every goddamn Monday morning, Chip thought to himself. He reflected that he felt like Pavlov's dog; he was conditioned to feel like screaming every time he saw an e-mail with Rajiv's name next to it. Unlike the dog, however, he would not get a treat for reading it, just that sick feeling. The message, of course, was flagged as a priority. The mail read:

E-MEMO
TO: Sales and Marketing Team
FROM: Rajiv Chopra
SUBJECT: Personal Time

Team:
   I will be out the office the first part of next week on personal business.

The message was dated Sunday at 8:00 p.m. Writing e-mails on a Sunday night, how typical. Despite the date and timing, the message seemed odd to Chip. It was brief, to the point, not caustic, and didn't entail any work on Chip's part, so unlike anything he had ever read from Rajiv.
   "Did you hear?" Kelly said, rounding the corner and bursting with information.
   "No, what?" Chip questioned back.
   "He's gone!" Kelly said.
   "Who?" Chip said, somewhat puzzled.
   Kelly continued with her exuberance. "Gandhi! Rajiv got canned!"

Chip was taken back. He was staring intently at Kelly now, searching for the punch line. "You're kidding, right?" Chip asked, hoping she wasn't.

"Nope. He's gone," Kelly said.

"I don't get it. What do you mean? He just quit?" Chip inquired skeptically.

"I mean… I had a beer last night with Tracy, you know, Hans' Admin. She said she got a call Friday night at home from Linda, all crying and hysterical. Linda told her that Rajiv had cornered her in one of the conference rooms and tried to force himself on her. Tracy said she was crying and didn't know what to do. So Tracy told her to call Hans and report the situation immediately. She did, and then Hans gave her Janice's number and told her to call Human Resources directly and explain the situation. Which again, she did."

Kelly continued as Chip struggled to make sense of this new turn of events. "Now you can imagine what happened when Janice got a hold of this. She went ape shit! She lives for this stuff. By Saturday afternoon they've got Rajiv in here under the spotlight, questioning him about the incident. By Sunday afternoon, they ask him for his resignation," Kelly explained, all the while beaming with excitement.

Chip sat with his mouth open, staring in utter disbelief at Kelly.

"Say something my man, you are free! The man is gone!" Kelly said, slapping Chip's arm.

The situation slowly began to sink into Chip's mind. "No more priority e-mails?" Chip asked jokingly.

Kelly laughed. "Not from Rajiv."

A huge weight immediately seemed to lift off Chip's shoulders. He felt an overwhelming sense of freedom, of relief. No more priority tasks. No more priority e-mails. No more of Rajiv's games and nonsense. He felt like he could do anything.

Then the exuberance was gone. As quickly as it came, it disappeared. He tried desperately to get it back. He told himself things had gotten better; Rajiv was gone.

So what, he answered himself. Had the situation changed that drastically? Would life really be that different? Didn't he still have the same decisions to make, the same questions to answer: Should I leave the company or stay? If I go, where will I go? Where will I end up? If I stay, what will happen? What do I want to do? What am I passionate about? What direction should I set sail? These questions still needed to be addressed. These issues still needed to be resolved.

No, nothing of substance had changed. Despite Rajiv's departure, the cause of his struggle remained. Certainly the day to day grind wouldn't seem as bad with his former boss now gone, but the essence of the problem remained, the central question still burned: How do I want to spend the hours, weeks, and years of my life?

Once that question was answered, he decided, he could finally leave the beach.

It was with this realization that the sense of freedom returned. He felt in control of his destiny, not chained by an organization, circumstance, or individual. He had no answer to the question, but knowing the problem seemed to minimize the problem. He felt confident the question could be answered, after all, it was such a simple question.

Take this job and...

"I got a call from Paul today," Chip said, staring at his dinner plate.

"Your old boss?" Stacy replied, taking a seat at their kitchen table.

Chip nodded. "He moved to a bigger company and he's running Sales and Marketing now. He needs a Marketing Manager," he said, looking for some response from Stacy.

She offered no input other than to nod that she had heard what he said.

"It's a little more money and I would have two people working for me. I would pretty much be in charge of Marketing for the entire company," Chip offered.

"You should never have left working for Paul. You could have just followed him out and avoided the whole GIT fiasco," Stacy said.

"I wouldn't be at the pay that Paul is offering if I had stayed where I was," Chip defended.

Stacy appeared unmoved by his argument. "The first move was risky. Now you're making another move with more risk just as we're going to buy a house. Are you sure you just don't want to stay at GIT? You weathered the storm, Rajiv is gone. Just do the job and make something of the work you're doing. Your new boss, whoever that turns out to be, has got to be better," she said.

"Staying where I am has risk too, you know," Chip said. "Staying put could be more risky than moving. GIT looks like it could be sold in the next month or two and the job I'm doing isn't all that important. My position could easily be eliminated."

"I just don't like all this turbulence, not now," Stacy replied.

"The turbulence is going to happen whether I move or not. At least by taking this job, I can control the change. If GIT is sold and new management comes in, I have no idea what could happen. Look, in the end, you weigh the risk, set sail and see what happens. You jump and you see, that's life. It may not work out exactly like we want but so what. No telling what might happen if I sit still and do nothing," Chip said.

"Don't give me that crap about everything being relative and it all depends on how you look at it," Stacy responded between bites of her dinner.

"There's no denying that the job itself added little or no value to my skills; six months wasted. It was an emotional roll-a-coaster. On the other hand, something good came out of all this; things certainly worked out well financially. Believe me, I don't want to stay at GIT. This is a move for the better. I know Paul, I know the company, the money is better…trust me, it's a move for the better," Chip said with conviction.

"Okay. If you're sure that you're going to be happier moving, then do it," Stacy sighed.

"Well, it's probably not what I want to do with the rest of my life, but it will be good for now." There was no doubt in Chip's mind; the move was a good decision. Too much had gone on at GIT to go into work with anything but a negative attitude. The entire experience had left a bad taste in his mouth. He knew he could probably make things work in the long run, but there would be a risk in that path, like any other. And considering he really didn't want it to work, it was best to leave. He was sure he was right. There was no way he could make a financial jump like this staying where he was. Besides, everyone had to do something and why not be well paid for it. So what if you had to compromise a little; make a few jumps. So what if you had to keep your mouth shut once in a while in order to collect a nice salary. So what if you weren't passionate everyday going into work; who was? You still got paid. You still had the ability to support your family. And while you got paid and paid your bills, nothing precluded you from searching for your passion.

The following Monday, Chip turned in his resignation to Human Resources. Although he thought he would, Chip again found no joy in the act. Despite the stories and desires for dramatic departures, what was the point? The company wouldn't crumble. They would continue on and forget Chip ever existed. Chip would also move on and GIT, in a very short time, would be a distant memory. No sense in burning bridges. The entire experience wasn't bad, he thought to himself. Despite the constant hammering from Rajiv, he felt stronger, better prepared for the future. He knew more about himself and what to do and not to do when jumping to a new job. He knew this move wasn't the final destination, just another adventure. Another voyage had begun.

After the Storm: A Peaceful Sea (for some)

6 months later at a restaurant

"How is everything at the old farm," asked Chip, part of him secretly wishing it was collapsing. "I understand they were sold."

"Yes, they were," Kelly smiled. She knew what he was looking for; a summary of how GIT collapsed without him. "Okay. Linda quit right after you left. She went to a competitor. You remember your last week of work when she called in sick that whole week?"

"Yeah," answered Chip.

"You're not gonna believe this. She was getting breast implants!" giggled Kelly.

"You're kidding," Chip said, astonished.

"Yes! Can you believe that! After all that talk about wanting to be taken seriously and not wanting to be an object," Kelly said. Chip recalled Linda mentioning that a number of times.

"That is unbelievable," Chip said. However, he was thinking to himself, very believable. Despite Rajiv's completely despicable behavior, Linda always seemed to want to call attention to herself; skin tight shirts, very short, very revealing skirts...

"What about Ted? How's he doing?" Chip inquired further. "I talked to him once or twice after I left but we kind of lost touch."

"Good, I guess. You know he retired right?" Kelly asked. Chip nodded to the affirmative. "Yeah, that's right, you were there when that happened. I remember now. I think his retirement started when you picked a fight with Janice because she wanted to do something nice for someone and you pissed all over the idea," Kelly said, prodding Chip.

"I'll ignore that and kindly ask you to move on, thank you," Chip said, smiling.

Kelly laughed. "Anyway, I think he works at a seminary or monastery or something," Kelly said with a touch of scorn. "They should have got rid of him a long time ago. Don't get me wrong, I liked him and everything. He was a nice guy…and funny, even when he was being a pig. But he was a big zero when it came to the job."

"Come on, he was a good worker, even at the very end when they treated him like a dog. Do you know he hadn't gotten a raise for almost three years? You or I wouldn't stand for that," Chip said with conviction. Imagine that, Chip thought to himself. I'm beginning to sound more like Ted everyday. The irony was amusing.

As usual, Kelly defended with calm, cold professionalism without missing a beat. "Then why did he? He could have left. The difference is, you and I know when to move on. I'm not buying that he's just a helpless victim. He's free to make choices like the rest of us."

"I'm not saying he's a victim, he's just part of a different generation. You know that. Loyalty to the company. Loyalty to the end, till death do us part. He took his loyalty seriously. And when being loyal to his family and loyal to his job conflicted with each other, he did what he thought he should do." Chip said.

Kelly refused to soften. "He should have focused that loyalty on his wife and kids and not on his stupid employer."

"You're right. He made a judgment error that seriously cost him. But that decision is fairly consistent with people of his generation. He shouldn't be punished forever," Chip said.

Ever the rock, Kelly refused to back away. "Well…I don't know."

Seeing that he was not gaining any ground and not wanting to push further, Chip changed the subject.

"How about you? What are you doing these days?"

Kelly brightened. "That's right, I didn't tell you. I gave my two weeks last week. Tomorrow is my last day. I got a new job as a Sales Manager. 15% increase in my base, a $9,000 signing bonus, a car, and up to a 20% bonus at the end of the year. Of course, that's based on company profitability and it's not guaranteed, but they've paid an average of 15% a year for the last 4 years. It's an awesome job," Kelly said, beaming with pride.

Chip was impressed. That kind of money would certainly be nice. "Very impressive. Congratulations," he said, shaking her hand.

"How is your job?" Kelly asked in return.

"Good. It's not the money you're getting, but it was a nice bump from GIT. I enjoy it. We've been pretty busy lately so the days blur together," Chip said.

"Is it the passion you were looking for?" Kelly asked.

Chip hadn't thought about those types of questions for some time: What was he passionate about? What did he really want to do? He hadn't thought about those questions since leaving GIT.

So much had gone on over the last six months. He had finished his MBA; he had gotten married; he and Stacy had bought a new house and to his surprise, Stacy was pregnant. Time was flying by. There were so many things to take care of now, so many things to handle. There was just no time to think about another new direction, like starting a business or switching jobs again. No, this job was fine for now. The job was challenging and going well. No problems with the work itself, the people he worked with, or his boss. Typical bump and grind, but no real issues. And like he had said, the money was good and with the new house and the baby on the way, there were real bills to pay, real situations to plan for. He reminded himself that he was lucky to have a job in today's climate; not everyone was so fortunate.

"Maybe not all the passion I had ever dreamed of, but it's a good job. The company is good and the money is good," he said, and although his eyes were looking directly at Kelly, his heart was still gazing longingly at the sea.

"Is Janice still running the show?" Chip asked, wanting to switch topics.

"You know after all her flag waving and motivational speeches about being devoted to the company and how women's careers are so important and any woman that stays home is doing an injustice to other women? Well, about four months ago, she dropped a bombshell that she was three months pregnant and that she would be leaving GIT to be a stay at home mom."

"You're kidding me. I didn't even know she was married," Chip said.

"She is. Oh! And I have to tell you this. You remember that room that Linda got cornered in? Janice turned it into a lactation room!" Kelly said, laughing.

"A lactation room?" Chip asked curiously.

"Yeah, a lactation room. For working mothers who are breast-feeding. There's a daycare center next door and any mom who is breast-feeding can get her baby and bring it to this room on lunch or breaks. Isn't that just like her? She did that a week or two after you left I think," Kelly said.

"What about Rajiv? Any word on what he's doing these days?" Chip couldn't resist asking.

Kelly smiled again, "You don't want to know. Let's just say that sometimes shit floats. And you know what the pisser is? After all that bullshit from Janice about intolerance, I think GIT helped him stay afloat."

6 months later at a competitor of GIT

E-MEMO
To: All Employees
From: Human Resources
Subject: Personnel Announcement

Michael F. Goyette

We are pleased to welcome Rajiv Chopra as the new Director of Sales and Marketing. Rajiv has an EE and an MBA. He comes to us with a tremendous amount of experience in our industry. Please stop by his office, he can't wait to properly introduce himself to each of you.

---

6 months later at a monastery

A sunny September day. Mostly blue skies, a few clouds here and there. A slight breeze created the perfect temperature. The sound of birds singing to the background of a running creek created a symphony of tranquillity. The smell of freshly cut grass permeated the air. A riding mower sat in the shade of a large oak tree, still warm from its recent work. The mower's captain sat next to it on a folding chair. He sat peacefully, taking in every sensory gift his newly found environment would offer.

So much life to experience, he reflected, so much beauty.

"Beautiful job on the lawn, Ted," commented two of the sisters as they passed the mower and its captain.

"Thank you, sisters," replied Ted.

It occurred to Ted that each lawn cutting seemed to bring more satisfaction and create more peace than the past forty years of work combined. There was no unquenchable thirst pushing him to move on to the next lawn, no voice at the back of mind screaming for more effort, no internal demon demanding more. Just an easy calm.

The Sisters found his services invaluable. Although they could find someone else to cut the lawn and act as the general handyman, he was left with the feeling that the monastery would crumble without his help. He felt at home.

Sitting there in the calm of the late afternoon on that day, much of the last four decades seemed to fade away. The decades of effort blurred together under one heading called 'Work'. A certain few events however, stood out painfully. They came in no particular order, randomly pummeling him from the past. He couldn't really remember why he worked that weekend twenty years ago, but he distinctly remembered missing his daughter's track meet to work it. He vaguely remembered the two week business trip he went on six years ago, although he did remember with vivid accuracy that it happened during the birth of his first grandchild on June 8 of that year. He couldn't quite recall the project he was involved with that made him late for dinner that one night fifteen years ago. But he did remember that it was on a Thursday night and it was the straw that broke the camel's back, at least that's what his wife said when she left him. It was their anniversary if he remembered correctly. It's amazing what sticks out in your mind after all this time, Ted thought.

But that was all in the past, water under the bridge. It didn't help to lament about those times now. He forced himself back to the present, to today, to the beauty surrounding him. Later that evening, he would see his grandchildren and spend hours talking to them about all kinds of silly things, the kinds of things that Ted would forget the next day but the kids would dine on for years to come. Then again, Ted thought, maybe he would remember them.

Ted meant the world to his children and grandchildren. He knew that now, with his new life, he had finally decided to reciprocate the sentiments.

It was time to fill the emptiness and loneliness with something meaningful as opposed to hours of endless labor that left him hungry. Chip was right, Ted decided. This was the meaningful stuff in life: the time with the kids, the time with the family, and the moments of peaceful reflection. All the stuff had a lot of meaning and all the meaning was good.

Life was good.

6 months later at a small bar in Detroit

Three lonely figures sit at a bar staring into space, each wallowing in their own self-pity. Mere months ago, Airline Titans, a Dream Team, now, two hollow men and one hollow woman searching for an answer to their demon question – How did this happen?

The perceived source of their pain is identified and announced at intermittent intervals by one of the three, not making the pain any less painful.

"All over a goddamn comma! Marketing solutions, my ass! Those fucking marketing people!"

The other two can only shake their heads and continue to stare...and wonder... How did this happen, how did this happen?

The End

Acronym Reference Summary

AADC	African American Diversity Coalition
Admin	Administrative Assistant
BHC	Better Health Committee
CADA	Chinese American Diversity Assembly
CADAVRE	Computer Assistance Desk and Anti-Virus Resource Employees
CAT	Computer Assistance Team
CCV	Corporate Core Values
CEP	Career Enhancement Program
CMC	Change Management Counselor
CMC	Career Management Counselor
CIP	Cultural Integration Plan
COB	Close of Business
CPPV	Committee for Promoting Progressive Values
CRASH	Computer Resource And System Help
CRDCMT	Career Resource Development And Change Management Team
CRDCMT - PMT	Career Resource Development And Change Management Team – Progressive Movement Team
DDOD	Don't Drool on Desk
DITWOP	Diversity In The Workplace
DWA	Designated Work Area
DWE	Designated Work Environment
ER	Expense Report
FGS	Feel Good Saying
FM	Magic
GIT	Global Instruments Technology
GLEE	Gay and Lesbian Employee Empire
GM	Germ Management
GM	General Manager
HR	Human Resources

HRC	Health Resource Center
MTT	Mountain Top Tone
RFQ	Request For Quote
RFC	Request for Check
RFC	Request for Circulation
RFC	Request for Certification
SCEG	Strategic Career Enhancement Group
SCEM	Strategic Career Enhancement Manager
SIMM	Strategic and Implementation Management Meeting
TACOS	Together All Contribute to the Organizational Structure
TEAM	Together Everyone Achieves More
TGR	Things Gone Right
TGNQRBNEW	Things Gone Not Quite Right But Not Entirely Wrong
TGW	Things Gone Wrong
TR	Trip Report
VILU	Valuable Interchangeable Labor Unit
ZIP	Zero Intolerance Policy

Printed in the United States
20845LVS00001B/217-219